Dream On

BY KERSTIN GIER

THE SILVER TRILOGY
BOOK TWO

DREAM ON

KERSTIN GIER

Translated from the German
by Anthea Bell

SQUARE
FISH

HENRY HOLT AND COMPANY
NEW YORK

SQUARE FISH

An imprint of Macmillan Publishing Group, LLC
175 Fifth Avenue
New York, NY 10010
fiercereads.com

Square Fish and the Square Fish logo are trademarks of Macmillan and
are used by Henry Holt and Company under license from Macmillan.

Our books may be purchased in bulk for promotional, educational, or
business use. Please contact your local bookseller or the Macmillan Corporate and
Premium Sales Department at (800) 221-7945 ext. 5442 or by
e-mail at MacmillanSpecialMarkets@macmillan.com.

Library of Congress Cataloging-in-Publication Data
Names: Gier, Kerstin, author. | Bell, Anthea, translator.
Title: Dream on / Kerstin Gier ; translated from the German by Anthea Bell.
Other titles: Zweite Buch der Traèume. English
Description: New York : Henry Holt and Company, 2016. | Series: The Silver trilogy ;
book 2 | Originally published in Germany in 2014 by
Fischer Verlag GmbH under the title Das zweite Buch der Traèume. | Summary:
"Romance, secrets, and new dream-world dangers follow Liv Silver into
Book II of The Silver Trilogy"—Provided by publisher.
Identifiers: LCCN 2015026290 | ISBN 978-1-250-11528-7 (paperback) |
ISBN 978-1-62779-655-2 (ebook)
Subjects: | CYAC: Dreams—Fiction. | Demonology—Fiction. | Supernatural—
Fiction. | Schools—Fiction. | Love—Fiction. | London (England)—Fiction. |
England—Fiction. | Horror stories. | BISAC: JUVENILE FICTION /
Love & Romance. | JUVENILE FICTION / Fantasy & Magic. |
JUVENILE FICTION / Horror & Ghost Stories.
Classification: LCC PZ7.G3523 Ds 2016 | DDC [Fic]—dc23
LC record available at http://lccn.loc.gov/2015026290

Originally published in Germany in 2014 by Fischer Verlag GmbH under
the title Das zewite Buch der Träume.
First published in the United States by Henry Holt and Company
First Square Fish Edition: 2017
Book designed by April Ward and Liz Dresner

Square Fish logo designed by Filomena Tuosto

1   3   5   7   9   10   8   6   4   2

For Leonie. I'm so proud of you.

If you can dream it, you can do it.

WALT DISNEY

1

CHARLES REALLY HADN'T made it hard for me to find his dream door: it had a life-size photograph of Charles himself printed on it. The photo showed him wearing a broad grin and a pristine white coat, with the words *Charles Spencer, DDS* on its breast pocket, and under that: *The best dentist you can find for your teeth.*

However, I wasn't expecting the photo to burst into song when I touched the doorknob.

"Working hard to keep teeth clean!" it warbled with great ardor in a fine tenor voice, to the tune of "Twinkle, Twinkle, Little Star." Startled, I looked around the corridor. Good heavens, couldn't it turn the volume down? I already felt I was under observation, although there was no one in sight except for me and the photo of Charles, only doors stretching down the corridor as far as the eye could see. My own door was just around the next corner, and in fact, there was nothing I'd rather have done than run back there and call off this whole operation. My guilty conscience was almost killing me. This was kind of like reading someone's secret diary, only much

worse. And I'd had to commit theft to embark on it, although opinions might vary on whether or not that was as immoral as it sounded. Legally speaking, yes, it was theft, but the kind of fur-lined trapper's cap with earflaps that I'd taken from Charles suited very few people indeed. Most anybody wearing one would look like an underexposed photo of a sheep, and Charles was no exception, so in that light, I'd even done him a favor. I only hoped no one would come into my room and see me lying in bed with that silly cap on. Because that was what I was really doing: lying in bed asleep. With a stolen trapper's cap on my head. But I wasn't dreaming anything nice; I was spying on someone. Someone who might well be in the process of breaking Lottie's heart, and Lottie was the best creator of crazy hairstyles, baker of cookies, dog whisperer, and comforter of susceptible teenage girls in the world. And as no one had a softer heart than Lottie (who officially was our au pair, by the way), that absolutely mustn't happen. So in this case, hopefully, the end justified the means. Didn't it?

I sighed. Why did everything always have to be so complicated?

"I'm not doing this for me; I'm doing it for Lottie," I said under my breath, just in case an invisible observer was listening in, and then I took a deep breath and pressed the door handle down.

"Now, now, no meddling!" The photo of Charles wagged its forefinger and broke into song again. *"Working hard to keep teeth clean, front and back and . . . ?"*

"Er . . . in between?" I suggested.

"Perfectly correct! Even though it sounds much nicer if I sing it!" And as the door swung open, Charles went on warbling cheerfully. *"If I brush for quite a while, I will have a happy smile!"*

"I really can't think what Lottie sees in you," I murmured, slipping through the doorway, not without one last glance at the corridor. Still no one else in sight.

Luckily I didn't find a dental practice waiting for me on the other side of the door, but a sunlit golf course. And Charles as well, in 3-D this time, wearing a pair of check pants and swinging a golf club. Greatly relieved that I hadn't landed in some improper dream (according to studies, over 35 percent of dreams are about sex), I quickly adjusted my outfit to the scenario: polo shirt, linen pants, golf shoes, and—because I simply couldn't resist it—a peaked cap. I strolled closer as casually as possible. The door to the corridor had closed gently behind me and now stood in the middle of the grass like a surreal work of art.

After landing, Charles's ball went straight into the hole with a single elegant movement, and his companion, a man of his own age with strikingly good teeth, cursed softly.

"What do you say about that, then?" Charles turned to him with a triumphant smile on his lips. Then his eyes fell on me, and he smiled even more broadly. "Hi, little Liv. Did you see that? It was a hole in one. Which means I've won our match by a huge margin."

"Wow, that's great," I said.

"Yup, it is, isn't it?" Charles chuckled and put an arm around my shoulders. "Let me introduce you. The guy there looking so grim is Antony, my old friend from university. But don't worry, he's all right—he's just not used to losing to me."

"Too true." Antony shook hands with me. "I'm the kind

of friend who's simply better at everything: I had better marks when we were training, I drive trendier cars, I run a more successful practice, and I've always had prettier girlfriends." He laughed. "And unlike Charlie here, I still have all my hair."

Ah, so it was that kind of dream. I felt even worse about having to disturb it.

As Antony ran the fingers of one hand through his luxuriant hair, the triumph disappeared from Charles's face. "Some women find a man with a bald patch very attractive," he murmured.

"Oh yes," I quickly agreed. "Lottie, for instance."

And my mom. After all, she was in love with Charles's bald brother, Ernest. Although presumably in spite of his bald patch, not because of it.

"Who's Lottie?" asked Antony, and I was just as interested in the answer as he was. Now we'd see if Charles was serious about Lottie.

At least he was smiling again when he said her name. "Lottie will—Hey, what's that?" He had been interrupted by a high-pitched sound suddenly ringing out over the golf course.

Now, of all times! "It's too early for the alarm clock," I murmured, and when Antony added, "Sounds more like a smoke alarm to me," I made for the door in a slight attack of panic. If Charles woke now, the whole dream would collapse, and I'd fall into a void, a very unpleasant experience that I wasn't keen to repeat in a hurry. As the high note went on swelling, while cracks were already appearing in the sky, I sprinted back to the door and grasped the handle just as the ground threatened to give way beneath me. With one last stride, I was safely through the doorway and out in the corridor, closing the door behind me.

Done. But my mission had obviously failed. I still didn't know how Charles really felt about Lottie. Even though he had smiled at the mention of her name.

The photo of Charles on his door struck up its tooth-brushing jingle again.

"Oh, shut up," I snapped, and the photo of Charles fell silent, looking hurt. And then, in the sudden hush, I heard it: a familiar, unpleasant rustling only a few yards away.

Although there was no one in sight and a sensible voice in my head told me that, after all, I was only dreaming, I couldn't hold back my fear. The feeling was as nasty as that rustling sound. Without knowing exactly what I was doing or who I was running away from, I took to my heels.

MY BREATHING WAS so loud that I couldn't hear anything else, but I felt sure the rustling was right behind me. And coming closer. I scuttled around the corner into the next corridor, where I'd find my own dream door. To call the sound a rustling wasn't quite right—that sounds more like a harmless rat, and this rustling was anything but harmless. It was the most mysterious rustling I'd ever heard, like a curtain being drawn back to reveal a hollow-cheeked chainsaw murderer with a bloodst—

I slowed down abruptly. Because there was already someone waiting for me beside my door. Luckily not a hollow-cheeked chainsaw murderer, someone much better-looking.

Henry. My boyfriend for the last eight and a half weeks. And not just in my dreams but in real life too. (Although it did seem to me that we spent far more time together in our dreams than when we were awake.) He was leaning back against the wall, as he so often did, with his arms folded, and he was smiling. The very special Henry smile that was just for me and always made me feel I was the luckiest girl in the whole world. Normally I'd have smiled back (with what I hoped was an equally special Liv smile) and flung myself into his arms, but at the moment there wasn't any time for it.

"Nocturnal fitness training?" he inquired when I stopped in front of him and hammered on the door with my fist, instead of kissing him. "Or are you running away from something?"

"I'll tell you inside!" I gasped, still hammering. The flap of the mailbox opened, and someone pushed out first a piece of paper and then a pen, infuriatingly slowly.

"Kindly write down today's password, fold the note correctly, and post it back through the flap," my friend Mr. Wu said in dulcet tones from the other side of the door.

I cursed quietly. My security system was brilliant at fending off unwanted strangers, not so good when I wanted to get to safety in a hurry myself.

"There really are more effective methods than running away in a dream, Liv." Henry had taken a good look around the corridor and now reappeared beside me. "For instance, you can simply fly out of danger, or turn into something so fast that no one could catch up with it. For instance, a cheetah. Or a moon rocket . . ."

"Not everyone thinks it's as easy to turn into something else as you do, especially not into a stupid moon rocket," I snapped at him. The pen in my hand was shaking slightly, but my fears had subsided a good deal in Henry's presence. I didn't hear any more rustling. All the same, I was sure we weren't alone. Hadn't it turned darker? And colder?

"You were such a cute little cat the other day," said Henry, who didn't seem to notice anything different.

Yes, very true. But in the first place, I'd wanted to turn into a large, dangerous jaguar, not a cute little cat, and in the second place, no one had been following me. Henry and I had just been trying a few things out for fun. It was a mystery to me how you could concentrate and turn into something quickly if you were threatened by a terrifying, invisible creature and your knees were knocking with fright. I guessed Henry was so good at all that transformation stuff because he was never afraid. Even now he was grinning, without a care in the world.

Gritting my teeth, I had finally scribbled *Felt slipper pom-pom* on the piece of paper, folded it into a triangle, and posted it back through the mailbox.

"Not as neatly written as it might be, but correct," said Mr. Wu from inside the door, and it opened. I grabbed Henry's arm, hauled him in through the doorway, and slammed the door behind us. Then I breathed a sigh of relief. We'd made it.

"Could you be a bit faster next time?" I hissed at Mr. Wu. (I'd never have dared to hiss at him in real life.)

"The tortoise can tell us more than the hare about the road it travels, Miss Olivia." Mr. Wu bowed to me (and the real Mr. Wu would never have done that) and gave Henry a brief nod. "Welcome to Miss Olivia's Dream Restaurant, young stranger with shaggy hair."

We really did seem to be in some kind of restaurant, as I couldn't help noticing, a rather unattractive one with black Formica tables, bright-red runners on them, and orange lanterns dangling from the ceiling. But there was an enticing smell of fried chicken. Only now did I notice how hungry I was. It had been a stupid idea to go to bed without any supper, because that made it harder for me to control my dreams.

Henry was staring at Mr. Wu, baffled. "Is he new here?"

"I am the guardian at the gate tonight," explained Mr. Wu solemnly. "I am called Wu, the Tiger's Claw, protector of orphans and the needy. Give a hungry man fish, and he will satisfy his appetite. Teach him to fish, and he will never be hungry again."

Henry chuckled, and I realized that I was blushing. My dreams were sometimes rather embarrassing. The proverb-quoting Mr. Wu also wore shiny black silk pajamas with a tiger's head embroidered on them, and a three-foot-long ponytail hung down from the back of his head. His real-life model, my first kung fu teacher, would never have gone around like that, even at Halloween.

"Okay," said Henry, still chuckling.

"Thanks, Mr. Wu," I said quickly, abolishing Mr. Wu and the entire restaurant with a wave of my hand. Instead we were now standing in the little park in Berkeley Hills, California, where I'd taken Henry in my dreams a couple of times before. It was the first place to spring to my mind. You had an excellent view of the bay from here. The sun was just setting over it, flooding the sky with wonderful colors.

All the same, Henry looked rather annoyed. "It smelled delicious in that restaurant," he said, "and now my stomach's rumbling."

"Mine, too, but however much we'd eaten we wouldn't have felt full." I let myself drop onto a bench. "After all, this is only a dream. Damn it, I ought to have given Mr. Wu a new password. Who knows—someone might have been looking over my shoulder just now when I wrote today's down."

"I was. *Stuffed kipper coupon* is a very creative password."

Was Henry laughing at me again? "I mean, no one would guess it easily."

"It was *Felt slipper pom-pom*." But now I was laughing myself.

"Honestly? Your handwriting's a terrible scrawl," said Henry, sitting down beside me. "And now I'd like to know what you were running away from. And why I didn't even get a kiss."

I sobered up at once. "It was that . . . that *rustling* sound again. Didn't you hear it?"

Henry shook his head.

"Well, it was there. An invisible, evil presence." I realized, listening to myself, that I sounded as if I were reading a bad horror story aloud. Too bad. "A rustling and whispering that came closer and closer." I shuddered. "Just like that time when it followed us, and you got us to safety through Amy's dream door."

"And where exactly did you hear the sound this time?" Unfortunately Henry's expression didn't tell me what he was thinking.

"In the next corridor on the left." I gestured vaguely toward the sea. "Do you think it was Anabel? I'm sure she's brilliant at turning invisible and making nasty rustling noises. Or maybe it was Arthur. There's nothing he'd rather do than scare me to death." Not that I could blame him. After all, I'd broken Arthur Hamilton's jaw almost exactly eight and a half weeks ago. I know that sounds bad, so I'll just say (to avoid getting too long-winded and complicated) that he deserved it. Although I'm afraid it didn't do me much good at the time, because out of our whole group of friends at school, his girlfriend, Anabel, was the rotten apple in the barrel. Or anyway, as it turned out, the crazy one. To be politically correct, I should say she suffered from "acute polymorphic psychotic disorder with symptoms of schizophrenia," which was why she was now in a closed psychiatric hospital well away from London, where she couldn't do any more harm to anyone—except in her sleep. Anabel was firmly convinced that a demon had given us the ability to meet in our dreams and shape those dreams deliberately—an evil demon from pre-Christian times with nothing less in view than ruling the world. Luckily for me, however, its attempt to take over the world had failed in the nick of time, just as Anabel, assisted by Arthur, was about to shed my blood as part of the necessary ritual. (I told you it was a long, complicated story!)

Belief in the demon was part of her sickness, and I was very glad that this demon existed only in Anabel's deranged imagination, because I had a problem with supernatural phenomena in general and demons in particular. Not that I could really come up with a conclusive explanation for the entire dream business. For the sake of simplicity, I mentally filed it away under the heading of "psychological and scientific phenomena that are perfectly capable of logical explanation, but can't yet be fully understood in our present state of knowledge." At least that made more sense than believing in demons. Even if my conviction had been slightly shaken again by that rustling sound just now . . . But I wasn't going to mention that to Henry.

He was still waiting for me to go on with what I'd been saying. "In the next corridor on the left," he repeated. He didn't mention Anabel and Arthur. He hated talking about those two, because until that incident on the evening of the Autumn Ball eight and a half weeks ago, they'd been among his best friends. "And you were there because . . . ?" He gave me an inquiring glance.

"Because there was something I had to do." Feeling uncomfortable, I rubbed my arm and automatically lowered my voice to a whisper. "Something totally immoral. I wanted to . . . no, I *had* to spy on someone's dreams."

"That's not immoral, just very practical," said Henry. "I do it all the time."

"You do? Whose dreams? And why?"

He shrugged his shoulders and briefly looked away from me. "Well, it can sometimes be useful. Or entertaining. It all depends. And whose dreams did you . . . er . . . *have* to spy on?"

"Charles Spencer's."

"Grayson's boring old uncle, the dentist?" Henry looked rather disappointed. "Why him, for goodness' sake?"

I sighed. "Mia"—my little sister—"saw Charles in a café with another woman. And she swears they were exchanging soppy glances and almost holding hands. I know that Lottie and Charles aren't officially an item, but he flirts with her like crazy, and they've been to the cinema together twice. A blind person could see that Lottie's head over heels in love with him, even if she won't admit it. She's been making him a pair of felt slippers for Christmas, so that in itself . . . Don't grin in that silly way! This is really serious. I've never seen Lottie in such a lovelorn state over a man, and it would be terrible if he's just toying with her feelings."

"Sorry!" Henry was trying, unsuccessfully, to keep the corners of his mouth under control. "At least now I know where your password . . . Okay, carry on."

"I had to find out what Charles really feels for Lottie—it was urgent. So I took his silly trapper's cap and broke into his dream tonight." It struck me, yet again, that at this very moment I was lying in my bed with the cap on—probably my hair was all sweaty by now. And presumably, also at this moment, Henry was thinking what I must look like in the trapper's cap with earflaps. He was going to start laughing again, I knew he was, and who could blame him?

But he responded to my glare with an innocent look suggesting that butter wouldn't melt in his mouth. "I get that. So how did you do it?"

I didn't see what he meant, and frowned. "Well, I went through his dream door."

"Yes, but as who or what?"

"As myself, of course. I had a peaked cap on because the dream was on a golf course, so I had to wear the right outfit. I'd just brought Charles to the point where he was going to say something about Lottie, only then his stupid smoke—" Horrified, I clapped my hand over my mouth. "Oh, shit! I completely forgot! The smoke alarm! It went off, and all I thought of was how to get out of the dream super fast before Charles woke up. I'm a terrible person! I ought to have woken myself and called the fire department."

The idea that Charles's apartment might be on fire didn't seem to worry Henry. He smiled at me and stroked my cheek with his fingertips. "Liv, surely you realize that in their dreams people don't necessarily have to be honest, right? In my experience, most of us tell even more lies in dreams than in real life. So if you want to find out the truth about someone, it's no use just strolling around in his dream and asking questions, because he'll tell you exactly what he'd say if he was awake."

That did sound plausible, of course, and to be honest the idea had occurred to me already. Looking at it that way, I'd stumbled into Charles's dream without any sensible plan, no subtlety in my approach at all, simply because I wanted to protect Lottie. "But how else could I have done it? And don't tell me I ought to have turned into a moon rocket."

"Well, it's always best if they don't notice you're there at all. As an invisible observer, you can learn a lot about people in their dreams, just from watching and listening. In fact, with a little patience, you can find out all about them."

"But I don't want to know *all* about Charles," I said, disgusted at the mere idea. "I only want to know if he's serious about Lottie. Because if he isn't, then . . ." I clenched my fists. No way were Mia and I going to let anyone hurt Lottie, certainly not Charles. Mia already thought it would be better to marry her off to the good-looking veterinarian in Pilgrim's Lane. "On the other hand—maybe poor Charles is dead of smoke inhalation by now because I didn't call the fire department, so in that case everything's settled."

"I love you," said Henry abruptly, pulling me closer, and I immediately forgot Charles. Henry didn't exactly throw those three magic words around lavishly. He'd said them exactly three times in the last eight and a half weeks, and for some reason, every time he did I felt terribly embarrassed. The only proper, universally valid reply to that was *I love you too*, but somehow I could never get it out. Not because I didn't love him, far from it, but because *I love you too* doesn't carry nearly as much weight as an *I love you* coming out of the blue.

So instead I replied, "Even though I can't turn into a moon rocket or make myself invisible?"

Henry nodded. "You'll learn all that. You're immensely talented. In every possible way." Then he leaned forward and began kissing me, so it turned out to be a really nice dream after all.

THE DISADVANTAGE OF these lucid dreams by night—dreams when you were fully conscious—was that you never really felt you'd slept well in the morning. However, over the last few months, I'd developed methods of making up for my lack of sleep: a hot shower, then gallons of cold water for my face, and finally a quadruple espresso for my circulation, disguised with a topping of frothed milk so that Lottie wouldn't go lecturing me on the sensitivity of young people's stomachs. The Italian coffee machine that ground fresh beans and frothed milk at the touch of a button was one reason why living in the Spencers' house wasn't so bad. Lottie might think that no one should drink coffee until they were eighteen at the earliest, but for Mom there were no such age limits, so I had unlimited access to caffeine.

Halfway to the kitchen, I met my sister. She had been out walking our dog, Buttercup, and put her ice-cold hand to my cheek. "Feel that!" she said cheerfully. "They said on the news it might even be a white Christmas this year, and the coldest January for eleven years . . . and silly me, I've gone and lost a glove. One of my gray polka-dot pair. You haven't seen it anywhere, have you? Those are my favorite gloves."

"No, sorry. Have you looked in Buttercup's hidey-hole?"

Buttercup had rolled over on the floor in front of me and was looking as cute and innocent as if she'd never dream of dragging gloves, socks, and shoes away and bringing them out again only after they were chewed to bits. I tickled her tummy at length and talked to her in baby language (she loved that!), before getting up and following Mia toward the kitchen, or rather toward the coffee machine. Buttercup followed me, not that she was after coffee. She had her eye on the plate of cold roast beef that Ernest had just put on the breakfast table.

We'd now been living in London for almost four months, in this large, comfortable brick house in Hampstead, but although I really liked the city and for the first time in years I had a large, pretty room all to myself, I still felt rather like a guest.

Maybe that was simply because I'd never learned to feel at home anywhere. Before Mom met Ernest Spencer and decided to spend the rest of her life with him, she'd moved house almost every year, along with Mia, Lottie, Buttercup, and me. We'd lived in Germany, Scotland, India, the Netherlands, South Africa, and of course in the United States, where Mom came from. Our parents had divorced when I was eight, but Papa was no keener than Mom on staying in one place. He was always glad when his company sent him to a new job in a country that he didn't know yet. Papa was German, and at the moment he and his two suitcases (he used to say no one needed more stuff than would fit into two suitcases) were living in Zürich, where Mia and I were going to stay with him for the Christmas holidays.

Was it surprising that all these years we'd wanted nothing more fervently than to settle down in one place? We'd always dreamed of a house where we could stay put and have all our things around us. A house with plenty of space, a room for each of us, a garden where Buttercup could race around and play, and an apple tree to climb. Now we were living in a house almost exactly like that (there was even a tree to climb, only it was a cherry tree), but it wasn't quite the same, because it wasn't *our* house: it belonged to Ernest Spencer and his two children, the seventeen-year-old twins Florence and Grayson. As well as the twins, there was also a friendly ginger cat called Spot, and they'd all three lived their whole lives here. But however often Ernest repeated that this house was now our house, it didn't feel like it. Possibly because there were no notches in any of the door frames with our names beside them to show how we'd grown, and because we couldn't connect any stories with the dark patch on the Persian rug or the cracked kitchen tile. Because we hadn't been here seven years ago, when a napkin suddenly caught fire while the family was eating fondue, or in the case of the tile, when Florence, aged five, had been so furious with Grayson that she threw a bottle of fizzy water at him.

Maybe it would just take a little longer. But we certainly hadn't left any traces behind us or created any family stories in the short time we'd been here.

Mom was already working on that problem, however. She'd always insisted on the three of us having a big breakfast together early on Sunday mornings, and she'd lost no time in introducing the same custom to the Spencer household, much to the annoyance of Florence and Grayson, particularly today. Judging by Florence's expression, she was in the mood to throw another bottle of water at someone. The twins had been out at a party until three thirty in the morning and couldn't stop yawning, Florence with her hand in front of her mouth, Grayson with no such inhibitions about yawning widely in front of us all and making sounds of exhaustion. At least I wasn't the only one having to fight off my weariness, although our methods of dealing with it differed. While I gulped great mouthfuls of coffee and waited for the caffeine to get into my bloodstream, Florence spiked orange segments on a fork and carried them elegantly to her mouth. She obviously thought vitamin C was the answer to tiredness. I felt sure the shadows under her caramel-brown eyes would soon go right away and she'd look as immaculate as ever. As for Grayson, he was shoveling mountains of scrambled eggs and toast into himself and had no shadows under his eyes at all. But for the yawning, no one would even have noticed how tired he was. He badly needed a shave, all the same.

Mom, Ernest, and Lottie had obviously slept well and were beaming at us cheerfully, and for once Mom was fully dressed and had done her hair, instead of coming down to breakfast all a mess in a revealing negligee, as she often did on a Sunday morning. Relieved, I smiled back.

Maybe I also smiled back because Mom's happiness was kind of infectious, and everything was so homey and Christmassy. The winter sun shone through the bay windows, which had wreaths decorating them; the red paper stars shone in the sunlight; there was a scent of melted butter, orange, vanilla, and cinnamon in the air (Lottie had been making a great mound of waffles that were smiling at me from the middle of the table); and Mia, sitting beside me, looked like a rosy-cheeked little Christmas angel in glasses.

Not that she behaved like an angel.

"Are we at the zoo here or what?" she asked as Grayson almost dislocated his jaw for about the eighth time, yawning.

"Yes," said Grayson, unmoved. "Feeding the hippos. Pass the butter this way, would you?"

I grinned. Grayson was another reason why I liked living in this house; in fact, he was an even better reason than the coffee machine. First, he could help me with my math when I got stuck (after all, he was two classes above me); secondly, he was a really cheering sight, even when he hadn't had a good night's sleep and was yawning like a hippopotamus, and thirdly . . . well, he was just nice.

His sister wasn't quite so nice.

"What a shame Henry didn't have time for the party last night . . . again," she said to me, and although her voice was dripping with sympathy, I could hear the malice behind it. It showed in the way she left that little pause before saying *again*. "You two really missed something. We had such fun, didn't we, Grayson?"

Grayson just yawned again, but my mother leaned forward and examined me in concern. "Liv, darling, you went to your room without having any supper yesterday evening. Should I be worried?"

I opened my mouth to reply, but Mom just went on. "Anyway, it's not normal to spend a Saturday evening hanging around at home, not at your age, and going to bed early. Just because your boyfriend doesn't have time to go to a party, you don't have to act like a nun and stay home yourself."

I cast a dark glance at her through my glasses. That was typical of my mom. We were talking about the birthday party of a guy two years ahead of me at school. I hardly knew him, and anyway, I'd been invited only as Henry's companion, so I'd have looked pretty silly going on my own. Aside from the fact that, whatever Florence said, I probably hadn't missed much. Parties were all the same: too many people in a small space, too much loud music, and not enough to eat. You couldn't talk except in a shout, a couple of people always drank too much and made fools of themselves, and if you danced, other people were poking their elbows in your ribs the whole time—it really wasn't my idea of fun.

"What's more," said Mom, leaning a little farther forward, "what's more, if Henry has to babysit his little brother and sister, which naturally I think is very nice of him—who's to say you can't go and help him?"

To my annoyance, she'd hit the bull's-eye, right at my most sensitive spot. In the eight and a half weeks of our relationship, Henry had often come here to see me: we'd spent time in my room, in the park, at the movies, at parties, in the school library, in the corner café, and of course in our dreams. But I hadn't been to his house once.

The only member of Henry's family that I knew was his little sister, Amy, aged four, and I knew her only from dreams. I knew that he also had a brother called Milo, who was twelve, but Henry didn't often talk about him, and he almost never mentioned his parents. Recently I'd wondered whether Henry was keeping me away from his home on purpose. I'd found out most of what I knew about his family not from him, but from Secrecy's blog. I'd learned that his parents were divorced, his father had already been married three times, and he was now planning to make a former lingerie model from Bulgaria wife number four. As well as Milo and Amy, according to Secrecy, Henry also had a whole crowd of older half brothers and sisters.

Mom winked at me, and I hastily thought about something else. When Mom winked, it was usually suggestive, and therefore embarrassing.

"I always had no end of fun babysitting. Particularly when the babies were asleep." She winked again, and now Mia put her knife down in alarm. "In particular I remember the Millers' sofa. . . ."

So much for a homey, nearly Christmassy mood.

"Mom!" said Mia sharply, and at the same time I said, "Not now!" We already knew about the Millers' sofa, and no way did we want Mom talking about her experiences on it over breakfast.

Before she could take another deep breath (the worst of it was that she remembered not just one embarrassing experience, but she had an almost inexhaustible supply of them), I added quickly, "I stayed home last night because I felt like I was coming down with a cold, and anyway, I had a lot of work to do for school." I could hardly say that I'd wanted to go to bed early on a secret mission, wearing the incredibly ugly trapper's cap that I'd stolen from Charles. Of course we hadn't told anyone what we did at night in our dreams—and presumably no one would have believed us, anyway. We'd have been carted straight off to join Anabel in the psychiatric hospital. Of everyone at the breakfast table, only Grayson knew about the dream business, but I was fairly sure that since the events of eight and a half weeks ago, he hadn't once gone through his own dream door, and I also guessed he thought we'd all keep away from the dream corridors. Grayson had never felt happy going into other people's dreams; he thought it was all creepy and dangerous, and he'd have been horrified if he knew that we simply couldn't leave it alone. Unlike Henry, he'd definitely have condemned my operation last night as immoral.

Incidentally, I'd had to wash my hair twice to get rid of the smell of sheepskin from that cap, but there was still something the matter with it. When Lottie, who had gone to get herself a second helping of scrambled eggs, passed behind me, my hair crackled audibly and stood on end, only to lie back against Lottie's pink angora sweater. Everyone started to laugh, one by one, even me once I'd glanced in the mirror above the sideboard.

"Like a porcupine," said Mia as I tried smoothing my hair down on my head again. "We really might as well be at the zoo this morning. Speaking of zoos, who's the extra place for?" She pointed to the empty plate beside Lottie. "Is Uncle Charles coming to breakfast?"

At the sound of his name, Lottie and I jumped almost at the same time. Lottie presumably in excitement; mine was more of a guilty start. As if on cue, we heard the front door open, and I tried to prepare myself for the worst. But the singed smell that suddenly rose to my nostrils came, to my relief, from my slice of toast.

And the energetic footsteps click-clacking along the hall didn't belong to Charles either, but to someone else. They were unmistakable. Mia groaned quietly and cast me a meaningful look. I rolled my eyes. I'd really rather have seen a singed Charles. So long as he was only slightly singed at the edges, of course.

The last of the warm Christmassy feeling seemed to leave

the room, and there she stood in the doorway: the Beast in Ocher. Also known as "the she-devil with the Hermès scarf," in ordinary life Philippa Adelaide Spencer, or Granny, as Grayson and Florence called her. Apparently her friends at the bridge club knew her as Peachy Pippa, but I wasn't going to believe that until I heard it with my own ears.

"Oh, I see you've started without me," she said instead of *hello, good morning,* or anything like that. "Are those American manners?"

Mia and I exchanged another glance. If the front door hadn't been left unlocked, then the Beast in Ocher had a key to it. Alarming.

"You're over half an hour late, Mother," said Ernest, standing up to kiss her on both cheeks.

"Really? What time did you tell me?"

"I didn't," said Ernest. "You invited yourself yesterday, remember? You said you'd be here for breakfast at nine thirty."

"Nonsense, I never said anything about breakfast. Of course I had it at home. Oh, thank you, darling."

Grayson was helping her off with her (ocher) coat—a fox had given its life for the fur collar—and Florence beamed and said, "Oh, you're wearing your (ocher) twinset; it really suits you, Granny!"

Lottie, sitting beside me, had tried to get to her feet as well, but I held her firmly down by the sleeve of her sweater. Last time she had bobbed the Beast a curtsy, and no way was I having her do that again.

Mrs. Spencer Senior was a tall, slender woman who looked a good deal younger than her seventy-five years. With her graceful, upright posture, long neck, elegant short hairstyle, and the cool blue eyes that she turned on each of us in turn, she'd have been the perfect casting for Snow White's wicked stepmother—in a Thirty Years Later special.

I'd better explain that we hadn't always been so hostile. At first we'd seriously tried to like Ernest's mother, or at least understand her. At the end of August, she'd set off on a three-month around-the-world cruise, and when she got back at the end of November fit and well, with a good tan and loaded with souvenirs, she found that her favorite son had moved his American girlfriend into the house, along with her daughters, their au pair, and their dog. It wasn't hard to see why Mrs. Spencer had been horrified at first, and so surprised that it rendered her speechless. But unfortunately not for long, because then she let fly, and to this day she hadn't stopped.

Her main object in life seemed to be insinuating that Mom was after Ernest for his money and had used all sorts of nasty tricks to catch him. She combined that with attacks on Americans in general; she thought they were uncivilized, stupid, and vain. She wasn't a bit impressed by Mom's two academic doctorates. After all, she'd gained those degrees in the United States and not in a civilized country. (She studiously ignored the fact that Mom was now teaching and lecturing at the University of Oxford.) The only people that Mrs. Spencer thought were worse than Americans were Germans, because Germany had started the Second World War. Among other things. So she thought Mia and I were not just uncivilized, vain, and stupid (on Mom's side) but also naturally nasty and underhand (on Papa's side). As for Lottie, who was German on both sides of her family, she was just nasty and underhand, and when it came to our dog, Buttercup—well, Mrs. Spencer didn't really like any animals at all unless they were on her plate, cooked and covered in gravy. Or if she was wearing them around her neck.

We really did try hard to overcome her resentment and get her to like us—but it was no use. (Okay, maybe we didn't try all *that* hard.) And by now we'd given up the attempt. What was it Lottie was always saying? Call out into the forest, and the same sound comes echoing back. Or anyway, she had a proverb along those lines. We were part of a pissed-off forest, anyway, or at least Mia and I were. Mom was still hoping for a miraculous change of heart in Ernest's mother, and as for Lottie—well, Lottie was a hopeless case. She firmly believed that there was good in everyone, even in the Beast.

The Beast now stared at Lottie and said, "I'll just have a cup of tea. Earl Grey. Black, with a dash of lemon in it."

"Coming right away!" There was no holding Lottie now. She jumped up, and the sleeve of her sweater almost tore because I was still clutching it firmly. Grayson did say, "I can make you a cup of tea, Granny," but Lottie pushed past him. We had already explained to Mrs. Spencer, several times, that Lottie was not our maidservant (and besides, she had every Sunday off), but our explanations had fallen on deaf ears. It was her opinion that if you paid someone a salary, she couldn't be your friend at the same time.

"In a proper teacup, please, not one of those thick mugs that you all use for your horrible coffee." Mrs. Spencer sat down. As usual, in her company, I suddenly felt that I didn't have enough warm clothes on. I wanted a nice thick cardigan. And some more coffee, in one of those thick mugs.

"*Boker*," Mia whispered to me.

"What?" I whispered back.

"Short for *the Beast in Ocher*. Let's just call her the Boker."

"Okay." I giggled. It really suited her.

The Boker glared at us. So did Mom and Florence—and it was true that whispering and giggling at meals didn't exactly suggest we were well brought up. But then, I guess the Boker decided it wasn't worth her while to tell us off.

"Grayson, darling, where's dear little Emily?" she asked instead.

"Still in bed asleep, with any luck." Grayson helped himself to yet more scrambled eggs, and spread butter on another slice of toast. At a rough estimate, it was his seventeenth slice. It was incredible how much he could shovel into himself without ever putting on an ounce of weight. "Dear little Emily," he said quietly.

Did he sound a tiny bit sarcastic? I stared at Grayson with interest. Emily was his girlfriend, also in the top class at school, editor of the school magazine, a prizewinning dressage horsewoman, and she was neither dear nor little. The Beast in . . . er, I mean, the Boker had obviously taken Emily to her heart. When she mentioned her, and she often did, it was obvious that she thought Emily was the bee's knees, and she was always praising Grayson, too, for his excellent taste in women, which, apparently, he hadn't inherited from his father.

Now she sighed indignantly. "Oh, I was hoping to see her here. But obviously the only guests you've invited to breakfast today are the domestic staff."

"Lottie lives here," said Mia, not going to the slightest trouble to sound friendly. "Where else would she eat breakfast?"

Mrs. Spencer raised her eyebrows again. "As far as I know,

my granddaughter has had to give up her rooms on the top floor to your au pair—goodness knows there's more than enough room there."

Here we went again.

"Mother, surely we've discussed that quite often enough. Can we *please* talk about something else?" Ernest wasn't looking at all happy anymore. And Mom was clutching the tablecloth as if she were afraid that if she didn't, she'd jump up and run away.

"All right, I'll change the subject: you must come and put new batteries in my fire alarms, Ernest," said Mrs. Spencer. "Charles's alarm went off in the middle of the night last night because the battery had run out." (Oh, good. Then he was still alive!) "I'd have a heart attack if such a thing happened to me." She ostentatiously put her hand to her ocher twinset at roughly the spot where her pacemaker would have been fitted if she'd had a weak heart, which she didn't. She had the constitution of an ox.

"A nice cup of tea." Lottie put the teacup down in front of her. "Earl Grey, with a dash of lemon."

"Thank you, Miss . . . er?"

"Wastlhuber."

"Whastle-whistle?" repeated Mrs. Spencer.

"Oh, just call me Lottie," said Lottie.

Mrs. Spencer stared at her, horrified. Then she said, "Certainly not!" emphatically, and began rummaging in her handbag, probably looking for smelling salts.

"Oh, loosen up, Boker," muttered Mia under her breath.

The Boker let a little sweetener drop into the tea from her personal pillbox and stirred the cup. "Why I'm really here is . . . well, as you know, I always have a little Twelfth Night tea party in January."

"*Little* is good," murmured Grayson, but his remark was drowned out by Florence's enthusiastic, "Oh, I just love, love, *love* your Twelfth Night tea parties, Granny!" As if they were the grooviest occasions of all time.

Mrs. Spencer smiled faintly. "Well, I was hoping that I wouldn't have to, but as my friends are always asking, and clearly none of you here are going to come to your senses"— at this point she cleared her throat and looked sadly at her son—"I can see I have no option but to extend my invitation to your new entourage, Ernest."

When no one reacted—Mia and I because we weren't sure what *entourage* meant, and were trying to work out whether it was something nasty—she added, sighing, "That means that I would"—once again she cleared her throat, and this time she fixed her eyes on Mom—"that I would be very glad, dear Ann, to welcome you and your two daughters to my house."

It was remarkable the way she managed to make that sound like an order. And you could bet that no one had ever looked less happy than she did when she uttered the words *very glad*.

Ernest thought so too. "If you . . . ," he began, frowning, but Mom put her oar in before he could go on.

"That's so nice of you, Philippa," she said warmly. "We'd love to accept your invitation, wouldn't we, girls?"

It took us a couple of seconds, but because Mom was looking so hopeful, we finally managed to smile and nod.

Okay, so we'd be going to an English tea party on Twelfth

Night, to have a lot of old ladies look at us curiously. We'd been through worse.

Mrs. Spencer, satisfied, sipped her tea. She'd certainly have swallowed the wrong way if she'd known that Twelfth Night was to be the day when Mr. Snuggles died, and she had just invited his murderers to her house. The murderers themselves hadn't the faintest idea who Mr. Snuggles even was. Without any forebodings at all, we reached for the cinnamon waffles.

TITTLE-TATTLE BLOG

The Frognal Academy Tittle-Tattle Blog, with all the latest gossip, the best rumors, and the hottest scandals from our school.

ABOUT ME:
My name is Secrecy—I'm right here among you, and I know *all* your secrets.

25 December

Merry Christmas, everybody! Enjoying the holidays? And did you find exactly the presents you wanted lying under the Christmas tree this morning? Not in the Porter-Peregrin household, I'm afraid. Persephone wept buckets because she unwrapped a little Cartier watch instead of her heart's desire. But what were her poor parents to do? I mean, they could hardly have done Jasper Grant up in gift wrap for her, could they? In fact, I can understand her. I miss Jasper myself. It simply won't be the same without him! A whole term in France, just to get a better French mark on his final school report—did he spare a thought for us? Who, may I ask, is going to provide the really good scandals at parties now that he's not here? And how are the Frognal Flames going to win their games without their second-best man? They're already suffering because Arthur Hamilton was voted out as team captain. And no, I still haven't the faintest idea what exactly happened after the Autumn Ball, or why Arthur argued with Jasper, Grayson Spencer, and Henry Harper, so do stop sending me e-mails about it. I'll soon find out—and when I know, I'll tell you right away. That's a promise!

It's fairly quiet in London at the moment. Mrs. Cook, the headmistress, is in Cornwall, like half the school (hey, is there anyone who DOESN'T have a holiday cottage in St. Ives?), and Mrs. Lawrence has flown to Lanzarote. Just like Mr. Vanhagen, by the way. Funny coincidence, don't you agree?

How about the rest of you? How are you spending the holiday season? Are you staying home in the warm, like the Spencer twins? I'd love to tell you what I'm doing, but then you'd only go trying to find out who I am again—and that would be such a bore. You'd better reconcile yourselves to the fact that you'll never know.

See you soon!

Love from your very Christmassy-feeling Secrecy

PS—Speaking of Christmas: Liv and Mia Silver are away with their father in Zürich for a whole ten days—but I doubt Henry is missing his girlfriend much. I guess it's more of a platonic relationship between those two—they've been an item for months, and they still haven't slept with each other. Only making out and holding hands . . . Hmm, what do you make of that? Seeing that we all know Henry Harper isn't exactly famous for holding back, it must be something to do with Liv. Is she a prude? Frigid? Or does she belong to some kind of religious community where sex is forbidden before marriage? Then again, maybe she's just a little slow for her age, poor thing.

4

I FELT FOR Mia's hand as the plane prepared to land, because as we came in, losing height, it did a couple of violent little jumps suggesting it was about to crash. But then we slid through the clouds and saw the Thames below us, and London in the snow, and the queasy feeling inside me turned to anticipation.

Mia pressed my hand. "Don't worry, nothing's going to happen to us. But next time you're welcome to make a will leaving everything you possess to your little sister, if it makes you feel better."

"First, if we crash, you'll be as dead as me, and second, I'm afraid I don't have anything to leave."

"You're forgetting your guitar and Aunt Gertrude's Christmas present." Mia giggled.

"No, sorry, I want that buried with me in my casket."

Our American great-aunt had excelled herself with this year's choice of presents: she had given Mia a Barbie coach (suitable for Shaving Fun Ken?) drawn by a pink Pegasus, and me a set for breeding primeval crustaceans. We could really use those things.

However, we'd long ago given up expecting much in the way of Christmas presents. For some reason, Santa Claus didn't seem to like us very much. Once again he hadn't brought the smartphones we so urgently needed to replace our Stone Age cell phones. Although we did get very stylish Stone Age cell phone cases, handmade out of felt by Lottie.

"I wonder why I have to write that stupid wish list every year, when we never get what we wish for," said Mia. "At least, I don't remember putting *plastic horse with wings* on my list. Or *near-death experiences on a ski lift*."

"Or *bruises all over me*," I added.

"What's so difficult to understand about *night-vision aid*, *bugging set*, and *red wig with bangs?*" Mia snorted sadly. "Instead we get sweaters, pillows, DVDs, and a skiing trip! And then we have to pretend to be grateful! Think how many smartphones Papa could have bought for that amount of money!"

"One would be enough for me," I said. You couldn't even phone to another country with my cell phone. Which meant I hadn't heard Henry's voice for ten days. At least, not on the phone.

The last time Mia and I had been on skis was eight years ago. So it was exciting when Papa took us to the top of the slope on our very first day. He thought skiing was like riding a bicycle: you never forgot how to do it. We could now refute that theory. I guess I was the first person ever to come down the entire World Cup slalom course at Adelboden on my behind. Papa had laughed like crazy and kept on asking solicitously about my poor bruised bum. That reawakened my ambition, so on the second day I spent only half as long lying in the snow. By the end of the vacation, I could ski faster than Papa, but I'd paid a high price for it.

At least I wasn't still limping as we came through the arrivals gate with our baggage. My stiffness was beginning to wear off.

We heard Mom's cries of "Yoo-hoo! Here we are!" before we saw her, and funnily enough it didn't bother me at all to see that Ernest was with her. By this time, I'd obviously not only gotten used to the idea that he was part of our lives now— at some point in the last four months I must have begun to like him. I was only a tiny bit disappointed that Henry wasn't there, when he'd said that he would meet me at the airport.

"You two look as if you've had a good time," said Mom after she'd hugged us. "As fresh and rosy-cheeked as two Swiss girls straight from the Alpine pastures."

"That's frostbite," said Mia. "With luck, we'll never need to use blush again."

Mom laughed. "Oh, how I've missed you!" she said. She looked fantastic, even though she'd been back to the hairdresser who gave her a style like Camilla, Duchess of Cornwall's. I hoped I'd look as good as Mom did at her age—aside from the hairstyle, of course.

But however hard I looked for Henry, there was no sign of his untidy shock of dark-blond hair anywhere. I was now more than just a tiny bit disappointed. Maybe he was waiting at the wrong airport.

Ernest, very much the English gentleman, took charge of our suitcases. "Haven't you brought any Swiss cheese back this time?" he inquired with a twinkle in his eye.

"We did get some Toblerone for you and Mom, but Mia ate it while we were waiting for our flight."

"Tattletale!"

"Better a tattletale than a greedy pig!"

"Watch out or I'll kick your poor bruised bum," said Mia.

Mom sighed. "Now that I come to think of it, it's been really peaceful without you girls. Come along! Lottie was going to bake sweet rolls filled with jam, her granny's recipe; they're called *Buchteln*, and she says they're best eaten warm."

We'd missed Lottie's food, so we hurried to the car. Eating cheese fondue every evening can be boring. While we'd been in Switzerland, Lottie had gone to visit her family and friends in Bavaria, and whenever she came back from there, she always had lots of wonderful new recipes and couldn't wait to try them out. We were happy to taste them for her.

On the way home, Mom and Ernest told us all the news (there wasn't actually any of that, but they talked thirteen to the dozen all the same), and Mia told them all the adventures we'd had skiing. She exaggerated a bit—we hadn't been stuck in the ski lift for half a day, only fifteen minutes, and it hadn't been dark by the time the mountain rescue outfit got it going again with a winch; the lift had started moving again in the normal way of its own accord. And there hadn't really been any avalanche dog coming to our rescue. But, hey, it was more interesting than what Mom and Ernest were saying, so I let her talk away while I switched on my cell phone and looked for any texts from Henry. I found a message from my network provider telling me that I was now back in the United Kingdom, and eleven texts from Persephone wittering on about Jasper, not yet her boyfriend but maybe he would be someday, and calling down curses on all the French school-girls he'd be meeting. But nothing from Henry.

Hmm. Did that mean I ought to worry?

We hadn't met in our dreams as often as we'd agreed to over the last ten days. That had been my fault, or at least the fault of my unaccustomed mixture of exercise, fresh moun-tain air, and Swiss cheese, all of them taken in large doses. I'd usually slept so soundly that in the morning I couldn't even remember seeing my own dream door. Henry might well be mad about that. On the other hand, I'd also waited outside his door and never seen anything of him. You couldn't agree precisely when you'd meet in a dream—I mean, who dreams a detailed timetable?

He'd given me one of those Japanese lucky beckoning cats for Christmas. Which would have been fine if I hadn't spent about a thousand hours laboriously making him a music box that played "Dream a Little Dream of Me" and had a photo of me stuck inside the lid. It was star-shaped. Maybe that had been a bad idea. The music box was as good as shouting *I love you!* while I wasn't so sure what a battery-driven souvenir costing six pounds ninety from the Asia shop said.

I stared through the window and thought of sending Henry a text—*I'm here, where are you?*—but then I decided not to. From the plane, London had looked like a scene in one of those kitschy snow globes, with glittering white powdered sugar all over the rooftops, trees, and streets—down here, however, there wasn't any glittery sugar to be seen. Slush isn't in the least romantic, and if I'd had to describe my mood, *slushy* would have been the right word for it. I'd arrived at the airport feeling cheerful and full of anticipation, and I got out of the car in a really bad temper when Ernest finally parked it in the drive of his house—I mean, our house. Matters didn't improve when the front door was opened by Grayson's girlfriend, Emily. She was the last person I wanted to see at that moment.

"Oh, there you are," said Emily, looking about as pleased as I felt. Objectively considered, she was a very pretty girl with gleaming, smooth brown hair, nice skin, a tall and athletic build, but I couldn't help it: to me she always looked like the stern governess in an old movie, like the one in *Heidi*. And like a horse. A kind of governess horse or horsey governess. She seemed much older than other eighteen-year-old girls, and it wasn't just because of her high-necked, severe clothes, but also because of the superior, know-it-all expression that she turned on everyone. For a split second I was tempted to turn around then and there and march away again. But then Buttercup came into the front hall with her ears flapping, and behind her were Grayson, Florence, and Lottie.

And someone with bright-gray eyes and dark-blond hair standing out in all directions. I almost burst into tears of sheer relief.

Henry.

He simply pushed Emily aside and took me in his arms.

"Hey, there you are again, my cheese girl," he murmured into my hair. "I've missed you so much."

I wound my arms around Henry's neck and held him much closer than was strictly necessary.

"You smell nice," I whispered. It wasn't precisely what I wanted to say, but it was the first thing to come into my head.

"That's not me; it's the stuff with the unpronounceable German name that Lottie's been baking." Henry made no move to let go of me again, and as far as I was concerned, he never had to, but stupidly we weren't alone.

"You're all invited to try them," cried Lottie. She was wearing the felt slippers she'd originally made as a Christmas present for Charles, but at the last minute she'd decided not to give them to him after all. Because there are many people who don't appreciate the value of a homemade present, she'd said. And that had been a wise decision, because the day before Christmas Eve, Charles had given her a foil-wrapped chocolate Santa Claus. A *small* foil-wrapped chocolate Santa Claus. My beckoning Japanese cat was a one-carat diamond by comparison.

"It's a surprise welcome-home party for you snow bunnies!" Lottie beamed at us. If she was suffering from unrequited love for Charles, she hid it well.

"And we'd have made up a welcome song, I'm sure," said Emily, not bothering to hide the sarcasm in her voice. "Only, what on earth rhymes with *snow bunny?*"

"Jar of honey?" suggested Grayson.

"Don't be silly!" said Emily, and without even looking, I could tell what kind of face she was making.

"No, *silly* doesn't rhyme with *bunny*. But *very funny* does," said Grayson, and I chuckled into Henry's sweater. Oh, it was good to be home. "And *plenty of money.*"

"Wrapped up in a five-pound note, like the Owl and the Pussycat when they went to sea," added Mia, "in their beautiful pea-green boat." She patted me on the back. "Hey, you two are getting between us and Lottie's jam buns."

Lottie's new recipe did indeed turn out to be for large, fluffy, very light yeast buns with a plum jam filling and a crisp crust, and life was downright perfect for the next twenty minutes. Sitting in the kitchen with the people I loved best in the world, drinking hot chocolate and eating the delicious jam buns—at that moment I couldn't imagine anything better. Everyone was talking at once, Mia telling more tall tales about our skiing expeditions, Florence planning the party she and Grayson would have for their eighteenth birthday in February, and Lottie describing the Bavarian cream pudding she was going to conjure up for us tomorrow. I didn't even have to let go of Henry, because we went on holding hands under the table, laughing and exchanging meaningful looks with each other, and after the second jam roll, I felt sure I was about to burst with happiness. Well, maybe not just happiness—those rolls might seem as light as a feather, but once inside you, they swelled to twice their original size. I felt a blissfully satisfied smile spreading over my face entirely of its own accord.

And then the perfect twenty minutes came to an end.

"I'm really impressed to see how sporting you are, Liv," said Emily, who was sitting opposite me. She had eaten only half a jam roll, with a knife and fork, which showed that she and Grayson had *not* been holding hands under the table. "I'd really never have thought it of you. My respects."

What was she talking about? "Well, we Silvers have our good points," I cautiously replied. "But I don't think I can manage a third yeast roll. It's Grayson you should be impressed by. If I've counted correctly, he's on his fourth."

"My fifth," said Grayson with his mouth full. "I already had one before—"

Emily cut him short. "I wasn't admiring you for the number of calories you can consume, Liv, I was admiring your nonchalance."

Nonchalance—the Boker had used that word recently (when she complained that she didn't have any herself these days, in view of the fact that Ernest and Mom were an item), so I knew what it meant; it meant being casual and unconcerned, not minding. Hmm. "Nonchalance about what?" I asked suspiciously.

Henry held my hand a little tighter and started getting to his feet. "Why don't we go upstairs and . . . well, unpack your suitcase?"

Emily returned my glance without batting an eyelid, totally unimpressed by the fact that Grayson was looking at her as if he'd like to jab his fork into her.

"Em," he said menacingly.

"What? I'm only saying I admire her." Emily was still looking me straight in the eyes. "I don't think most people would be so happy to have their sex life discussed in public." She added with a thin-lipped smile, "Or rather, their lack of a sex life."

Henry groaned quietly and stopped pulling at my hand, and Grayson dropped his fork on his plate with such a loud noise that Mom, Lottie, Florence, and Ernest, who were all deep in conversation at the other end of the table, fell silent. For a second you could have heard a pin drop.

Then Mia, speaking instead of me, said, *"What?"* I was very grateful to her for taking over. "Who's been discussing Liv's sex life where?"

"Sex life?" Mom echoed her. It was always a cue for her to be wide awake.

"Oh, I suppose someone at Frognal Academy." Emily leaned back, crossing her arms. "Someone with nothing else to do. If it's any consolation, most people don't think you're really frigid."

"What?" said Mia again. And once again Mom, too, echoed Emily: "Frigid?" I swallowed with difficulty.

Florence sighed. "Em! Presumably Liv hasn't seen it yet." She was looking at me sympathetically. "Or did you go on the Internet while you were away skiing?"

I shook my head slowly. Nonchalantly, you might say.

"Oh, I see." Emily allowed herself to give that thin-lipped smile again. "I thought Henry would have told you about it ages ago."

No. He hadn't. Whatever *it* was.

"I haven't had a chance yet," said Henry. "And by the way, Liv is standing right here. It's only silly gossip. No one will be interested."

"No, of course not. Secrecy only let two hundred and forty-three readers add comments to her post," said Florence.

Mia jumped up and snatched Lottie's iPad off the sideboard. She was right. It was about time I gave up my wonderful nonchalance as well. I let go of Henry's hand and stood up.

"Like I said, it's only uninteresting gossip," Henry repeated.

"Dead boring," agreed Grayson. "May I have another of those jam bun things, Lottie?"

"Oh," said Mia, staring fixedly at the iPad. "Oh no. Oh. Bloody. Hell."

I took the thing from her and skimmed Secrecy's post. One nasty dig after another, which was typical of her blog. There was the bit about Henry and me at last, in the postscript: *they've been an item for months, and they still haven't slept with each other.*

Well, in fact, that was true. How did she know? Or was she simply guessing?

Only making out and holding hands . . . Hmm, what do you make of that? Seeing that we all know Henry Harper isn't exactly famous for holding back, it must be something to do with Liv.

What did she mean, Henry wasn't exactly famous for holding back? I didn't think he'd been all that restrained. Or me either. But you didn't have to go rushing into things.

Is she a prude? Frigid? Or does she belong to some kind of religious community where sex is forbidden before marriage? Then again, maybe she's just a little slow for her age, poor thing.

Oh well. Huh. If that was all. Maybe I really was a little slow for my age. So what?

Almost relieved, I raised my head and grinned at Henry. "You and Grayson are right. It really is dead boring, uninteresting gossip."

Henry grinned back, and with a cheerful grunt, Grayson helped himself to another roll. Emily's thin-lipped smile was looking a little sour now, but maybe I was wrong there—after all, her natural expression was grumpy. And Florence, Mom, Ernest, and Lottie went back to their conversation as if nothing had happened. I was so relieved that my appetite came back. Surely another little jam bun wouldn't do any . . .

"Don't rejoice too soon," said Mia, putting her forefinger on the screen. Among all the other comments, Secrecy had spoken up again. *Don't be too hard on poor Liv—she's new to the role of a girl in love. Not so long ago she was still the kind of student who got her head dunked in the toilet. Poor thing, she could*

tell you all about the insides of the toilet bowls at her school in
Berkeley, California. . . .

"How does she know about that?" asked Mia quietly.

"No idea." But I wasn't grinning now. Secrecy and the
whole school could assume whatever they liked about my sex
life, for all I cared, but the Berkeley story was a secret. Apart
from the four girls who had attacked me in the toilet, only Mia
and Lottie knew about it.

And . . . *Henry.*

As I slowly turned my head to look at him, his cell phone
began to ring.

IN MY DREAM, I was walking through Frognal Academy with everyone staring at me, giggling and whispering. Emily, looking elegant on a purebred bay horse, trotted past me in the stairwell and called, "Don't be too hard on poor Liv. She can't help it if Henry doesn't want to sleep with her."

Luckily I spotted a green door in the wall of the corridor at that moment, so I knew I was just dreaming.

"She's simply rather underdeveloped physically and mentally," said Emily. It annoyed me that she had the nerve to insult me in my own dream. Fundamentally, didn't that mean that my own subconscious mind was saying these mean things about me? I wasn't letting it get away with that. With a wave of my hand, I abolished the horse, and Emily fell to the stone floor with a thud.

"Ouch!" she said indignantly.

"Are you crazy, Liv?" Florence helped her friend up. "She could have hurt herself."

"My dream, my rules!" I said, reaching for the doorknob. "And I really couldn't care less what people think about me."

A snap of my fingers, and Emily, Florence, and all the rest of them turned into soap bubbles. They floated through the stairwell and burst, one by one, with a series of quiet pops. Satisfied, I slipped through the green door into the dream corridor outside.

"Activate Security Protocol Mr. Wu mark three," I said quietly. If no one was listening, I liked talking to the door as if I were on the starship *Enterprise*. Weirdly, and although I hadn't done anything to it myself, it had changed quite a lot over the last few weeks. While at first, it had looked like the door of a cozy cottage in the Cotswolds painted deep green, it now had two columns, one on each side, and an extra skylight above it. It was still green, but not such a dark green, more of a fresh minty color, and as it now looked, it suited a mysterious Victorian villa rather than a cottage in the country.

I connected the changes that had happened to the door with those I had gone through myself. I'd noticed the same thing happening to other doors in this labyrinth. Some just changed their color; the paint on others was peeling away; some changed their size and shape entirely. I suspected it had something to do with the owners' states of mind. It was impossible to keep it all straight, because in addition, the doors were always changing places with one another.

However, the doorknob in the shape of a lizard was still there, and it winked at me when I quietly closed the door behind me. Just in time to see Henry's untidy blond hair disappear around the next corner. I was going to call his name, but then I didn't—who knew how loud the echo might be in these corridors, and who or what might be enticed into investigating? Furthermore, where on earth was Henry off to? His door was directly opposite mine, and we'd been going to meet each other. Right here. And if I had my way, right now.

I decided to go after him. After all, I had better things to do than stand around here looking stupid and waiting for him. Like finally talking, for instance. And really talking, not just canoodling.

Keeping quiet—I was barefoot—I followed him. We hadn't had a chance to discuss how Secrecy could know the story of the school toilets in Berkeley. Henry's cell phone had rung, and he had left in a hurry to go and collect his little brother. From a friend's house, he had said.

"Can't your mum do it?" Emily had asked, and I was really glad I hadn't asked that question, because I don't think I'd have survived the cold, contemptuous look that Henry gave her.

Not that it bothered Emily at all. When Henry had left, she turned to Grayson. "I thought Mrs. Harper had dealt with that problem?"

"Em!" said Grayson with a strange sideways glance at me.

"What's the matter?" Emily had shaken her head as if baffled, while Grayson took her by the elbow and led her into the next room.

"That problem"? What problem?

That was when I realized it was high time for me to talk to Henry. It was one thing that I knew so little about my boyfriend. Or rather that he told me so little about himself. But the fact that even Emily was better informed than I was hurt me more than I liked to admit. Now and then I'd thought of probing, asking Henry all the questions that had come into my head as time passed, but then I didn't ask them after all. In movies and books, the hero's girlfriend who always wants to know everything usually turns out to be a silly cow and a control freak, and pretty soon she's the hero's ex-girlfriend. Or, depending on what kind of story it is, she's the victim of a terrible crime and everyone is secretly pleased. But control freak or not, I was beginning to feel I just had to know where I stood with Henry.

The corridor into which he'd turned seemed to be empty, but I thought I heard footsteps in the corridor branching off to the left behind an imposing red door, so I went faster. I'd soon catch up with him.

Talking, no making out, I reminded myself again to be on the safe side. Repeating it like a mantra couldn't hurt.

"Ouch!" I'd bumped into something hard, or rather into someone turning the corner, just like me but in the opposite direction. At first I thought it was Henry.

"Good heavens, Liv!" exclaimed the someone, obviously as startled as I was.

It wasn't Henry; it was Arthur Hamilton. The Arthur Hamilton whose jaw I had broken and whose crazy girlfriend had tried to cut my throat last fall. The Arthur that I'd seen only at school since the disaster in the cemetery, and then I'd kept my distance. If our paths did happen to cross, we'd stared at each other like two enemy generals meeting off the battle-field, demonstrating strength and lasting hostility.

I jumped away from him as quickly as I could. However, it was too late to assume an intimidating expression—I was afraid I was gawping at him more like poor scared Bambi.

Arthur had recovered from the shock faster than I had, because he was smiling.

No doubt about it, he was still the best-looking boy in the universe, with his symmetrical features, big blue eyes, his porcelain complexion, and his angelic golden curls, but something in him had changed. Not outwardly; there wasn't even a scar left from his injury, although his jaw had been wired for several weeks. No, the damage was under the surface, as if last fall's events had affected the mysterious aura of a born winner that used to surround him. And his smile had clearly lost something of its hypnotic charm. "Very smart outfit, Liv Silver."

I didn't have to look down at myself to know what I was wearing—it was what I actually had on at that moment: a pair of baggy pajama bottoms with blue polka dots on them, and an old T-shirt of Grayson's that I had rescued from the donation bag because I thought the panda in a pink tutu on the front of it was funny. The wording under the panda said TOO FAT FOR A BALLERINA.

Hell. Why was I roaming around these corridors in pajamas? I ought to have turned into a jaguar. Then maybe Arthur would have shown a little more respect. "Thanks," I said with all the dignity I could muster up. "Have you seen Henry? He ought to be somewhere around here."

"I wonder why I'm not surprised to find you still haunting this place?" Arthur smiled faintly. "Well, it was obvious that you weren't going to give that up. What are you after? Getting into your teachers' dreams in the hope of better grades?"

Not a bad idea. "As a matter of fact, I'm not so fond of spying on other people." I could sound condescending myself if necessary. Even in pajamas. "How about you? What are you doing here yourself? Paying a visit to your old friend the demon? What was his name again? Something beginning with *L*. Sounded like *more water on the sauna stove* in Finnish. Lelula? Lilalu? Luleli?"

That was really funny—*löylyä* actually does mean "pour more water on the sauna stove," as I knew from a nice Finn called Matti who was friends with Lottie when we were in Utrecht. He taught us any number of things that we didn't really need to say in Finnish. But Arthur wasn't laughing anymore.

"Oh, I remember," I said slowly. "Of course, the demon wasn't real. Just an invention of Anabel's."

"Anabel," repeated Arthur, and he sounded as if saying her name hurt him physically, "Anabel is sick."

"You don't say!" I replied as callously as possible. I mean, was I supposed to feel sorry for Anabel? When she'd lured me into a trap and hit me over the head with an iron torch holder? Never mind that after that she'd tied me up so that she could cut my carotid artery at her leisure. The stupid thing was that I *did* feel sorry for her. As we now knew, Anabel had spent the first years of her life with a weird sect that worshipped demons, along with her mother, who had committed suicide later in a psychiatric hospital. No wonder Anabel herself was totally mental.

Arthur was inspecting me attentively, as if he could read my thoughts. I swallowed and tried to look extra grim. All I needed now was Arthur thinking I could understand his ex-girlfriend. Or him, come to that. Although—well, he had loved Anabel, and everyone knows what crazy things you can do when you're in love. And now she was in a psychiatric hospital herself, his friends weren't speaking to him, and he wasn't captain of the basketball team anymore. Poor Ar— no, stop that! The hell with poor Arthur! Next thing I knew, I'd be feeling guilty about breaking his jaw.

"She did some bad things, but . . ." Arthur hesitated for a

moment, and once again I felt a surge of sympathy. "But she didn't write that book herself."

He meant the grubby old notebook where Anabel had found her rituals for conjuring up demons. The book had been burned on the night when Arthur and Anabel had lured me to the Hamiltons' family vault in the cemetery, intending to free Anabel's imaginary demon from the underworld with the help of my own far-from-imaginary blood.

Whether Anabel was traumatized or not, her knife would have killed me if Henry and Grayson hadn't turned up in the nick of time. So that was quite enough sympathy and understanding, thank you.

"True. Someone just as nutty as Anabel wrote the book," I said firmly.

"Could be," admitted Arthur, and he said no more for a second or so. Then he made a gesture that managed to be helpless and arrogant at the same time as it took in the whole corridor. "So how do you explain all this, then?"

I'd asked myself the same question often enough. I shrugged my shoulders as casually as I could. "Well, how can I be here in London and talk to my grandma in Boston at the same time? How come the garage door will open if I press a button while I'm still a mile away? How can people visit each other in their dreams? So far as I'm concerned, to be honest, those are all phenomena I can't explain. But just because I don't understand them, it doesn't mean they have to be the work of demons. There's a scientific explanation for everything."

Now Arthur had his superior smile back. "Oh, is there? Think what you like if it makes you feel better, Liv Silver. My regards to Henry."

"Thanks, and mine to the demon Lilliburlero when you next see him," I snapped back with my most hostile enemy-general expression as I turned to walk away. "I must be going. See you sometime—I'm afraid."

Arthur nodded. "Yes, I guess that can't be avoided." And he added under his breath, "But be careful, Liv. We're not alone in these corridors."

I resisted the temptation to turn around and tell him what he could do with his pretended concern and/or concealed threats, and I marched away, well knowing that he was watching me, probably with his eyes fixed on my polka-dot pajama bottoms. For a moment I was tempted to make a more elegant departure by turning into a jaguar, even at this late stage, but there was always the danger that once again it wouldn't work, and I'd be scurrying away as a silly little kitten, so I didn't run the risk.

And where the hell *was* Henry? He was never around when you needed him.

SO AS NOT to give myself away to Arthur by walking back the way I'd come, I marched as purposefully as possible farther along the corridor, and then turned off it again to be right out of his field of vision in the unlikely event that he was still keeping an eye on me. Then, to be on the safe side, I repeated the maneuver again. When I finally stopped and took a surreptitious look around, none of the other doors struck me as in the least familiar. Where on earth had I ended up? I'd never before strayed so far from my own corridor. Maybe I should have made chalk marks on the walls to be sure of finding my way back. I felt goose bumps rising on my arms, but I forced myself to wait a little longer. Then I turned around, and three minutes later, I was cautiously peering down the corridor where I had met Arthur. Not that there was any trace of him now. No trace of Henry either.

I remembered Arthur's warning. So what if I wasn't alone here? This was worse; I was lonesome as they come, not a soul I knew in sight.

I quickly set off on the way back, half expecting the damn

corridors in this maze to change direction—after all, you never knew here—but thank goodness they stayed where they were. Not so very much later, with a sigh of relief, I turned into the corridor where my own door lay.

There was still no sign of Henry. Now what? Did I stand around waiting for him, or stand him up so that at least I could get a bit of sleep? No, I'd made up my mind to talk to him, and I wasn't going to let another night go by.

With my own door less than forty yards away, I felt safe enough to try turning into a jaguar again. You never knew, practice might make perfect. Sad to say, I couldn't concentrate properly, so once again it went wrong. My pajama bottoms now had a jaguar pattern, but that was all. Oh, and I saw a tail too. Oops! I waggled my behind a bit, giggling. It wasn't a bad jaguar tail, but I'd better get rid of it. However, before I could do that, someone put his arm around my shoulders from behind.

"Making yourself beautiful just for me?"

Henry. Now, of all times.

I hated it when he came quietly up behind me. And I hated myself for not hearing him. Who knew how long he'd been watching me while I fooled around with my jaguar tail?

He drew me close, and I almost went weak at the knees, it felt so good. So familiar, and right, and as if there weren't any problems at all.

"Where've you been?" I tried to put a little distance between us, but I failed miserably. "I met Arthur just now. On my own." I hoped that last bit came out in a suitably accusing tone.

Henry covered the top of my head with kisses. That felt good, too, I'm afraid. In between, he murmured, "What a good thing my beautiful, clever girlfriend can do kung fu in a tight spot. And you'd have everyone scared to death with that cheetah tail, anyway. So what did Arthur say?"

"Jaguar," I corrected him. "It's supposed to be a jaguar tail. And Arthur didn't say much, just made a couple of cryptic remarks. And of course he didn't laugh at my jokes. Do you know what *löylyä* means in Finnish?"

Henry laughed and took my face between his hands. "Kiss me?" he suggested with a gleam in his gray eyes.

"No!" I pushed him away from me. *Talking, no making out*, that was my new mantra. Although right now it seemed to me a pretty stupid mantra.

However, that was no help with all the questions I had.

For instance, *Where were you going in such a hurry just now? Or How come we've never met at your house? Are you serious when you say you love me, and if so, why don't you tell me what's weighing on your mind? How is it that Grayson and Emily know something about your mother and her problems? And what was the idea of giving me that beckoning Japanese cat?*

None of them passed my lips. Instead I asked, "How did Secrecy know what happened in the school toilets at Berkeley?"

He shrugged his shoulders. "Honestly, Liv, you don't want to worry what that silly cow writes about you."

"But that's the point. She wouldn't write about things that she can't really know, unless . . ." I stopped.

"Unless what?"

"Unless someone told her about them."

"That makes sense," said Henry, shrugging again.

"Does it? But I haven't told anyone but you, Henry." It

came out much more seriously than I intended, maybe a little too dramatically. "So . . ." I bit my lower lip.

For a moment Henry looked puzzled, and then his eyes widened. "Are you saying that I'm hand in glove with Secrecy?"

I didn't answer that. I just chewed my lip as eloquently as I could manage.

Henry's eyes widened a little farther. "Oh—unless maybe you think I could actually be Secrecy myself?" And although he was obviously struggling not to, he burst out laughing. His laughter came spilling and gurgling out of him in his own typical way, and unfortunately it was infectious. I felt the corners of my mouth beginning to twitch. Henry leaned forward to kiss me. "You're so sweet! I love you, Liv! I love you so much."

Then we didn't say anything else for some time, while I sent that silly mantra off to Nirvana, or wherever mantras go when you've finished with them.

Until . . . yes, until we heard the laughter. Someone else's laughter. Like something out of an old horror movie, deep and echoing, with a good deal of craziness in it. It was rolling down the corridors toward us, so much of a cliché that I didn't feel at all afraid as I moved away from Henry's arms to look for the cause of it. If this was Arthur's way of proving that we weren't alone here, it didn't work very well.

Far down the corridor, we saw a figure that seemed to grow a little as we stared at it.

"What's that supposed to be?" asked Henry.

I didn't know either. For a moment I thought of the demon, but at the same time I felt sure that a demon would never go around wearing a cloak and a slouch hat, if only for fear of looking ridiculous. Or was I right? The figure in the slouch hat—judging by its outline and the depth of its voice, it was a man—laughed again, this time really rumbling laughter, and the echo was thrown back and forth from wall to wall of the corridor.

I was torn both ways. I was curious to find out who this character was and what he wanted. After all, I was still dreaming, and furthermore, Henry was standing right beside me. So what could go really wrong? On the other hand, a little voice inside me whispered that it would be a good idea to make for the wide blue yonder.

However, it wasn't until the man was only a few doors away and began to speak—"Who are you who venture to roam in the haunts of Senator Tod Nord?"—that I decided to listen to the little inner voice. *Tod*, which in German means "death," didn't sound good.

"Senator Tod *Nord?*" repeated Henry as I seized his arm and tried to haul him away. The figure wasn't far from our doors now.

"Did he say *Nord?* As in *north?*" Henry was still looking back behind us. "Is that some kind of zip code or what?"

"Could you put off finding out to another time?" I cried.

"Wait! What do you make of this?" Unfortunately Senator Tod decided to follow us, while declaiming something that made no sense at all. "Rodents at rondo!"

For some reason, that seemed to interest Henry enormously. "Rondo?" He was reluctant to let me lead him on. "What do you mean?"

I couldn't believe it! Now he was stopping to have a conversation with this character! Didn't he know that the best way to deal with lunatics is to ignore them? I wouldn't be surprised if the man behind us produced a scythe from under his cloak any moment now, to suit his first name.

Once again he laughed his deranged laugh. And this time it really scared me.

"Don't just stand there!" I hissed at Henry, who was slowing down no matter how I tried to hurry him.

There! Grayson's door was ahead of us. It looked the same as ever, a perfect copy of our front door at home, painted white, with plant containers outside it and the chubby stone statue known as Frightful Freddy barring our way. A place to take refuge! "Wait—stranded on root!" cried Senator Tod, or at least that was all I could seem to make out in the confusion of the moment. Not for the world was I going to do as he said and wait, that was for sure.

I just hoped Grayson, like me, hadn't changed his safety precautions. If he had, then Senator Tod Nord was going to grab us. I bent down to Freddy and whispered, "Ydderf, Ydderf, Ydderf" into his ear (he had the head of an eagle, so it wasn't easy to make out just where his ear was supposed to be, but I didn't have time for such details now). "And hurry up about it! There's someone after us!"

"You may come in," squeaked Freddy, sounding slightly insulted, as I flung the door open, pushed Henry through it, and let it slam before the character in the slouch hat could catch up.

"That was a close thing!" I gasped.

Henry didn't reply. My hand went out to him and met empty air.

"Henry? This isn't funny!" Horrified, I looked around. But there wasn't a sign of Henry anywhere.

7

"EXPLAIN AEROBIC ADB production in human cells with regard to a gross equation with the balance of ADB contained in them."

At first I thought Senator Tod had slipped into Grayson's dream, confused ravings and all, but the speaker had been Grayson's biology teacher, Mr. Bridgewater. We were in a classroom in Frognal Academy, where Grayson was sitting at a table on his own, in front of four teachers, looking rather pale. Obviously this was some kind of exam.

"Aerobic ATP production, do you mean?" asked Grayson, casting me a glance of annoyance.

"ADB," Mr. Bridgewater corrected him, and Grayson turned even paler.

There were a few chairs for onlookers by the wall, and I tiptoed over and sat down beside Emily, carefully coiling my jaguar tail up beside me.

I didn't know whether to be worried about Henry or cross with him, but mainly I felt cross. Maybe he had simply turned into a breath of air. He could do that sort of thing. Or maybe he had woken. Whichever it was, I didn't much care for being left here on my own. Especially as I thought he really ought to have taken that guy in the slouch hat more seriously.

"How's Grayson doing?" I whispered to Emily.

Emily put a finger to her lips. "Shh. Other people are trying to learn something!" My jaguar tail twitched with annoyance. Even in Grayson's dreams, Emily was a terrible spoilsport.

"ATP is produced by . . . ," Grayson began, but Mr. Bridgewater interrupted him. "Not ATP. ADB! Don't try to get out of it by changing the subject, Grayson!"

"But . . . but it really is ATP. Adenosine triphosphate. I've learned all about ATP and its uses. Would you like me to give you a rundown on . . . ?" Grayson sounded desperate now.

"Young man, that's very laudable, but today we are examining you on ADB," said the examiner next to Mr. Bridgewater. "So carry on, please, we don't have all day."

"ADB . . . ADB . . . Aaaaaadeeeeebeeee . . ." Grayson ran his hand through his short fair hair.

Poor boy. He still had those dreadful dreams of failure. I longed to intervene, but then he might have realized that he was only dreaming and—even worse—that I'd slipped into his dream without permission. No, it was better for me to keep my head down and slip out again as soon as the air was clear.

"I'm afraid I'm not up to date with ADB," Grayson finally said.

Beside me, Emily sniffed. "Typical," she said, not even under her breath. Grayson promptly looked at us. His expression was so unhappy that my heart lurched sympathetically. I gave him an encouraging smile. Sad to say, I had no idea what ATP was, or ADB either, or I might have been able to help him.

"So you're not up to date with ADB?" repeated Mr. Bridge-water, exchanging sorrowful glances with his colleagues. "Well, think it over again. . . . What could it mean?"

Ancient daft Bridgewater. Apes devour bananas. Alternative drippy baboon . . .

Grayson sighed. "I really don't know." He added pitifully, "What is it, then?"

"Oh, good heavens!" The stout woman teacher to Mr. Bridgewater's left shook her head pityingly. "ADB—Anti-diet-butter! Everyone knows that!"

"Anti-diet-butter?" Grayson stared at her incredulously. "What's anti-diet-butter supposed to produce in human cells? And what does it have to do with biology, anyway?"

He was so right. This really was the silliest dream of all time. Anti-diet-butter—couldn't Grayson's unconscious mind come up with anything better?

"Impertinent into the bargain!" The stout woman clicked her tongue and turned to her colleagues. "Well, I for one can't waste any more of my time on this candidate. As I said before, I fear we can't pass him."

"I'm afraid I feel the same," said Mr. Bridgewater. "I'm very sorry, Grayson, but you've failed this exam."

Grayson looked as if he might burst into tears. "But . . . but . . . ," he whispered desperately.

"I said all along you ought to study more," said Emily sternly, with a touch of satisfaction in her voice. "Not so much partying and basketball. You should think more about your future!"

I was about to contradict her when everything around us suddenly turned pitch dark. The ground gave way beneath my feet, and I fell into a gaping void.

Grayson had woken, and I did the same, to find myself in bed with a thudding heart.

Gasping, I sat up—I hated it when this happened. It was a terrifying feeling to fall into the dark, as if oxygen would be in short supply there and I'd choke to death as I plunged into space—I was sure dying must feel just like that.

The glowing numbers on my alarm clock said it was ten past four. Sunday the sixth of January. The last day of the school holidays. Unfortunately not to be entirely devoted to doing nothing, because this afternoon the Boker's famous Twelfth Night tea party would take place, and I didn't have anything to wear yet. I just hadn't had time to go through my wardrobe, and Mom's and Lottie's, in search of something suitable. All the same, I had a chance to catch up on my sleep now, and that seemed to me far more important than the wardrobe question. But first I must go to the bathroom.

With a sigh, I rolled out of bed and groped my way to the door of my room. It was almost a full moon, and quite light here on the second floor, but by now I was so used to this house that I could have found my way to the bathroom with my eyes closed—and even without stepping on the creaking floorboard in the corridor that Ernest had been meaning to replace for ages. It made a rude noise if you put too much weight on it, "Like Aunt Gertrude when she's had bean soup," Mia always said, and she liked to tread on it on purpose. I made an elegant detour around the floorboard; after all, I didn't want to wake anyone. But just as I was putting my hand out to the bathroom door handle, I heard the toilet flush inside the room. My reflex action was to turn and run away, but I didn't because it occurred to me that this was the real world and I was in no danger of meeting Senator Tod or anyone like him. Apart from the fact that I felt sure the Senator didn't bother to wash his hands very thoroughly. Rather impatiently, I stepped from one bare foot to the other, until at last the bathroom door swung open and Grayson came out, bare-chested as usual (whatever the temperature outside) and in only his pajama bottoms. But who was I to complain? Anyway, I didn't have my contact lenses in or my glasses on at this time of day, and my view of him was rather blurred.

"You awake too?" I said in friendly tones, and Grayson let out a small squeak of alarm. He was obviously still half asleep, and hadn't seen me. Now he was trying to squint at me through his half-closed eyes.

"Liv! What a fright you gave me!"

"Sorry."

"I was just dreaming about you."

"How sweet of you."

He sighed. "No, it wasn't a nice dream. More of a horrible nightmare. I made a terrible mess of my oral biology exam! When they told me I'd failed, I woke up in a fright. My heart's still thumping like mad."

Because you didn't know anything about anti-diet-butter, you poor little sensitive plant! Whereas I met Arthur and Senator Tod tonight, and do you hear me complaining?

"How about you?"

"Hmm?"

"Why are you awake?"

"Oh. Full moon," I said. "And I need the bathroom."

"You're wearing my old T-shirt." By now Grayson's eyes must be accustomed to the moonlight. "You were wearing it in my dream as well."

Uh-oh . . . dangerous ground. I held my breath for a moment.

"But you also had a tail in my dream," Grayson went on thoughtfully.

"A *tail?*" I repeated, trying to sound as disapproving as Emily. I could have sworn that Grayson was blushing. Although you couldn't really see in this dim light.

"A leopard's tail," he said.

No, damn it, a jaguar's tail! "How peculiar!" I shook my head. "I wonder what Freud would have to say about that? Was there a squirrel in your dream as well?"

Grayson didn't reply. Then he said quietly, "You're not doing that anymore, are you, Liv?"

I swallowed. "What do you mean?"

"The dreams, the doors . . . You and Henry aren't still exploring that corridor, are you? Isn't all that over?" He sounded so serious and anxious that I couldn't lie to him. I really don't know what I'd have told him if an Aunt-Gertrude-after-bean-soup noise hadn't echoed down the corridor just then. Someone had trodden on the loose floorboard. It was Mia, unlike me looking neat and cute in the pleated white nightdress that Aunt Gertrude had given me for Christmas three years ago. I'd never worn it, but Mia loved it because she felt like a boarding-school girl from a Victorian adventure story in it, and Lottie loved it, too, because she thought it made Mia look like an angel. She used to iron every pleat and frill devotedly.

"I'm going into the bathroom first," I said as Mia came closer. She didn't say anything, just went past us toward the stairs, looking fixedly ahead of her.

"Hey!" I said a little louder. No reaction.

Where was she going? To the toilet on the first floor? Or to help herself to one of the remaining jam buns, although Grayson had staked his claim to those in advance.

"Mia?" Something seemed wrong with her.

"She's sleepwalking," whispered Grayson. "It's supposed to happen when the moon is full."

He was right, of course—she was sleepwalking. I'd done it, too, as a child. Swaying slightly but as if she knew where she was going, Mia went downstairs. Grayson and I followed her.

"Should we wake her?" I whispered.

"Better not. Or she might fall down the stairs."

Once at the bottom of the stairs, Mia stopped and stared at nothing for a while. Then she went straight to the front door of the house.

"Now I think we really had better wake her," said Grayson. Mia was already pressing the door handle down.

I put an arm around her shoulders. "Mia, darling, it's seventeen degrees outside—it's not a great idea going for a walk barefoot."

Mia was looking my way, but her eyes seemed to go straight through me.

"Creepy," I said.

Grayson snapped his fingers right in front of Mia's nose a couple of times, but she didn't even bat her eyelashes.

Nothing about her strangely empty expression changed, but at least she let me lead her up the stairs again. I kept on her right, Grayson on her left, and between us, we steered the little Victorian-boarding-school girl back to her room. When Mia was finally in bed again and I had covered her up, her eyelids, wide open until then, closed at once, and she murmured, "I know you, Mr. Holmes. You will solve this case."

"You can be sure of that, Watson," I whispered, and laid my head beside hers, just for a moment.

"I'd better go and lock the front door just in case she goes down again." Grayson was yawning.

"Thanks." Obeying an impulse, I snuggled under the covers beside my sister. I was just too tired to go back to my room. Even too tired to need to go to the bathroom. "You're really nice, Grayson."

"Don't push, Sherlock," muttered Mia, and Grayson said, "You're really nice yourself." But maybe I was just dreaming that bit.

OF COURSE LOTTIE hadn't been invited to Mrs. Spencer's traditional Twelfth Night tea party, and just as well. First, the Boker had picked today to try getting Charles together with her friend's just-divorced granddaughter, so Lottie would only have been in the way. And second, she'd have been anything but proud of us, because we did no credit at all to the good manners she'd tried to teach us.

It all started well. Dressed perfectly for the occasion, we rang Mrs. Spencer's doorbell on the dot.

I felt well rested, and therefore ready for another fencing match with the Boker. Mom hadn't woken me until midday, when Henry called to tell me that he had not been assassinated by Senator Tod in his dream. In fact, his little sister, Amy, had roused him, just as I rescued us by going into Grayson's dream. And after that there was no chance of dropping off to sleep again, because Amy had thrown up on Henry's bedside rug. She had a tummy bug and was well on the way to recovery now, but Henry thought he'd caught the same thing.

All the same, we made a date for the coming night—the

advantage of these dreams was that you could meet people even if you were sick in bed and not feeling too good. Even better, you couldn't infect another person however much you kissed. Although first, of course, there'd be things to discuss that we hadn't gotten around to last night.

However, before all that I had to survive this tea party.

The Boker's house was much closer than I'd thought, at the end of a quiet road up near Golders Hill Park. It was a very pretty, old house, redbrick like most of the others here, the doors and window frames painted white. Although it wasn't enormous, it had a very upmarket sort of atmosphere, and seemed to me much too big for an elderly lady living on her own. But maybe she had a household help. Or two household helps. And a butler. Anyway, she must employ a gardener. In the front garden alone, there were countless box trees and yews with the snow knocked off them, trimmed into globes and pillars, and as accurately clipped as if someone had gone over them with a pair of nail scissors first thing this morning. There was a bird in the middle: from the front it looked like a giant running duck or a fat stork, from behind it was something like a peacock, and although it was only topiary, made of clipped box bushes, it seemed to me to be giving us a definitely nasty look.

"The gardener here must have his hands full," said Mom.

"Yes." Ernest's smile was slightly forced. "Yes, the gardener here changes quite often—it's tough living up to Mother's expectations." He pointed to the duck, stork, and peacock creature. "That's why no one but Mother herself is allowed to touch Mr. Snuggles here."

Honestly, the British! They even give their plants pet names.

"It's really a very artistically clipped . . . er, vulture," said Mom.

For a moment Ernest's smile was genuine, not forced. "It's a peacock," he said, kissing Mom on the cheek. "Look, that's its tail."

"Oh. Of course. If that's part of it, then yes, it's obviously a peacock." Mom nervously straightened her hair. It was clear that she was scared stiff of Mrs. Spencer and her girlfriends, but she'd never have admitted it. She acted as if she were having a lovely time. Mia and I were a little bit scared, too, but only because as we left the house, Grayson had asked, kind of casually, whether we knew all the verses of the national anthem by heart. It seemed another of his Granny's old Twelfth Night customs was for everyone to salute the portrait of the Queen, put their hands on their hearts, and belt out the entire anthem with all its verses.

"But don't worry—that's right at the end when everyone's tanked up on orange punch," Grayson had added. That didn't really reassure us. If I'd known about singing the national anthem earlier, I could at least have looked up the text on the Internet. In our haste, however, all that came to mind was the opening of the Dutch national anthem, "*Wilhelmus van Nassouwe ben ik, van Duitsen bloed.* William of Nassau am I, and of Dutch blood." But I wouldn't score with that unless the Boker had invited a Dutch guest.

I'd wasted an hour finding an outfit that satisfied Lottie, and another hour trying to fend off her attack on my hair— no use. In the end I gave in and let Lottie construct a complicated set of braids on my head. Although she claimed that Scarlett Johansson had worn her hair just like that at the Oscars ceremony, I thought my head looked like a fruit basket minus the fruit. No wonder the peacock was giving me such a funny look.

"*Oh, say can you see, by the dawn's early light* . . . ," sang Mia beside me. "That's not right, is it?"

"Definitely not. Don't you dare sing that!"

Mia grinned. "I feel just like in *Pride and Prejudice*. The first visit to Lady Catherine de Bourgh . . . I mean, Boker," she whispered. In spite of last night's little outing, she looked fresh and pink-cheeked—the effect was still of a girl straight from the high Alpine meadows. Her pale-blond hair was brushed to fall smoothly over her shoulders; Lottie had just combed the fringe back and pinned it up in a little circlet over her part. I'd happily have changed places with her. And even more happily with Florence, whose chestnut locks flowed over a pale-green dress that Lady de Boker and her friends thought "perfectly charming." They were right.

Mrs. Spencer sighed deeply when she opened the door to us. "Oh, so you've all come," she said with a note of barely concealed disappointment in her voice. "But at least you've left that badly mannered mongrel at home."

"Buttercup is not a . . . ," Mia began, but Mom's elbow landed in her ribs and silenced her.

"Of course none of us wanted to miss your Twelfth Night tea party," said Mom. "We're so happy to be here."

Exactly. So happy that we almost had tears in our eyes.

From the inside, the house was just what the outside promised: full of well-tended antique furniture, with Christmas decorations on the mantelpiece, a spinet (it really was like *Pride and Prejudice*!), and an impressively spread table covered with plates of little tarts, scones, and sandwiches. I saw no sign of the orange punch that Grayson had mentioned, but there were pretty flower arrangements, plenty of tea in large round teapots, and elderly ladies with friendly smiles and lips painted coral. And—oh no!—Emily, cooing, "Surprise, surprise!" as Grayson stared at her, taken aback. Weren't we safe from Miss Spoilsport anywhere?

Probably not, if the Boker had anything to do with it. It turned out that she had invited Emily especially for Grayson's sake, and "because after all, she's one of the family too."

Neither Emily nor Grayson contradicted her, which made me roll my eyes again and go on looking around—surely that punch must be here somewhere. I was feeling more and more in need of something to fortify me.

The whole point of this so-called party was obviously to stand around with a cup of tea, sipping it now and then, chatting to the other guests, and smiling. Only people who'd had a lot of practice managed to eat something at the same time. I could do the rest of it all right.

I did find it rather difficult to smile at Emily, particularly when she poked a finger into my hairstyle and said, shaking her head sympathetically, "You know, Liv, less is sometimes more when it comes to style."

I could have snapped back with at least four crushing retorts, but my jokes were wasted on Emily, anyway. So I turned to the other guests instead. Not that there were all that many of them. The ladies wearing coral lipstick were Mrs. Spencer's bridge-playing friends, she'd known them since their schooldays, and if I'd heard correctly, they were called Bitsy Bee, Tipsy, and Cherry. (I hoped those weren't their real names.) Cherry had brought her granddaughter, a young woman called Rebecca who looked as if she was secretly longing for some orange punch as well. No wonder, because Cherry (Sherry? Chérie?) was letting everyone know that Rebecca was only recently divorced and urgently needed a new husband, this time one who would also be acceptable to her granny and her granny's friends. A dentist, for instance.

The old ladies themselves were all singles again, except for Tipsy, who wasn't widowed yet and had a husband in tow, a grouchy-looking old gentleman who was talking earnestly to another old gentleman. The Boker introduced the other old gentleman to us as "the Admiral." The Admiral had a white beard, terrifying bushy eyebrows, and a very military bearing; in fact, he looked as if he might turn to the portrait of the Queen any moment now and strike up the national anthem. But where was the portrait? The only picture above the mantelpiece was an oil painting of dead pheasants picturesquely lying beside a bowl of grapes. While I was examining the picture—the pheasants really did look very dead—Charles came out of the kitchen. I tried to look at him kindly, through Lottie's eyes, so to speak: broad-shouldered, with bright eyes, dazzling white teeth, little laughter lines around his mouth, sticking-out ears like a tribute to the Prince of Wales, bald patch even though he was only in his late thirties, terrible knitted sweater-vest with a pattern of lozenges. . . . Okay, right, I'd have to get in some more practice at looking at him through Lottie's eyes.

Charles was carrying an enormous bowl over to the table, and as I studied his ears, I remembered that I still had his hideous trapper's cap hidden in my room. I felt a brief pang of guilt.

"Is that the punch?" I asked, to take my mind off my guilty conscience.

Charles nodded. "Mother's famous hot Twelfth Night punch. Would you like some?"

I took a quick look at Ernest and Mom, but they were deep in conversation with Bitsy Bee, so I let Charles pour me a mug of punch. Mom wouldn't have minded, anyway. It tasted delicious—of orange, cinnamon, and a touch of cloves. You didn't notice the alcohol at all. What you did notice were the looks being cast at Charles from the spinet, where Tipsy, the Boker, Cherry, and the newly divorced granddaughter were standing. The attention they were paying him didn't escape Charles either. He smiled and waved to them, whereupon they all giggled like mad except for the granddaughter.

I coughed, and Charles turned back to me.

"How is Lottie?" he asked. "It's a pity she didn't come with you."

A pity, was it? And how about the woman in the café that he'd practically been holding hands with? And Cherry's granddaughter, who he'd been checking out only a second ago?

Nope, this time Charles wasn't going to get away from me with an excuse about a fire alarm gone wrong. I took another sip of punch. "Lottie's just fine," I claimed, adding, "She's gone to the cinema with a boyfriend."

"Oh." Charles plucked at his lower lip. "That . . . that's good."

"Yes, I think so too. Jonathan is such a nice guy."

"What Jonathan?" asked Mia, popping up beside me like a jack-in-the-box.

The Jonathan I've just this minute invented, dummy. "Lottie's Jonathan," I said, watching in alarm as Grayson and

Emily also came strolling over to us. And right behind them the Boker and the divorced granddaughter.

"Oh, *that* Jonathan—yes, he's a great guy." Mia snapped up two of the delicate little sandwiches at once. "And ever so romantic," she went on with her mouth full. "He gave Lottie one of those funny Japanese beckoning cats for Christmas."

I shot her a dark glance.

"One of those plastic cats?" asked Emily scornfully. "What's so romantic about that?"

"It . . . it can be very romantic," I murmured. Oh God, I needed more orange punch. In short order, and ignoring the fact that the Boker had joined us now, I snatched the ladle from Charles's hand and helped myself.

"A plastic cat isn't romantic, just cheap," said Emily.

No, it wasn't! It was a symbol. Not directly a symbol of love, but of happiness, a symbol with a wealth of tradition behind it going back to the famous *maneki-neko* cult. I'd read that on Wikipedia, and I wondered whether to tell Emily so. But know-it-all that she was, she might have read it on Wikipedia herself, and then she'd know that Hello Kitty had been inspired by the same cult too.

"What did Grayson give you, then, Emily?" asked Mia. Good question.

Emily pointed to her neck. "This lovely pendant."

"A figure eight lying on its side—the sign for infinity." The Boker smiled, much moved. "How very pretty."

The sign for *infinity*? Had Grayson lost his marbles? I drained my mug of punch in a single draft and tried to dart scornful glances at him.

"Yes, my grandson has a great sense of style." Mrs. Spencer patted Grayson's cheek, and he turned slightly pink. "When it comes to his girlfriend too." With a heavy sigh, she left Grayson alone and placed her hand on Charles's shoulder. "Would you show Rebecca the garden while it's still light, Charles dear? Rebecca is so interested in plants. She has a degree in biology. And she plays golf, don't you, Rebecca dear? Maybe you two could play a round of golf together sometime! But off you go into the garden, now! And do smile, Rebecca, so that Charles can see your beautiful teeth."

Rebecca managed to come up with a brave smile. I felt really sorry for her. Particularly as Charles didn't seem a bit interested in her beautiful teeth.

"Mother, it hasn't been properly light all day," he said. "And a garden isn't exactly an attraction in winter. What film have they gone to see?" He looked at me expectantly. "She doesn't like action films. I hope this Jonathan knows that."

Punch. Where was the ladle? It did smell delicious. While I was about it, I handed Rebecca a mug of punch too. She gave me a grateful smile.

"Who doesn't like action films?" asked Mrs. Spencer Senior, adding with a touch of pique, "My garden is worth seeing all the year round."

"He's talking about Lottie," Mia helpfully explained. "But I wouldn't put it that way. Lottie likes action films just fine when she has someone to hold her hand in the exciting scenes."

Charles swallowed convulsively. I was feeling sorry for him again. But it was his own fault. He'd had his chance. Now it was Jonathan's turn. Only, unfortunately Jonathan didn't exist.

"Oh, we can always see the garden another time," said Rebecca.

"Lottie? Isn't that the German nanny's name?" The Boker's eyes were wide with astonishment, and she didn't even notice Rebecca unobtrusively making herself scarce, along with her glass of punch. "What, may I ask, do you think you're doing associating with your brother's inamorata's nanny?"

"First . . . ," said Charles, looking around for Rebecca, but she was out of earshot, beginning a conversation with Florence and the Admiral. "And secondly . . ." He took a deep breath. "And thirdly, I'm not letting you tell me who I can like and who I can't."

Mrs. Spencer looked as if she might fall down in a faint right away. "Do you mean to say that you *like* that . . . that stupid, uneducated German girl?"

Mia indignantly gasped for air. Emily and Grayson were looking shocked as well. I was the only one keeping my cool. It must be because of the punch. Great stuff. I'd have to get the recipe.

Charles nodded. "Yes, I do like Lottie. Not that there's anything going on between us . . ."

I warmed to him again at that moment, so I forgave him for not putting Mrs. Spencer right about the words *stupid* and *uneducated*.

"Then you'd better make sure it stays that way." Mrs. Spencer compressed her lips. "It's bad enough your brother breaking his heart over that Wallis Simpson look-alike, and now my younger son shows a perverse liking for the servant class. I don't think I'll survive it." She was struggling for air. "I can hardly breathe!"

"Because you're choking on your own nasty nature," said Mia, not quite as quietly as maybe she thought.

"I could do with a little fresh air myself," Emily

intervened. "And I'd very much like to see around the garden, even in the twilight." She exchanged a glance with Grayson and took the Boker's arm. "And my mother wants me to ask what fertilizer you use on your hydrangeas."

Her diplomacy worked. Mrs. Spencer let herself be led away. "You're an angel, Emily," we heard her saying, and even if I wouldn't necessarily have agreed, I had to say that for once Emily was doing something sensible.

"Can I borrow your iPhone?" Mia had already taken it out of Grayson's pocket. "I have to Google 'inamorata.' And find out about this Simpson woman. And then I must read up on crimes of passion."

She was so angry she'd gone pale all over. I'd probably have felt the same if the punch hadn't made me feel nice and woozy.

"I'm thirty-nine years old, and I really don't need my mother telling me what to do anymore," Charles exploded, if a little late in the day.

"Lottie isn't stupid, and she's not after anyone's money either," hissed Mia at him, while her fingers flew over the display.

"I know that," said Charles.

"She's clever and beautiful—why would she want anything to do with a dentist? I mean, she could have anyone!"

"I know that," Charles repeated.

"Would you like some of the hot punch, Mia?" asked Grayson. "I think it would do you good."

"Are you crazy? She's only thirteen." I snatched the ladle from his hand. "Do you want her dancing on the tables? It's enough for one of us to be drunk. I feel sort of muzzy. I can't be responsible for my actions."

"You can't?" Grayson was grinning. "Very interesting."

"I never usually drink alcohol," I defended myself. "But your grandmother is really . . . and if I'm supposed to be singing the national anthem . . . oh, help, am I slurring my words already?"

"No!" Grayson was laughing uproariously now. "Liv, there isn't any alcohol at all in that punch—it's just hot orange juice with spices."

"What?" Wasn't I drunk after all? Not even a little tipsy? But then why had they made such a fuss about this famous punch? Famous! I ask you! But okay, that explained why you couldn't taste the alcohol in it.

"And as for the national anthem, I was only joking," Grayson went on, sounding pleased with himself. "No one has any intention of singing, I assure you. Either drunk or sober. And do you see any portrait of the Queen around here?"

I stared at him. "You made it up? You were just tricking us?" Reluctantly, I had to admit that he'd done it pretty well. "I'd never have expected you to show so much imagination and abject cunning," I said with an appreciative grin.

"Well, you underestimate me." Grayson took the ladle away from me again. "Now you know that it won't get you drunk and you don't have to sing, would you like a little more?"

"No, it wouldn't be any fun now." I looked thoughtfully at Grayson. With the expression on his face at the moment, I could imagine what he had looked like as a little boy, cheerful and perfectly happy with himself, nothing to worry about. "Did you really give Emily a symbol of infinity?"

Grayson's smile turned several degrees cooler.

"I mean, do you know how long infinity lasts?" I asked. "Longer than a lifetime."

He didn't answer.

"Bad news!" Mia handed Grayson's iPhone back. "If you want to get away with a crime of passion, you have to be quick about it!"

"Who are you telling?" muttered Charles.

"This time, the Boker won't get off scot-free," said Mia. "This time we must defend Mom's honor. And Lottie's. And our own. We can't put up with this kind of thing any longer."

Grayson raised his eyebrows. "What on earth," he asked, "is a Boker?"

LATER. WE ARGUED over who had thought it up. Mia insisted that it was her idea. But one thing is certain: on the way home from the tea party, we were racking our brains for ways to teach the Boker a lesson. This afternoon had been the last straw, and we wanted to hit her where it would hurt. And what occurred to us—or as Mia insisted, to her—was that clipped topiary bird standing in her front garden, Mr. Snuggles, whom no one was allowed to touch except Mrs. Spencer herself. It was obvious that she loved that box tree more than anything else in the world.

Yes, Mr. Snuggles was her vulnerable point. And on educational grounds, we had to strike that vulnerable point. Or rather clip it. Mr. Snuggles's hours as a peacock were numbered.

We spent the rest of the evening planning our coup, unobtrusively collecting all the equipment we'd need, and waiting for everyone else in the house to go to sleep at last. Just after midnight, we slunk out of the house. I'd have liked to go by bike, but the garage door squealed so badly that we'd have woken everyone. Anyway, it took us only ten minutes to walk to the Boker's house, and we passed the time by arguing over what creature we were going to turn the peacock into. Mia wanted it to be a penguin; I was in favor of a skunk, because for a skunk we wouldn't have to sacrifice the entire peacock tail—we could reuse parts of it.

However, the fact was that we'd greatly overestimated our ability to clip a box bush. Even in easier conditions—and it was dark, it was cold, we were in a hurry, and we hadn't been able to get hold of suitable tools on the spur of the moment—it probably would have been difficult to give the peacock a completely different shape. What was more, we set about it with different ideas in mind—"A penguin!" "No, a skunk!"—and Mia was working on Mr. Snuggles from the front with Ernest's handsaw, while I was clipping his rear end with the big household scissors.

At least no one disturbed us. We hadn't met anyone on the way here (and this was supposed to be a big city!), and everyone in Elms Walk seemed to be sleeping peacefully too. Although the moon was full. The *snip-snap* of my scissors and the *critch-cratch* of Mia's saw were the only sounds to be heard. Apart from our hissed curses.

"These scissors will only cut thin twigs," I complained. "If I carry on at this rate, the skunk won't be finished until Christmas next year!"

"And this saw will only get through what it's not supposed to! This is where a night-vision aid would really come in useful. Oops!" Mia held her breath for a moment. "There goes his beak."

"Never mind, skunks don't have beaks. . . . Come on, let's

change places. Heavy engineering is what we need back here."

At this point, we really knew that we wouldn't manage to give Mr. Snuggles a new identity—as either a penguin or a skunk. All the same, we went on sawing and snipping. When we finally stepped back and looked at our handiwork in the moonlight, we had to admit that what was left of the peacock didn't resemble any known form of life. Or any form at all, to be honest. It was just a heap of leaves and shredded branches.

Mia was the first to begin again. "Well, if we'd managed a suspiciously perfect penguin, I suppose the Boker might even have been pleased."

"Exactly, and that's not the point," I agreed. "Still, we could try clipping what's left of his midriff into a frog. . . ."

"There's a car coming." Mia pushed me down into the flower bed, and as the car drove past and turned into an entrance a few houses farther on, she said, "Forget the frog, we'll never do it, anyway. Let's get out of here."

She was right—we were hopeless gardeners, but all the same, we'd carried out our mission. So we'd better clear off before anyone saw us.

But there was no need to worry. Nothing moved in the streets on the way back either. Only a cat crossed our path, and a cat couldn't tell on us. Drunk with our victory, we crept into the house, where I took the saw back to Ernest's workshop—after cleaning off any give-away box leaves—while Mia hung the scissors up in their usual place in the kitchen. No one saw us except Buttercup, and good dog that she was she didn't bark, but followed us upstairs wagging her tail.

"That was fun," whispered Mia outside her room, and I had to agree. I felt a little like Zorro, avenger of the weak and disinherited, and with that sense of elation, I fell asleep.

I don't know why I didn't dream of anything nice, only of a man with a slouch hat and a huge knife in his hand chasing me through the deserted streets of Hampstead. Something seemed to be wrong with my feet; I could hardly raise them from the ground. And the man with the knife kept coming closer. I wanted to call for help, but no sound came out. Instead my leaden feet stumbled toward the nearest house. I might be able to get help there. When I saw the mint-green front door, I knew I was only dreaming. Of course. Hopefully, Henry was waiting on the other side of it.

Relieved, I turned to face my pursuer.

"I'll carve a Z into your forehead," he cried. It was Charles, and he wasn't wearing a slouch hat, but his trapper's cap. I looked at him, baffled. What was my unconscious mind trying to tell me this time?

"When I come out, I hope you'll be gone," I said. Then I cautiously opened the door.

"About time too." Henry looked around it. "Can I come in?"

"Sure," I said, trying to shoo Charles away with a gesture. "Just let me . . . er . . . tidy up a little first."

"No need." With a soft laugh, Henry closed the door. "Why are you so late? I thought you were never coming."

"Mia and I had something to do first. A little cosmetic alteration to Mrs. Spencer's front garden. She'd been saying horrible things about Lottie and Mom again today. So we chopped down her silly peacock."

"Mr. Snuggles?"

"You mean you know him too?"

Henry laughed. "Everyone knows Mr. Snuggles. You mean you and your sister really . . . ?"

"Chopped him up like matchwood, yup," I said proudly. "I'd like to be there when she looks out of her window in the morning."

Henry looked around, shivering. He rubbed his arms. As usual, he was wearing jeans and a T-shirt, and it was winter in my dream. "How about going somewhere else, let's say the London Eye?" And before I could answer, we were already in a glazed capsule high up on the giant wheel above the bank of the Thames, with London by night at our feet.

"You did that!" I said. I couldn't have imagined it in such detail myself, because while Ernest had brought us here on our sightseeing tour last September, the line of people waiting to ride on the Eye had been so long that we abandoned the idea.

"Yes, I did." Henry put his arm around my waist and pulled me close. "Romantic, eh?"

He was right. There was no one else in the capsule, and it wasn't moving. Glazed all around, it offered a fantastic view. Only, the green door didn't quite fit into this futuristic scene. I put my head back and looked up at the sky through the glass. The stars were sparkling so splendidly that Henry had probably given them an extra boost, but that made no difference.

"It's beautiful," I whispered.

"You're beautiful," Henry whispered back, sounding perfectly serious, and for a moment I forgot the stars and everything else. What in the world could be more important than kissing Henry under a glass dome high above the sea of lights that was London? Warmth spread through me, and Henry gave a little groan as I nestled closer to him. He kissed me harder, burying his hand in my hair.

Something hit the glass above us hard, and I jumped. There it was again. And again. It bounced off our capsule and fell to the depths below.

"What did that?" There were more and more of them. *Clonk. Clunk.*

"Not me this time," said Henry.

"Me neither," I assured him.

Henry stared up. "Too big for hailstones. They look more like . . . lucky cats?"

Now I saw them too. Beckoning Japanese cats made of plastic really were raining down from the sky and bouncing off the glass roof. A red-and-white one had just landed above us, and as it slowly slid over the domed roof and downward, it seemed to be looking straight into our eyes.

Henry let go of me. "Well, if you're not doing it on purpose, Liv, I'm afraid your unconscious mind is trying to tell us something."

I knew he was right: this was still my dream. I'd made it rain beckoning cats. Or rather, my worried unconscious mind was warning me not to go on kissing Henry but talk to him instead.

"Sorry," I said, dropping onto the seat in the capsule. The odd hail of cats had stopped falling.

"Didn't you like the cat?" Henry sat down at the other end of the seat, and I was glad of the distance between us. For the first time since he'd come through the door, I looked at him properly. He was even paler than usual, and there were dark shadows under his gray eyes.

"Has Amy given you her tummy bug?"

Henry raised an eyebrow. "You want to talk about stomach infections?" Was I wrong, or did I really hear a touch of annoyance in his voice?

"No, I only wanted to know how you are."

"Fine, thanks. I've drunk chamomile tea and taken a tablet, and right now I'm lying comfortably in my bed. With a bucket beside it just in case. So that the rug doesn't suffer a second time." He smiled a little wryly. "What's the matter, Liv?"

"Why haven't I ever been to your home? I don't even know what your room looks like."

"Well, we can easily change that," said Henry, and instead of sitting on the seat in a capsule on the big wheel I was perched on the edge of a bed. Henry was opposite me, sitting on a chair at a desk and grinning at me. "Voilà—my room. I just left out the bucket and tidied up a bit."

"I didn't mean it like that," I said, but all the same, I looked around with interest. There wasn't a lot of furniture. Just the broad bed, the desk, and its chair. I expected that his clothes were in the built-in wardrobe behind two white-painted slatted doors. My own green dream door beside them didn't quite fit into the red, white, and dark-blue color scheme.

Large quantities of books were simply stacked along the walls—obviously Henry didn't think much of bookshelves. There was a guitar leaning against one of the stacks. A basketball hoop hung above the bed, and the ball that went with it was lying on the rug, a soft version of the British flag. Textbooks and paper covered with Henry's handwriting towered up on the desk, and the music box I'd given him for Christmas stood there as well. He didn't have any pictures hung on the walls, only an enormous bulletin board over the desk with notes, postcards, and photos on it. Including one of me and Henry at the last Autumn Ball. I stood up to take a closer look.

"There are clean sheets on the bed," said Henry, reaching for my hand to pull me down on his lap.

My knees instantly went weak. Was this the time and the place to show Secrecy, Mom, and anyone else interested (me included) that they were wrong about my being sexually backward? Admittedly it was a great temptation, particularly as Henry's smile had never been more seductive, but then I remembered those lucky cats that my unconscious had brought raining down just now. Suppose that bombardment was only the beginning? Who knew what else my unconscious would do to make me talk to Henry and clear up a few important points? I pushed him away from me and tried not to let the glint in his eyes distract me.

"Henry, I don't want to know what your room looks like, or that your sheets have been changed," I began. "Or rather— well, yes, but then it ought to be your real bed. . . . Anyway, it ought to be real if we . . ." No, I wasn't getting anywhere this way. I stepped back and took a deep breath. "Why have I never been in your room for real? How come Grayson and Emily know about problems you've never mentioned to me? Why don't I know all those people in your photos when I'm awake?"

Henry sighed. "But you're here now."

"That's not the same!"

"Yes, it is," said Henry. A pair of basketball shoes fell on the rug out of nowhere, and there was a rain of socks, six in all, distributed picturesquely around the room. A pot with a dried-up houseplant in it appeared on the windowsill. "It's absolutely the same now."

"No, it isn't," I said firmly. "Because this is still a dream. My dream, to be precise. We never meet at your place—why not?"

"If that's the trouble, we can go there now." Henry pointed at the green door. "I'll show you all the photos, and you can tell me what your problem with the beckoning cat is."

"I'm talking about the real—"

I was interrupted by a scream. Someone shouted Henry's name. And at the same moment he disappeared, taking his room with him.

I was left alone with my green door on an enormous Union Jack flag, staring frustrated at the void.

ABOUT ME:
My name is Secrecy—I'm right here among you, and I know *all* your secrets.

7 January

Welcome back to the treadmill. So here we are: This is the first school day at the Frognal Academy minus Jasper Grant. And instead the kids at the Lycée Baudelaire in the little town of Beauvais, France, are meeting a new student today. According to my research, there's nothing at all interesting in Beauvais (apart from the wine they make with grapes from those parts. And the bus to Paris). The school doesn't even have a basketball team. So there won't be anything for Jasper to do but study.

Only joking. This is Jasper Grant we're talking about, let loose among French schoolgirls. You lucky girls in Beauvais, cheer up. Beauvais may be a dump in the usual way, but it's going to be a load of fun from now on.

However, it's not as if nothing was going on here at the moment—even without Jasper, I have one or two items of news for you. First: Ever since Mrs. Lawrence got back from Lanzarote, she's been throwing up every morning. And she's been seen buying folic acid supplements at the pharmacy—so let's congratulate her on her pregnancy, and we can assume that Mrs. Lawrence will soon be Mrs. Vanhagen. Well, as soon as Mr. Vanhagen is divorced from the present Mrs. Vanhagen.

Secondly—and if you ask me, this is much more of a scandal—vandals chopped down the big box-tree peacock in Elms Walk last night. I'm sure many of you knew it. It even had a name, Mr. Snuggles. Dear old Mr. Snuggles stands—sorry, stood—in Grayson and Florence Spencer's grandmother's front garden, and he'd won several prizes for topiary. I'll give you links below to a couple of articles about him in gardening magazines. Wasn't he a magnificent sight? But now he's only a sad little heap of leaves and twigs. Rest in peace, Mr. Snuggles. And may whoever did that to you burn in Hell.

Right, now I must run or I'll be late for lessons. And no, I'm not telling you what my next lesson is! ☺

See you soon!

Secrecy

10

WHEN MIA AND I appeared in the kitchen at seven the next morning, still sleepy, all the others were there already, and they seemed to be in a state of great agitation. Ernest was on the phone in the dining room next door, talking frantically, and Florence was sitting at the table in tears. Mom was patting her shoulder.

"What's happened?" I asked in alarm. Maybe a much-loved family member had died. Or a nuclear power plant had blown up? Even Grayson was looking kind of upset.

Lottie was squeezing grapefruit juice as she did every morning, but she, too, had cheeks red with emotion. "Guess what?" she said to us. "Someone chopped down a tree in Mrs. Spencer's garden last night."

I stared at her incredulously for a moment. Not a much-loved family member, then, not a nuclear power plant. My eyes went to Florence's face, which was wet with tears. Was she really crying over Mr. Snuggles?

Unobtrusively, I slipped past Lottie and over to the coffee

machine, put the biggest cup I could find under it, and pressed the cappuccino button. Twice.

"A tree? But why?" asked Mia with a perfectly judged mixture of curiosity and mild surprise.

"No one knows," said Lottie. "But Mrs. Spencer has already called in Scotland Yard. It was a very valuable tree."

I almost laughed out loud. Yes, sure. I bet they had a special gardening squad to investigate such cases. Scotland Front Yard. *Good day, my name is Inspector Griffin and I'm looking into the murder of Mr. Snuggles.*

"Why is Florence crying?"

"She's crying because she loved the tree so much," said Mom.

For goodness' sake—it hadn't even been a proper tree, more of a bush. A bush forced into an unnatural shape.

"It wasn't just any old tree. I've known Mr. Snuggles since I was a little girl." Florence sniffed. Her eyes were red with crying. "We practically grew up together."

Mia and I exchanged a quick glance. Oh God. I needed coffee, and fast! Was the machine really going slower than usual today?

"It really was a beautiful . . . er . . . example of topiary," said Mom, stroking Florence's hair. "I really do wonder what kind of people would do a thing like that."

Well, people like you and me, I'd say.

"Horrible, nasty people who are envious of everything beautiful!" Florence gave a loud sob.

What? No, we weren't envious. And we'd have turned Mr. Snuggles into a beautiful skunk if he hadn't been so darned awkward about it. I quickly looked past Mia at the kitchen scissors hanging on their hook on the wall. Had all that butchery blunted them? Maybe they even had notches in the blades. I glanced surreptitiously at the palms of my hands for welts and blisters. Yes, that sore place on my forefinger was new.

My double cappuccino was ready at last. I gulped it so greedily that I burned my tongue.

"It was probably some young louts on their way home from a party," said Ernest, coming in from the next room with the telephone. "Although Mother suspects an envious neighbor."

"Has she really called in Scotland Yard?" asked Mia.

Ernest smiled. "A friend of hers used to work there—you met him yesterday, the man with the big beard."

"The Admiral?"

Ernest nodded. "Mother is in such a state that she asked him to turn to his former colleagues. But I really don't see what they can do about it."

So I should hope. I drank some more coffee and wondered whether we'd left footprints in the flower bed, and they'd put the forensic department on our trail. Or fibers from our jackets . . . No, nonsense! First, the earth all around the clipped box bushes was completely covered with fine mulch, and second, Scotland Yard wasn't about to send its forensic experts out for a clipped box tree, Admiral or no Admiral. Why was he called Admiral, anyway, if he'd been in the police?

Someone touched my shoulder, and I jumped. But it was only Grayson moving me aside on his way to the coffee machine.

"Everything okay, Liv?" he asked.

"Yes. Yes, why?" I replied, quickly hiding my hand with

the suspicious sore place on it behind my back and almost dropping my cup as I did so. "I had a wonderful night's sleep. Long, deep sleep."

Mia clicked her tongue warningly, and I stopped at once, before I could sound even more suspicious. There was nothing left of yesterday's wonderful elation when I'd felt like Zorro. I was feeling like a criminal instead. Here in England maybe they sent you to prison for what we'd done. Particularly as Mr. Snuggles had obviously been no ordinary bush but some kind of local celebrity.

But the full extent of it became clear to me only when we arrived at Frognal Academy. Everyone there seemed to know Mr. Snuggles as well. And they all knew about his demise because Secrecy had put it in her blog first thing this morning.

Or so I heard at the school entrance from my friend Persephone Porter-Peregrin. I took her smartphone from her hand and read the blog entry. Rest in peace, Mr. Snuggles. An obituary for a topiary peacock. In a school gossip blog. Would you believe it?

Even more incredible, how on earth had Secrecy come by her information so soon? It was positively uncanny. I looked around for Mia, but she had already disappeared into the crowd. Florence's tears hadn't made her feel guilty, unlike me. I even got the impression that she rather enjoyed all the fuss. I wished I could feel the same, but Secrecy's obituary of Mr. Snuggles only made it worse. If even someone as fundamentally nasty as Secrecy was claiming the moral high ground . . .

Stupid gossipmonger! Suppose she lived in Elms Walk, and that was why she'd been able to take a look at the Boker's front garden so early in the morning? At least that would explain it. We'd have to check the addresses of the people on Mia's list of suspects as soon as we could.

A red-haired girl smiled at me in passing and said, "Don't let it bother you, Liv. I'm waiting until my wedding night too!"

Baffled, I stared as she walked away. Who on earth was she?

"Look, here's the link Secrecy gave to a report in a gardening magazine—wasn't Mr. Smithers just amazing?" Persephone had taken her smartphone back and was batting her long lashes dramatically. "He was even on a list of protected plants of the British Isles. . . ."

"Mr. Snuggles," I corrected her.

"Yes, that's what I said." She linked arms with me. "You really have to wonder who'd do a thing like that, don't you? They must be terribly disturbed!"

"Hmm," I said. "Maybe they had good reasons. If there was more than one of them, I mean."

"Hey, Liv! I think it's really mean the way they keep going on at you," said a girl I didn't know from Adam, or rather Eve. Persephone piloted us around her as if she were a pillar or something.

"It's typical—they always blame the woman. Whereas it could just as well be Henry's fault," said the unknown girl. "Just wanted to let you know I'm on your side."

"Er, thanks, very nice of you," I said.

"You're welcome. We girls have to stick together, and Secrecy's a slag and a disgrace to feminism."

Okay. This was getting stranger all the time. "Do you

know her?" I whispered to Persephone, but my friend's thoughts were still dwelling on Mr. Snuggles.

"What good reason could anyone have to murder an innocent tree?" She shook her head.

"Murder sounds so . . . well, excessive, don't you think? I mean, even if Mr. Snuggles were a person—which he isn't, he's a plant—then it would only be a case of injury because he still has his roots, so he can always grow again."

"A plant is a living creature too," said Persephone quietly.

Oh God. That made me a murderess.

"I thought Mr. Smithers—"

"Snuggles!"

"—was so cute. When I was little and we went to the park on Sundays, we always passed him, and he looked a little different every time." She heaved a melancholy sigh.

This was unbearable. So were all the curious glances cast at me even up on the next floor. And all the whispering. Persephone didn't notice. Her mind was entirely on Mr. Snuggles.

"Obviously nothing in this wicked world is safe from vandalism," she wailed.

I decided to change the subject. "I wonder how Jasper's getting along? On his own with all those French kids. And he never got good marks for French. I bet he can't even ask the way to the toilet, poor thing."

Guess what, my tactics worked. The mention of Jasper's name made Persephone forget Mr. Snuggles right away. "Yes, but that has its good points—he won't be able to chat up the pretty French girls," she said cheerfully. "I mean, it'll be difficult for him to flirt in a language he doesn't know."

Yes and no—intelligent conversation wasn't exactly Jasper's strong point, so his attempts at flirtation might actually be more successful if he just gave a dazzling smile, whereupon they'd probably overlook his language problems. But I didn't say so to Persephone. I was just relieved that we'd stopped talking about that silly box tree.

However, my relief lasted only until the lunch break. Even on the way to the cafeteria, I had a sinking feeling, and not just because everyone was staring at me again. It was as if there was something in the air, something nasty (and I don't mean the smell of steamed cabbage, which was on the menu for lunch today). The sinking feeling got even worse when a text from Mia arrived. Mia never usually texted me. Texting on the ancient numerical keypads of our phones was pure torture. It took you a full minute to type in *Hello*. Four twice, two once, five six times running but with a little pause in between them, then six three times. And too bad if you made a mistake, because then you had to begin again at the beginning.

Mia's text had only two words in it: *giy aaat*. I stared at the display, frowning. *Giy aaat?* What was that supposed to tell me? Was it an abbreviation? A secret code? Or had she just hit the wrong keys? I thought of texting her back, but given the time it would take me to type *What do you mean?* and send the text, I could just as well go over to the lower school canteen and ask her in person. Only, I didn't feel like it. I was so close to my own cafeteria now that I could smell the food, and I was hungry. Also I wanted to see Henry. I'd better simply call her.

"Hey, Liv!" A couple barred my way. "Is it true?" asked

the girl. I knew her—she was one of Persephone's friends. Itsy. Unfortunately that wasn't her real name any more than her best friend's real name was Bitsy, but for reasons I didn't understand, I could never remember what they were actually called. So I just said, "Hi!" in a friendly voice. "Is what true?" I added.

The boy with Itsy on his arm was Emily's brother, Sam. He and Itsy had been a happy couple since the Autumn Ball.

"Is what Secrecy writes true?" asked Sam. He didn't like me because last year Emily had made him ask me to go to the ball with him and I'd said no.

"You read Secrecy's Tittle-Tattle blog?" Even worse: Was he interested in my sex life? But maybe Sam and Itsy themselves were in a similar situation and were unsettled by the whole discussion. In which case, they just wanted my advice, which was . . . well, kind of nice. So I looked first Sam and then Itsy straight in the eye and said, "Yes, it's true. But it makes no difference at all. There isn't a set time for these things. Everyone can make up their own minds when and whether to do it. So don't let other people influence you— you just go your own way, never mind what anyone else thinks." That was the stuff to give them! I ought to be a speechwriter. Or a pastor. Stand by what you think is right! Dare to be yourselves!

But obviously Sam didn't agree. "You ought to be ashamed of yourself," he said, and Itsy added, "I'd never have thought it! Shame on you. Come along, Sam."

Shame on me? What was the matter with them? I turned back to my cell phone and almost collided with Arthur. Like me, he'd been staring at the display of his own phone.

With great presence of mind, I put on my enemy-general expression and raised my chin. "Arthur."

Oddly enough, Arthur's expression wasn't as cool and superior as usual, but almost a bit . . . could it be sympathetic? "Oh, hell, Liv," he said. "Maybe you'd better not go in there."

I raised my chin if anything a little higher. "First, I couldn't care less what other people say about me, and second, I'm hungry." *And third, I can do without your sympathy, thanks very much.*

Shaking my head, I pushed past him into the cafeteria. Henry was sitting there at the back, at our usual window table, along with Grayson, Florence, Emily, and a friend of Florence's called Callum Caspers. A plate of selections from the salad buffet stood at the empty place next to Henry, which meant that there was ground beef Wellington to go with the cabbage today. I hadn't been able to stomach the school's ground beef since I found a fingernail clipping in it one day, as Henry knew, so he had thoughtfully chosen me a plate of mixed salad in advance. That was really nice of him. I'd almost reached the table when the cell phone I was holding rang. Now Henry, Grayson, Emily, Callum, and Florence noticed me, too, and fell silent.

"With you in a minute." I put the phone to my ear. Mia. I could hardly make out her voice.

"Didn't you get my text?"

"*Giy aaat?* Yes, but what's it supposed to mean?"

"Get out!" snapped Mia. "It says *get out*! I was typing blind. They know. So get out!"

However, it was too late for that. Florence was already on

her feet, standing in front of me with her arms folded. "Is it true?" she asked.

"Er." Slowly, I lowered the phone. Where was I supposed to get out to, and why?

"Liv." Henry was the only one whose face looked friendly. And sympathetic.

"This is what Secrecy posted seven minutes ago." Emily had brought out her smartphone and was reading from it. *"PS—I've just found out who have Mr. Snuggles on their consciences. Liv and Mia Silver. Obviously it was a childish act of revenge on Grayson and Florence's grandmother because they don't like her. So a cultural feature of our part of town that took decades to grow has been the victim of their silly prank."*

Secrecy. She couldn't know—it was impossible! I felt weak at the knees.

"Is it true?" Florence repeated quietly, but all the same, everyone in the room seemed to hear her.

And they were all staring at me, every last one of them. "Because if so, I'm never going to sit at the same table as you, ever again." With a last, infinitely scornful look, she ran past me and out of the cafeteria. Emily and Callum followed close on her heels.

Grayson also got to his feet. The expression on his face hurt me almost physically. He looked so incredibly disappointed.

"Grayson . . . ," I began, without knowing exactly what I was going to say. The one thing I really wanted was for none of this to be really happening. Why couldn't it simply be a dream?

"I must go—I have to set up my experiment before

chemistry," said Grayson, avoiding my eyes. "See you later. Then maybe you can explain what you two thought you were doing."

Henry drew me down on the chair beside his and held my hand very tightly. "It's not so bad, honestly," he assured me. "Have some salad?"

AT LEAST THERE was one good thing about this whole ghastly business: I found that I could now turn myself into a perfect jaguar without a hitch. I looked so deceptively real that even Senator Tod showed proper respect when we unexpectedly met and faced each other.

In human form, I'd certainly have screeched with fright to see him suddenly coming around the corner like that. And then I'd probably have run away, like last time. But my jaguar self instinctively crouched, the hairs rose on the back of my jaguar neck, and I bared my sharp canine teeth.

That seemed to impress Senator Tod. He slowly took two steps backward, murmuring, "Take it easy, nice kitty, take it easy."

Aha! So he could speak in a perfectly normal way if he wanted to. At close quarters, he didn't look nearly as menacing as from a distance—the face beneath that slouch hat seemed to be perfectly human. It wasn't a skull or a zombie face crawling with maggots, as I'd secretly feared, just an ordinary man's face, the kind that you might see on any street:

rather round, a strong nose, lower lip slightly fuller than his upper lip, and pale-blue eyes, although there was a glint in them that I couldn't quite place, and it scared me. Apart from that glint, however, he had seemed quite harmless.

A deep growl emerged from my throat. No way was I a nice kitty! This was my corridor, and I was feeling like a really nasty kitty today. I'd not had a particularly good week.

"Okay," he said, taking another step back. "Then I'll come back another time." Only when there was plenty of space between us did he turn and disappear around the next corner.

I hissed after him. Then I strolled back to Henry's door, sat on the doorstep, and devoted all my attention to licking my paw. My own door was right opposite, but I didn't feel in the least like going back there, never mind how tired I might be.

I was being tormented by dreadful nightmares every night—nightmares in which Mr. Snuggles was alive and sobbing bitterly, or I myself put out roots and mutated into a bush, whereupon Mrs. Spencer, Florence, and Grayson all worked me over with a pair of scissors. Out here in the corridor, it was so much more peaceful than in my own dreams. And I had any amount of time to practice shape-changing.

With an elegant movement, I coiled the jaguar tail around my feet. Guilty feelings, shame, and rage were obviously just the thing to help with concentration, or my concentration, at least. The jaguar was one of my easiest tricks now, like the barn owl, and today I'd even managed to turn into a breath of air. Before that, I'd hovered invisibly along the corridors for some time, feeling pleased with myself. Past Mom's door (MATTHEWS'S MOONSHINE ANTIQUARIAN BOOKS— OPEN FROM MIDNIGHT TO DAWN) and Mia's door, which I recognized because at the moment it was guarded by a waist-high version of Fuzzy-Wuzzy. Fuzzy-Wuzzy was Mia's ancient cuddly toy, a floppy-eared rabbit that she had loved to bits when she was a little girl. He looked that way, too, with his nibbled ears, only one eye (the other had been left behind in Hyderabad, India), and wearing faded dungarees that had once been yellow. Unfortunately he wasn't at all cute blown up to his present size, but rather scary. The giant Fuzzy-Wuzzy was sitting outside a wooden door painted violet blue and, oddly, was holding a fox's tail in one paw, maybe to frighten visitors off. I looked at him hard, wondering at the same time how come I could see all this when I was just a breath of air, and of course a breath of air doesn't have eyes. I should have left that out (the wondering, I mean), because, oops, suddenly my sense of gravity was back and I dropped to the floor with a bump. Never mind, I knew now that I could do it, and I felt proud of that. When Henry came along, I'd show him right away.

Where was he this time? Hopefully no one was keeping him from sleeping again. In his family, his was always the first name to be shouted when they had a problem. And unfortunately they always seemed to have a problem just when Henry and I were embarking on a serious conversation. I stretched and began sharpening my claws on his doorpost. When Spot did that, someone always jumped up to let him out.

Henry had been a great comfort to me this week. To be honest, he was my only comfort. All the others were treating Mia and me like a couple of lepers, me even more than Mia because according to Mom and Lottie I was "the elder and more sensible sister and ought never to have allowed it." Mia said she'd have done it, anyway, even without me, and I was inclined to believe her. All the same, of course Mom and Lottie were right.

At school, all the fuss about the topiary peacock had died down a bit by now, but Mia and I were still getting nasty looks or remarks from total strangers usually keen to tell a moving story about how they'd known Mr. Snuggles all their lives. Fortunately Secrecy had changed the subject in her blog by now, and Henry assured me that grass would soon grow over the whole thing again.

For the others, maybe, but not for Florence.

She was refusing to sit at the same table as me, just as she'd said she would, and had ostentatiously picked a place at the other end of the cafeteria. Of course Emily had moved with her, and I couldn't say that really bothered me—on the contrary, it was good to have her leaving me in peace for once. The only trouble was that it meant Grayson didn't sit with us either.

In view of the new developments, Persephone wasn't sure whether going around with me would be bad for her own popularity, so at first Henry and I had our table all to ourselves at lunchtime, but on Wednesday we were joined by a couple of boys from Henry's basketball team.

And Arthur.

"Who'd have thought it—our Liv a professional killer? A paid-up member of the front-garden Mafia," he said, giving me a broad smile. "If you ask me, the general importance of clipped box is overestimated in this country. Why don't we sit down?" (That was a rhetorical question, since he was already sitting down.) "We're having a spot of trouble with a magnolia at home. Someone ought to teach it a lesson."

Although I didn't for a moment forget that he was the enemy general, the cunning, unscrupulous Arthur, I was kind of grateful for this gesture. Even Henry, who had no problem about sitting alone with an outcast like me, seemed glad of the company. I was sure he hadn't forgotten all the lies his former best friend had told, not to mention that nasty business in the mausoleum, but when he grinned at Arthur now, I knew he felt, like me, that this was nice of Arthur. We couldn't be friends again, but at least we'd settled on a kind of truce.

The other two boys, Gabriel and Eric, couldn't have cared less what I'd done. They didn't know Mr. Snuggles, they weren't interested in plants, and they thought Secrecy's blog was silly, girly stuff, so they never read it. I liked them both. On principle, Persephone adored all boys on the basketball team, so she joined our table again. (And for half an hour, she entirely forgot Jasper, far away in France.) To be honest, lunch was more fun now than it used to be with Florence and Emily.

It was only Grayson I missed. Not just at lunchtime. I missed our little conversations beside the coffee machine in the morning, or when we were arguing over who got the bathroom first in the evening. He was avoiding me and said only the bare essentials, if that, when we met. Instead he looked at me sadly, as if he couldn't put his feelings into words.

It was worst at home—where of course Florence also avoided sitting at the same table as Mia and me. She left the room without a word as soon as one of us came in. Mom, Ernest, and Lottie sighed when that happened, but they were full of understanding for Florence's feelings, whereas they didn't show any sympathy at all for the reasons behind our butchery in the Boker's front garden.

We'd tried hard to justify ourselves by listing all the horrible things the Boker had done, the unforgivable remarks she'd made, and, yes, they agreed that now and then she hadn't behaved too well, but they always ended up asking why poor innocent Mr. Snuggles had to pay for it. The crazy thing was that by now I myself didn't understand how we could have done it.

Mia did not feel the same. She still thought the whole thing would have been really cool if we hadn't been caught. And that brought us to the heart of the matter: Where the hell did Secrecy get her information? Mia and I hadn't even had time to tell anyone—and there it was in her blog already.

No one but Henry had known. But we'd had that conversation in my dream, where no one else could have been eavesdropping. Or could they? Maybe someone had slipped through the doorway with Henry disguised as a breath of air? Or an amoeba?

Of course it had occurred to me that Henry himself might have been the security leak, but I had suppressed the thought quickly—if I couldn't trust even Henry, then who could I trust? No, he wouldn't do a thing like that to me. At the very most, he might have passed on the information without knowing it would reach Secrecy. When I tackled him about it, for once he hadn't been amused but rather annoyed. And then he'd sworn that he had not told anyone about it, even by mistake.

I believed him.

Lost in thought, I scratched my ear with my hind leg. Of course I believed him, I loved him! Without Henry, the last week would have been unbearable. Mom's deeply disappointed glances ("I thought you two realized how important this relationship is to me"), Lottie's horror ("This isn't like you girls at all—you normally wouldn't hurt a fly!"), Grayson's bafflement ("I just don't understand why you did it!"), Florence's contempt (no words for it), and Ernest's efforts to blame it all on adolescence ("You're still children. Only the other day I read that when the brain is developing during puberty, short circuits are preprogrammed")—well, all that hit me much harder than I liked. If I could have turned time back by sacrificing a part of my body, I'd have done it like a shot.

When I told Mia so, she looked at me, shocked. "Are you serious? You'd give a toe for it never to have happened?"

I nodded. "Or a kidney. Or an ear."

"You're crazy," said Mia. "We wanted to pay the Boker back, and we did. If it hadn't been for stupid Secrecy, we'd feel like heroes now—and the hell with that silly bird. I'm going to crack down on Secrecy. Sooner or later she'll give herself away, and then I'll nab her."

So far, unfortunately, that didn't look likely—at least, Secrecy didn't live in Elms Walk, as I had been assuming. In fact, not a single student from Frognal Academy lived in Mrs. Spencer's neighborhood. We'd checked all the addresses.

As if all that wasn't punishment enough, Mom insisted that we must apologize to Mrs. Spencer and offer her financial compensation.

It was not a nice moment when we stood in front of her murmuring, "We're very sorry," with Mom's stern eye on us. I was only glad that Florence and Grayson weren't there— I'd probably have died of shame. The Boker refused to accept our apology, but she didn't turn down the financial compensation. Of course, she said, the value of Mr. Snuggles had been incalculably high, and sad to say our savings wouldn't bring him back, but she thought it essential to take our money. That way we'd learn that our malicious actions had consequences. In fact, the loss hit us hard: for the first time we'd saved up nearly enough for a really good smartphone—and now of course we could forget about that.

And as for the educational effects, they were limited to extending our English vocabulary with a few new terms like *insubordination* and *collateral damage* (both out of the Boker's lecture on the depravity of young people today).

"If there's one thing I'm proud of, it's my tendency to insubordination," announced Mia as we set off for home. As for me, I felt like a living case of collateral damage.

But don't they say that what doesn't kill you makes you stronger? Or as Mr. Wu used to put it, "When water has been poured away, you can't bring it back." In other words, what happened had happened, and life went on.

You just had to think of the positive aspects: not only had I expanded my vocabulary, I was really good at shape-changing now. With the Boker's face in my mind's eye, I could easily concentrate on turning from a jaguar into a small barn owl. And from a barn owl into Spot, the Spencers' fat cat. A moment of concentration, and I looked like Buttercup. Now I was a beckoning Japanese cat. A bottle of fizzy drink. A dragonfly with shimmering wings. Back to the jaguar again. A breath of air. Myself in a Catwoman costume. Great!

"Not bad!" said Henry's voice behind me, and I spun around. He had come out of his door unnoticed during my little performance, or at least so I supposed. "You're really getting good!"

"I know!" I said cheerfully, snapping my fingers and changing the Catwoman costume for jeans and a T-shirt. "Senator Tod ran away from me just now. What shall we do next? I fancy a bit of roller-skating." Another snap of my fingers, and Henry and I had Rollerblades on our feet. I turned a high-spirited pirouette.

"You're in a good mood." When Henry laughed, little lines formed around his eyes. "No acute attacks of guilt and self-hatred?"

"Nope. I've taken Mr. Wu's advice: never mind how hard the times are, he always says, carry a green branch in your heart and a songbird will settle on it."

"Wow—where on earth does Mr. Wu get all these hoary old sayings from?" Henry reached for my hand, and we skated down the corridor together. That was one of the things I liked about him—he was always ready to fall in with my feelings, and he asked no questions. "So Senator Tod came back, did he?"

"Yes, from over there," I said, pointing to the place beyond Mom's door where a corridor branched off sideways.

"Was he talking in riddles again?" Henry whirled me around in a curve. I laughed. This was really fun.

"Not really. He called me a nice kitty and said he'd be back in a . . ." I fell silent, because at that very moment, there was a loud bang, and a man in a tropical helmet and a safari outfit came around the corner, with a gun under each arm and three huge knives in his belt. I had to look twice, but yes, it was Senator Tod in another disguise. We came to a halt right in front of him, and he threw back his head and laughed his crazy laughter.

"Shall we change shape?" I whispered to Henry, who was staring, fascinated, at Senator Tod. "I can't see him shooting a dragonfly successfully. Or a fruit fly."

But Senator Tod didn't seem to be about to use his guns. "I set out to hunt leopards, and now I have a couple of teenagers on skates in my sights," he said.

Jaguars, for heaven's sake! Why did people always get them mixed up?

"I know you two," Senator Tod went on. "You ran away from me not so long ago—and I know your names. Henry Grant and Liv Silver."

My cheerful mood was gone. I didn't quite like a man whose name meant "death" knowing *my* name.

"Almost right," said Henry, raising his eyebrows arrogantly. It was all very well for him to talk; after all, the Senator had given him the wrong surname. Jasper's surname, to be precise. "And you are . . . ?"

"Him again," said someone behind us. It was Arthur—I hadn't noticed that we were skating past his showy metal door with the words CARPE NOCTEM engraved on it. Although it didn't look quite so showy now. It had definitely shrunk.

"Arthur Hamilton," stated the big game hunter. "The boy who looks like an angel but has a heart of stone."

"So you two have met before?" I was feeling a bit better when Arthur came and stood beside us, because the Senator knew his name too.

"Yes, this character's been wandering around acting strangely for some time." Arthur pushed a lock of fair hair back from his forehead. "Although he hasn't introduced himself to me yet."

"Then let me do it—this is Senator Tod," I said, and Henry added, "Tod Nord, as in North."

"North as in south?" asked Arthur.

Senator Tod nodded.

"And is that your only name?" asked Henry, although the obvious question, of course, would have been *How do you know our names?* Or *What do you want from us?*

Senator Tod laughed again. "Oh, no! I have many names, my boy. I told you some of them at our first meeting."

"You're not a demon, by any chance?" I inquired as casually as possible. "From ancient times, Lord of Shadows and Darkness and all that?"

Both Henry and Arthur shot me glances of annoyance.

"Well, I was only wondering . . . ," I murmured. "He talks in that high-flown way, he says he has many names—I just wanted to be on the safe side."

"A demon, no, I'm not a demon," said Senator Tod, and he sounded almost regretful. "But Dona dents rotor!" He pointed behind him. "Tornado, nerd, sot—I have all those in me!"

He was starting all that confused stuff again.

"And your door is in this corridor, is it?" Arthur pointed to a yellow wooden door. "Is it that one?"

"Nice try," said Senator Tod. He slowly took aim with his guns, fixing his pale-blue eyes on us. "What happens if you shoot people in here? Do they really die?"

"Of course not," I said, scratching my arm uncomfortably.

"They don't?" Senator Tod smiled. "But you're not sure, are you, Goldilocks? Why don't we try it? Bang bang." He cocked one of the triggers. "Which of you shall I take out first? The girl?"

Okay, so this was the moment to turn into a dragonfly. Or better still, a killer hornet.

"But you'd need a gun for that," said Henry before I'd made up my mind which. Taken aback, Senator Tod glanced left and then right. Instead of his guns, he was now holding two wriggling leopard cubs under his arms. And the knives in his belt had turned into long sausages.

"Wow!" I said admiringly. "Did you do that, Henry?"

"Bang bang," said Henry, and Arthur laughed out loud.

"Ouch, they have sharp claws, right? But do you know what's worse?" Arthur pointed behind him. "Here comes Mommy!"

Sure enough, a huge leopardess was prowling along the corridor toward us, growling even more fiercely than me just now.

Senator Tod was trying in vain to shake the leopard cubs off. "Get them away from here!" he cried, squeezing his eyes shut. But when he opened them, the little leopards were still there. And there was no sign of a gun anywhere.

"Come on, you guys, let's go," said Arthur, linking arms with both of us and leading us through his doorway. The last thing we saw before we closed the door was the leopardess crouching to spring.

12

I DON'T KNOW what I'd expected—maybe that we'd land in some kind of bat cave, or in Arthur's parents' grand house with its swimming pool and private cinema, but this surprised me. We were standing in a huge library. The place was flooded with light, and high above us was a mighty white-and-gold domed roof. The room was circular and surrounded by bookshelves three floors high, with galleries running around it for access to the books. Long tables with brass reading lamps and workstations, enough of them for dozens of school classes, branched out in a star shape from a central area where you presumably borrowed books. It all looked both modern and wonderfully old-fashioned, and a quiet "Wow!" escaped me.

"The Reading Room of the British Library," said Henry, obviously not quite as impressed as I was.

"Yup. I like having it all to myself." Arthur swung himself up on one of the tables. "So what do you think of our big game hunter?"

"Is he being torn to pieces out there at the moment?" I

asked. Glancing at Henry's feet, which were now in ordinary shoes, I switched from my Rollerblades to sneakers.

"Depends how far he's in control of himself," said Arthur, shrugging his shoulders. "He wasn't doing too well against Henry's and my powers of imagination—so now either he'll have accepted the leopards as real and is terrified, or he's taken over at the wheel and he's running things himself."

"Or he's waking up." Henry yawned and leaned against the table. "One way or another, I don't think he's particularly terrifying."

"Well, you should," said Arthur. "The fact that he knows our names and is out and about in these corridors shows that he's closer to us than we'd like."

I looked at Arthur. "You think he's someone we know in real life?" That was a creepy idea.

Arthur shrugged his shoulders again. "In any case, he knows who we are, and I don't like that one little bit."

"Nor do I," Henry admitted. "I'm pretty sure I've never met the guy before."

"But couldn't it just be coincidence? Maybe he eavesdropped on us and got to know our names that way? I mean, why would we be the only ones walking around in these corridors?" My theory was that anyone could be here who found his or her door in a dream, tried to open it and go through. Except that most people didn't seem to see their doors. Or simply didn't try to go through them. Otherwise this place would be teeming with crowds of people.

Arthur gave a snort of amusement. "So Senator Tod—someone we've none of us seen in our lives—just happens to be roaming around outside our dream doors, just happens to call us by our right names, and just happens to utter these mysterious threats of his?"

Er, well, presumably not. Someone who knew us must have shown Senator Tod the way here. And that could really be only one person.

Damn.

"Anabel!" I said. "She could have put him on our trail."

Arthur nodded slowly. "I've come to that conclusion myself. I just wanted to be sure it wasn't any of you. I guess we can rule out Grayson and Jasper. And it wasn't me either." He pushed a lock of hair back from his face. His hair was longer than usual and rather untidy—intriguing. I'd never known Arthur's hair to be anything but perfectly styled. But it didn't make any difference to his staggering good looks.

"Maybe he's some friend or relation of Anabel's, and she told him the whole story. Or a member of the sect who believed in that silly demon's handbook," I said thoughtfully, while Henry folded his arms and said nothing. But I could tell when his brain was working overtime.

"Friend? He's at least in his midthirties. And not at all Anabel's type." Arthur bit his lower lip, perhaps thinking of the time when *he* had still been Anabel's type. "He's not a relation either. She doesn't have many relations, and I know all of those she does have. As for the sect—she was out of there by the time she was three years old, and the community was broken up. She wasn't in touch with any of them after that. And her mother was in the nuthouse until her death. . . . No, I don't think it's anyone from her past."

"It's ages since I saw Anabel's door." Henry looked at Arthur keenly. "Do you know where it is now?"

Good question! Anabel's door had been very striking: a huge double door with gold fittings and a Gothic pointed arch, like a church porch. In the past, you could always rely on finding it opposite Arthur's door. But since Anabel had been in the psychiatric hospital, the door had disappeared without a trace, and there was another door where it used to be.

Arthur shook his head. "No idea. I assume that Anabel completely changed the look of it so that we won't find it. In principle, it could be any door."

"Including the door opposite?" I asked.

Embarrassed, Arthur examined the toes of his shoes. "That one belongs to my mum."

Oh. How . . . er . . . how sweet.

"You're not trying to tell me you aren't seeing Anabel anymore, are you?" Henry gave his former best friend a cool look.

"Well—well, I'm not. I've only seen her twice since she's been in the hospital. Right at the start." Arthur stared at the toes of his shoes again. "She turned up outside my door, but I'd changed the code of the lock." He raised his chin and looked first me and then Henry straight in the eyes. "Can you imagine what it's like being manipulated by your own girlfriend? How awful you feel knowing that you've been exploited and that she was telling you lies?"

"I hope that was a rhetorical question." Henry had raised one eyebrow.

"The second time Anabel and I met, I ended it," Arthur went on, undeterred. "Or rather . . . Well, the fact is, *she* ended it. Anyway, it wasn't an edifying occasion. She accused me of all sorts of things." He fell silent for a moment, before saying, "Don't look so suspicious, Henry!"

"Oh, you'll have to excuse me." Henry's voice was heavy with sarcasm. "I could never imagine what it's like being manipulated and told lies by your own friend, and how awful that makes a person feel."

Arthur raised both hands. "Please—goodness knows I've apologized often enough."

Really? Not to me. Still, maybe he thought that after I broke his jawbone we were even.

Henry and Arthur were staring fiercely at each other.

"There are some things that can't be forgiven," said Henry.

I sighed. Any moment now, they'd be at each other's throats. Or turning into animals of some kind to tear each other to pieces.

"Listen, you two, why don't you stop it and we'll think what to do about this Senator Tod instead?" I suggested. "What could make Anabel want to set him on our trail? And what can he actually do apart from running around in weird disguises and letting his deranged laughter echo down the corridors . . . Hang on a moment!" Excitedly, I gasped for air. "The man's out of his mind! He's a patient in the same hospital as Anabel! That would account for his ramblings about rotors and tornadoes and so on."

Arthur raised his head, and then nodded. "That could be right."

"Yes, it could," Henry agreed. "Although I get the impression that there's method behind his madness, if that's what it is. I just don't know what the method is yet."

"Even if he was a psychopathic killer—I don't feel there's any way he can hurt us here," I said. "He's just rather a nuisance."

"So far, maybe," said Arthur. "But you shouldn't under-estimate Anabel. She's still dangerous."

"She's been sectioned," I said. "She's in a psychiatric hospital in Surrey, and they'll be keeping her there."

"You've no idea what she's capable of, Liv," said Arthur.

"I don't?" I shot him a furious glance. "She was going to cut my throat with a hunting knife, so I have a very good idea what she's capable of. However, while she's in that hos-pital, I suppose we don't have to be afraid of her. Or of that weirdo outside the door. Right, Henry?"

But Henry's mind seemed to be on something else. "Rodents," he murmured. "Tornado . . . rondo . . . stranded on root . . . could that be a code?"

I sighed. "If so, we'll work it out. But what I was really going to say is—"

"Senator Tod may not know a lot about these things yet, but you yourselves know how quickly we've learned to deal with the situation," Arthur said, interrupting me. "I think I'm pretty good at it myself, and Henry could even be . . ." He hesitated, but it seemed like he couldn't bring himself to say that his ex–best buddy Henry could even be better at it than he was. "But the real point is: none of us are a match for Anabel."

"Dona dents rotor," Henry murmured. "Was that it? Or did he say *Mona*?"

"But—" I was going to point out, for the fourth time, that Anabel couldn't do anything to hurt us, but Arthur wouldn't let me finish my sentence.

"Don't you get it, Liv?" He slid off his table. "It's not about what happens in the real world. It's here"—and he pointed to his door, which was jammed between two bookshelves on the second floor, looking as if it belonged permanently in this Reading Room—"it's here that danger threatens. We know far too little about it. I guess we don't know even a fraction of the possibilities. Whereas Anabel has crossed boundaries that you two don't have the faintest inkling about. Believe me, this thing isn't over yet."

That, or something like it, was what Anabel herself had said at our last meeting several months ago. *It's only just begun*—those had been her words.

Henry seemed to have given up on puzzling out Senator Tod's peculiar remarks. "So what?" he said, looking at Arthur. "Even if Anabel is planning something, our doors are secure. We just have to go carefully outside them." He moved away from the table where he had been standing. "And by *we* I mean, in this case, Liv and me. To be honest, I'm not so interested in what happens to you." His gaze became if anything a little more piercing. "I don't trust you, Arthur."

"You don't trust anyone, Henry," replied Arthur heatedly. "That's why you can't give all this up." He made a sweeping gesture at the room around us. "You're addicted to slipping into the dreams of anyone you don't trust an inch. I know you're good at it. And I know you think you're ruthless. But compared to Anabel, you're an innocent choirboy."

It was Henry's turn to shrug his shoulders. "Compared to you too," he said coolly. "Come on, Liv, let's go. This is likely to be a short night. . . ."

He put his hand out to me, but when I was about to take it, it suddenly wasn't there anymore. It had disappeared, along with the rest of Henry.

I groaned. "Oh no, not again!"

Arthur looked at me. "Does that happen often?"

"All the time. His brother and sister wake him almost every night. They have some kind of stomach bug going around."

"And yet again his mother's in no fit state to do anything for them. Poor old Henry—my own family are a bit weird, but I really wouldn't swap with Henry." Arthur stretched his legs and gave me a broad grin. "Though mind you, he does have a cute girlfriend," he added casually.

"And this is the moment when, I'm very sorry to say, I really have to be going," I said, looking around for the door into the corridor. Yes, it was still hanging in the same place between the two bookshelves. I went up the steps to the gallery, with Arthur following at a suitable distance, very much the courteous host. If I'd had a coat with me, I'm sure he'd have helped me into it. I'll admit that I wouldn't have minded chatting to Arthur a little longer, particularly now that things were getting interesting. But for one thing, he suddenly had a rather arrogant glint in his eyes, and for another, it didn't seem fair to Henry to ask his former best friend questions about him.

I cautiously looked through the doorway and out into the corridor. I almost expected to see pools of blood on the floor, but the corridor was empty and spotlessly clean.

"Like me to escort you to your door?" asked Arthur. Light was falling directly on him from the domed roof, and only now could I see that he looked kind of exhausted. Not like the old Arthur, not quite so self-confident, although he still came out with the same smart remarks. And suddenly what he'd said about Anabel didn't seem to me quite so absurd. Okay, so I didn't trust him an inch myself—after all, this was Arthur, right?—but on the other hand, I didn't entirely understand why Henry had simply dismissed his misgivings like that.

"Well, how about it?" Arthur seemed to have noticed my hesitation.

I shook my head. All I wanted right now was to be in my bed. Even better, in my bed after a few hours of dreamless sleep. "I can make it on my own. I bet Senator Tod has had enough for today too. Thanks for . . . er . . ." Well, thanks for nothing, really.

"Okay," said Arthur, adding all the same, "Even if Henry doesn't agree, I think we should all stick together. Together we may be strong enough."

Yes. Maybe. Strong enough for whatever was going to happen.

"Good night." I was about to set off, but then I turned around after all, almost as if I was steered by remote control. I simply had to ask, even if it was Arthur I was asking, and that gave me a horrible sense that I was betraying Henry. "What did you mean a moment ago? About Henry not trusting anyone, and slipping into other people's dreams by night? Whose dreams?"

"Well, if he hasn't even told you *that* . . ." Arthur didn't finish his sentence. He didn't have to.

13

I WOKE WITH a start, bathed in sweat. Oh, damn it! I'd mutated into a plant again, right in the middle of the park. But one good thing was that I'd woken just as the Boker approached me with a huge pair of scissors. This really couldn't go on— I did need at least a few hours' sleep. Maybe I should try the herbal tea that Lottie swore by. Even if it had a nasty smell of valerian. (Which was probably why Spot the cat always sat on Lottie's lap while she drank it, gazing lovingly at her.)

A look at my alarm clock showed me there were only two hours left before it was time to get up, that was all, and I probably wouldn't get any sleep if I kept my sweaty things on. So I switched on the bedside lamp, got out of bed, and put on a clean pair of pajama pants and a clean T-shirt. Or rather, I was going to put them on, but as I reached for them, the door of my room opened. I let out a small squeak of alarm and crossed my arms over my breasts—heaven knows who I thought was coming in, but it was only Mia. And she didn't look at me, but walked slowly past me and toward my bed, staring at it.

"Yes," she said out loud. "Yes, she's lying there."

"No, she isn't," I said. "She's standing here. Right here in front of the wardrobe!"

But Mia didn't seem to hear me. She reached out her arms as if to feel for something. I quickly pulled the clean T-shirt over my head, went up to her, and cautiously touched her arm. "Hey."

"She looks just like you, Liv," whispered Mia, her gaze fixed on my pillow, which was all out of shape. She hadn't blinked once since coming through the doorway. "Yes, I'll do it," she added firmly, and before I could react, she had snatched up one of my decorative cushions (it had a squirrel on it) and was pressing it down firmly on my pillow with both hands.

"Mia!" I said, rather more sharply this time. This was crazy. My sister was trying to smother a pillow with a cushion. On the other hand—if I hadn't happened to be out of bed, she'd probably be in the middle of smothering me. "Wake up! At once!" I grabbed her by the shoulders and shook her hard. "Mia! That'll do, the pillow's dead now!"

She was breathing heavily, blinking in the light of my bedside lamp. Then she uttered a bloodcurdling scream. Well, maybe it was bloodcurdling only because she was screaming straight into my ear. Or loud enough, anyway, to bring Grayson on the scene. He rushed through the doorway in a pair of granddad flannel pants with a large check pattern, part of the granddad pajamas that the Boker had given him for Christmas. She didn't know that on principle Grayson wore no pajama top at night, so that the outfit didn't really look very grandfatherly at all.

"What's the matter?"

I was very glad I'd had time to get the T-shirt on, even if

it was back to front, as I now noticed. "She was sleepwalking again," I said.

Mia seemed rather confused, staring in turn at me and the cushion in her hands, and her breathing was still unsteady. "I've been sleepwalking again?" she repeated. "I had such a horrible dream. Liv had a clone, a sneaky creature who wanted to kill her and take her place . . . but you got away in time, Livvy, and I hid you in my room. All the others thought the clone was the real Liv." She looked reproachfully at Grayson. "Even you!"

"Er . . . should I apologize?" said Grayson. Luckily he seemed to be the only one we'd woken. I quickly closed the door so that it would stay that way.

Mia gulped. "Anyway, we had to wait until the false Liv was asleep. Then we came into your room and—" She broke off.

"And tried smothering the false Liv with a cushion," I went on in her place, shaking my pillow back into shape. "This pillow is lucky you didn't want to stab it with a knife. . . ."

"You mean I came into your room in my dream and picked up a cushion to . . . Oh God!" Mia stared at me, horrified. "That's terrible!"

"It's okay. Nothing happened."

"But if you'd been lying in bed . . ." Mia's eyes filled with tears. That happened so seldom—and when it did they were usually tears of rage—that I reached for her hand in alarm.

"Hey, it's all right, Mia." I gently pushed her down on the edge of my bed and sat down beside her.

"Nothing's all right," said Mia.

Grayson stood there in front of us looking undecided. "She tried to smother you with a cushion?"

"No, she smothered my pillow with a cushion, that's all." I darted him a nasty look. Did he have to go on about it now, when Mia was so upset, anyway?

But Grayson wasn't impressed by my nasty look. He sat down on the bed, too, on Mia's other side. "Can you remember whose idea it was in your dream for you to smother Liv?"

"She wasn't trying to smother me—it was my horrible clone, wasn't it? The one you thought was real," I said, still trying to meet Grayson's eyes over the top of Mia's bowed head, but he wouldn't look at me. "Anyway, to be honest, who cares? There are some dreams you don't want to analyze; you just want to forget them as soon as you can." For instance, dreams when there's a root growing out of your feet and branches and leaves out of your fingertips. "I suggest we take Mia back to her bed."

Mia shook her head. "No, I never want to sleep again. I do dreadful things in my sleep."

"I'll come to bed with you and keep watch," I said, glancing at the clock. "We don't have much of tonight left, anyway."

"Can I just stay here?" Mia didn't wait for my answer. She crawled under the duvet and snuggled under it.

"Yes, of course you can do that too," I said.

Grayson sighed. "Don't you think this sleepwalking is odd, Liv? And her trying to murder you in your sleep?"

"You're exaggerating." I straightened the duvet over Mia. "It was only my clone she was after."

"I really don't ever want to sleep again," murmured Mia, but she had already closed her eyes. "Only for a little while now, because I'm so tired. . . ." The rest of what she was saying turned into incomprehensible murmurs, and the next second she was breathing deeply and peacefully.

Grayson and I looked at her in silence. Suddenly I felt aware of how close he was, and I wished he'd put a T-shirt on. His bare chest was unsettling me.

"Isn't this the moment when you ought to leave the room?" I asked, realizing as I spoke that it sounded a little too snide. He hadn't really done anything except look at me with a disappointed expression, but all the same, I went on. "Or have you forgotten that Mia and I are under the Spencer family curse? No getting up close and personal with girls who murder bushes."

Grayson reached for my arm and forced me to look at him. "Liv, you have to take this seriously. Suppose Mia didn't have that dream of her own accord? Suppose there's someone manipulating her dreams to harm you?"

I swallowed. "That's . . ." Out of the question, I'd been going to say. But was it really?

"Think about it. How does Secrecy come to know so much about you?"

Yes, how? All the little hairs stood up on my arms, and Grayson saw it. "Things that only you knew," he said urgently. "You and Mia."

And Henry.

"No idea," I whispered. "Mia for one would never have given them away."

"Not of her own accord. But couldn't someone else have slipped into Mia's dreams at night and found out all those things?" Grayson's brown eyes looked much darker than usual in the light of my bedside lamp. He seemed to be seriously worried, and so sympathetic that I suddenly wanted to lean against him and have a good cry. I was so exhausted. But of course I didn't—on the contrary, I moved a little farther away from him.

"You think Secrecy was spying on Mia in her dreams?"

He shrugged his shoulders. "More likely someone who passed what they found out on to Secrecy."

"And that someone would also make Mia go sleepwalking?" I shook my head and stroked a lock of hair back from my sister's face. "I sometimes walked in my sleep as a child myself—it runs in our family. We all have vivid dreams."

"You certainly do." Grayson sighed. "Liv, please tell me honestly—you and Henry are still doing it, aren't you?"

Oh no, not that again. But Grayson wasn't letting me get away with just looking at him blankly.

"You're still roaming around that corridor, right?"

"Well . . ." This was really difficult. I'd have loved to keep the truth from him, if only to spare myself his disappointed look. "Not . . . er . . . necessarily," I stammered.

And there it was: the disappointed look. Grayson was better at it than anyone else I knew.

"I thought so. I could tell from the dark shadows under your eyes. Somehow I'd have been surprised if you two could leave it alone. Not Henry and not you either. Leaving Arthur out of this entirely . . ." With another deep sigh, he finally let go of my arm. "I just don't understand you—it's so unreasonable, and thoughtless, and . . . Well, it's not the way to behave! Dreams are like thoughts: they have to be free, and no one should go spying on them. Certainly not for fun."

"But . . . but we're not doing it, anyway," I said defensively. "We don't go slinking into other people's dreams." *Except in emergencies. When Senator Tod is chasing us and your door happens to be the only way of escape* . . . "We only meet in our own dreams. There's nothing bad about that."

"Apart from the fact that you two have no idea how and why this dream thing works, anyway? After all we saw last year?" Grayson's whisper was so loud now that it could hardly be called a whisper at all.

"I thought we'd agreed last year that demons don't exist either in general or in particular," I said.

"That doesn't change the fact that you don't know what you're getting yourselves in for. It's unpredictable, it's immoral, it's unhealthy, it's—"

"Shh!" I interrupted him. This argument at five on a Friday morning, combined with my inexplicable wish to throw myself in tears on Grayson's bare chest, was just too much for me at this moment. "You'll wake Mia again. She needs her sleep. And I need mine." I pointed to my bed.

"Exactly." Grayson went to the door—or stomped to the door was more like it. He was angrier than I'd ever seen him before. He turned back again on his way out. "Do you think I haven't seen the state you're in? Leaving aside the huge quantities of coffee you put away every morning. How much longer do you think you can go on like this?" He didn't wait for an answer, just added a distinctly unfriendly "Sleep well," and closed the door behind him. At least he didn't slam it.

"Same to you! And kindly put more clothes on next time," I muttered. Then I switched off the bedside lamp and lay down carefully under my duvet with Mia, feeling terrible.

Of course I couldn't drop off to sleep again. Instead I thought about what Grayson had said. Suppose someone really was stealing into Mia's dreams on the sly? But who could have any interest in doing that? Was it someone who wanted to hurt me, as Grayson suspected? The only person who really came to mind was Anabel. Maybe she could make someone start sleepwalking. But she'd have to possess some personal item belonging to Mia to open her dream door. And how could she have laid hands on that when she was in the hospital in Surrey? Or was the real explanation, as Arthur had suggested, that Anabel knew people who had it in for us in the real world? People we might even know ourselves?

Beside me, Mia moved slightly. She still looked totally relaxed. I gave up trying to go to sleep, carefully got out of bed, put on a thick woolen cardigan to keep warm, and sat down on the upholstered window seat, my favorite place for thinking ever since we'd moved in with the Spencers. It had a view of the garden that Ernest tended so lovingly. Not that it was a particularly pretty sight at this season, with its trees and bushes bare of leaves, but you could imagine what it would be like in spring, when the cherry tree and the magnolias were flowering, with a carpet of forget-me-nots spreading under them. Tonight, however, spring seemed to me infinitely far away.

Mia turned on her other side and made a happy sound. At least one of us was sleeping deeply. I sighed. I could just be imagining things, but no way was I going to let someone walk around in my sister's dreams. Only, how could I keep watch on her door? That was the question on which everything ultimately turned. Would I be able to increase the security precautions on it, or would I have to tell her what seemed to be going on so that she could protect herself?

I hadn't found an answer to that question by the time my alarm clock rang. The only certainty was that I was going to need an enormous amount of coffee again.

14

EVEN ON THE way downstairs, I could hear the argument going on in the kitchen. Mia was standing in the middle of the staircase, leaning over the banisters. When she saw me, she raised a hand in warning and put her forefinger to her lips.

"Really, Florence, this time you're going too far," Ernest was ranting down on the first floor.

"It's my eighteenth birthday, and I want this party to be special!" his daughter spat back. "I can't celebrate it in this house, not under the same roof as those . . . those monsters!"

"That's us," whispered Mia.

"So what do you have against holding the party at Granny's house?" Florence went on. "She offered to have it there herself, she has plenty of room, and she'd love to help with the preparations! It's all for the best so far as you're concerned, Dad—remember what this house looked like after our last birthday party?"

"But that's not your reason," said Ernest.

"No," Florence admitted at once. "I just want to celebrate my eighteenth birthday in a place where those creatures—"

"That's us," whispered Mia again.

"—where those creatures aren't welcome!"

"Florence Cecilia Elizabeth Spencer!" Ernest sounded really angry, listing all Florence's names like that. "I let you get away with a good deal, but this . . ."

"What about it?" snapped Florence. "You can't force us to have our party here. It's bad enough to have you making us live here with those foul *fiends*."

I almost whispered, "That's us," myself this time. Foul fiends? What century did she think we were living in?

At that moment Lottie came running down from the very top of the house, trying to get past us. "I overslept!" she gasped. "The first time in five years I—"

"Shhhh!" Mia barred Lottie's way and put a hand over her mouth.

"Muft fqueeth grapefruit!" said Lottie indistinctly, trying to free herself, but Mia wasn't letting go.

"No one down there is agitating for grapefruit juice right now, believe me!" I whispered, and then Lottie stopped struggling, squished herself in between us, and leaned over the banisters herself, straining her ears.

The argument in the kitchen was still going on.

"Grayson, say something!" Florence demanded.

Yes, exactly, I thought. *Say something, Grayson.*

"I can't say I fancy having a birthday party at Granny's," said Grayson. As he was the only one not shouting, we had to lean far over the banisters to hear him. Luckily the kitchen door was open. "You can't even turn around there without knocking something valuable over. Not a very cool location, if you ask me."

"Absolutely," Mia whispered.

"Eavesdropping isn't right," Lottie whispered back. "We ought to let them know we're here."

"No way!" said Mia and I at the same time.

"Of course we'll clear Granny's china collection away first," Florence was protesting in the kitchen. "And I'm not asking you, anyway. I made up my mind about this ages ago."

"Florence Cecilia Eli . . ." Obviously Ernest couldn't think of anything else to say.

By now Mom had joined us, and was leaning over the banisters herself a few steps higher up. Her face showed that she was suffering pangs of conscience, but she clearly didn't dare go any farther down the stairs with Florence shouting in that shrill voice. Or was she developing unsuspected mother-lioness instincts and staying with her babies to defend them tooth and claw if necessary?

"Oh yes?" Now we could hear Grayson perfectly well. "If that's so, then we'll just have separate birthday parties, little sister: you have yours at Granny's house and I'll have mine here. And we'll see which of us gets more guests!"

There was a brief silence. Then Florence cried furiously, "You wouldn't do a thing like that to me!"

"Yes, I would. You're just being silly."

"Me, silly? Did I go slinking out of the house by night to destroy a cultural monument?"

At this point, Mom gave us her familiar look, the one that said, *Now see what you've done.* So much for her mother-lioness instincts—she didn't have any.

"Oh, Florence, do shut up," said Grayson in the kitchen. "I'm sick and tired of all this fuss. It was only a tree, for God's sake!" He came marching out of the kitchen so fast that we didn't have time to take cover.

We must have been an odd sight, all four of us hanging over the banisters side by side (only Buttercup was missing, but she'd probably been sitting in the kitchen beside Ernest's chair for some time, waiting for the slice of cold roast beef he usually gave her). However, Grayson just glanced wearily up at us and then went to the coat stand to put on his jacket.

"Now see what you've done, Dad!" snapped Florence in the kitchen. The mixture of fury and tears in her voice was perfectly calibrated. Could you learn to do a thing like that? "You've managed to drive a wedge between us. Between me and my twin."

Now she too came rushing out of the kitchen, and with great presence of mind, we abandoned our listening position and acted as if we were all just that minute coming downstairs. In the process, unfortunately, Lottie and Mia bumped their heads together.

"Ouch," said Mia reproachfully.

Florence didn't favor any of us with a glance, but simply shot by on her way upstairs. We could hear the bathroom door slam and the sound of the key turning in the lock.

So at long last, the way to the coffee machine was clear.

Or no, not quite clear yet. Grayson was still standing by the coat stand. My guilty conscience forced me to stop in front of him while Mom and Lottie went into the kitchen.

"I'm sorry," I murmured, and I meant it. I was sorry we'd sawed Mr. Snuggles down. I was sorry they were quarreling because of us. And I was sorry that Grayson looked so unhappy.

"What for?" he snapped at me, sounding more like his twin sister than he presumably thought.

"Well, for being such monsters, creatures, and foul fiends," Mia replied instead of me.

I was pretty sure that Grayson didn't mean to, but the grim expression on his face gave way to a spontaneous smile. Relieved, I smiled back. He abruptly pulled up the zipper of his jacket and put a knitted cap on his head. He was the only one of us to cycle to school in the morning, come rain or shine. Ernest had been going the long way around on his way to work so as to drop Florence, Mia, and me off at Frognal Academy. But since Florence had been putting as much distance as possible between herself and us, Mia and I had taken to going by bus instead. After all, we didn't want the poor girl having to rush out of a moving vehicle just to escape our presence.

The next bus would leave in ten minutes, and if we wanted to catch it and get to school on time, we'd have to hurry.

Grayson had seen me look at the big clock on the wall, and his smile got wider. "Too bad, the foul, fiendish, monstrous creature will have to do without her coffee today," he said.

"Oh, that's okay," I said. "I have plenty of adrenaline running through my veins to keep me going."

Which was true, but unfortunately the effect lasted only until lessons began. I had great difficulty in staying awake during Mrs. Lawrence's French lesson. As an experiment, I put my head down on my arms. I'd just close my eyes for a moment. Now would be the perfect time for a little nap. I was left alone at last. That would be the solution: sleep during the day when everyone else was awake. Pure relaxation.

"Have you heard yet where Florence and Grayson are having their birthday party?" Persephone wasn't interested in Mrs. Lawrence's explanation of the *passé composé* tense either. She was more in the mood for one of those whispered monologues that she called "conversation," and that never came to an end until Mrs. Lawrence was standing in front of us, spitting nails and accusing *me* of disturbing the peace. How I hated that! "It's going to be at their grandmother's house. According to Secrecy, anyway." Of course, Secrecy knew everything, as usual. Sometimes it was almost a blessing not to have a smartphone. (And I probably wouldn't have one for quite some time, but I didn't go so far as to feel grateful to Mrs. Spencer for that.)

"I suppose that means you and Mia won't be coming. I mean, you're banned from their grandmother's house." A theatrical mini-pause for effect, and then she went on. "I hope you won't mind if I go all the same, will you? Grayson is sure to ask Gabriel, and when Gabriel asks me if I'll be there, too, I can't very well say no . . . and yesterday I saw that lovely Missoni skirt, perfect for a party, not a typical Missoni striped skirt but dark blue, not boring old navy blue but kind of stronger, not royal blue, though, more of a dark ocean blue, it's difficult to describe, maybe you can come and look at it again with me tomorrow, they have super dresses as well but you won't be needing one if you're not going to the party, on the other hand one can always use a new dress, and my sister says Missoni clothes are sort of timeless capital investments. . . ."

Persephone chattered and chattered or whispered and whispered. It was like sitting next to a defective compressed air system. But after a while I got used to it. Out in front was Mrs. Lawrence's monotonous but tuneful French, beside me was Persephone's soporific whisper—my head sank to my arms again.

". . . was caught? Henry had to go and fetch him from the police station."

Suddenly I was wide awake. "What? Who?"

Persephone looked at me, shaking her head. "You don't have to tell me if you'd rather not. But I'd love to know if that's true—I mean, it seems odd to me, a boy of twelve stealing expensive perfume."

"What boy of twelve?"

She stared at me, wide-eyed. "Oh goodness, you don't know about it, do you? Hasn't Henry told you?"

"No," I said. I didn't mind if I was showing my ignorance, I just wanted to know who Persephone was talking about.

Without further ado, she handed me her phone. And I could read it all there in black and white, while at the same time Persephone gave me a running commentary on the facts all over again.

Henry's little brother, Milo, had been caught stealing a bottle of perfume in a department store, and Henry had had to go and fetch him from the police station. They weren't going to prosecute, but Milo was banned from that store. Secrecy and Persephone could only guess at Milo's motives, but they were sure he didn't have any money to speak of, because as everyone knew, his father had been neglecting the children since separating from their mother, and he spent money only on his new girlfriend.

"It's so sad, don't you think?" Persephone took her phone back, never mind the fact that I'd been about to click on the link that Secrecy had given to the Bulgarian former lingerie model who was Henry's father's girlfriend. "The poor kid must have taken the perfume just to give his mother something nice. Isn't it terrible the way men always want younger girlfriends? It means a woman is either abandoned or she has to marry a very old man. . . ."

I was listening with only half an ear. Because all this had happened only last Saturday, the very day when Mia and I were on our way home from Switzerland. When Henry's phone rang and he said he had to go and collect his brother from a friend.

From a friend!

"Olivia Silver! Persephone Porter-Peregrin!" Mrs. Lawrence had obviously said our names several times already, because I saw the angry vein that always stood out on her forehead when she was about to enter someone in the register.

"*Oui, madame, pardon, madame*, I didn't understand the question," said Persephone like a good girl.

"The verb *devoir*," said Mrs. Lawrence. "*Fabien et Suzanne. Attendre une heure à la caisse du musée.*"

"They really had to wait for a whole hour at the museum ticket office?" Persephone clicked her tongue disapprovingly. "But I suppose it depends what the exhibition was. I'd probably have waited even longer to get into the Kate Moss exhibition; it was really super."

Now Mrs. Lawrence's vein looked as if it might burst any moment. "*Fabien et Suzanne ont dû attendre une heure!*" she cried. "*Ont dû!* They had to wait for an hour."

Well, that was their tough luck. But for now I couldn't care less about Fabien and Suzanne and the stupid museum.

15

THE JANUARY SUN shone through the high windows of the cafeteria, bathing everything in warm golden light that was out of kilter with the way I felt. Henry was already sitting at our table, talking to the boys. At the moment he was laughing at something Gabriel had said, and suddenly I didn't want to walk over to them. Instead I stopped in the middle of the room as if rooted to the spot. Originally I'd been going to grab Henry and shake him and ask why the hell he hadn't told me anything about his brother and the rest of it, but seeing him sitting there and laughing, I realized that I wasn't angry with him at all. I was . . . yes, what was I? Sad? Disappointed? Confused? Anyway, a bit of all those. He sat there in the sun, looking so familiar and at the same time so strange.

A shadow fell between us. "You're in my way." Emily had stationed herself in front of me with a laden tray and was acting as if she couldn't get past. I took a step aside. All the same, Emily made no move to go on.

"Didn't you do brilliantly with Florence and Grayson?"

she said. "I suppose you're proud of yourself. No one's ever managed to divide the twins before."

"I didn't . . ." I closed my mouth again. No way was I going to justify myself to Emily. "Your soup will get cold," I said instead.

Emily shook her head. "I wouldn't like to be you," she said. "It must feel dreadful inside your head . . . so sick! First that business with Mr. Snuggles and now . . . Hey! Put that down at once!"

I had taken the bowl of soup off her tray and sniffed it. "Yummy, cream of leek—supposed to be really good for the hair."

"You *are* sick!" said Emily, but I could see that she was scared of what I might do.

I raised the soup bowl. "More gloss, fewer split ends . . . Want to massage it in yourself, or shall I do that for you too?"

"Don't you dare!" Since Emily was stuck holding her tray with both hands, she decided to go on without her soup. "Absolutely, totally sick," she said over her shoulder as she walked away.

"Talking about herself, is she?" asked Henry. I hadn't noticed him leaving our table during my little spat with Emily. "Do you want help?"

"No. Do you want some soup?" I offered him Emily's bowl.

Henry grinned, took the soup from me, and put it down on the nearest table. Then he put his arm around my waist and drew me close. "Hey, you're late today, cheese girl. I really must tell you what I've found out."

I stiffened. "Why didn't you tell me about your brother? Why did you lie to me?" I spoke very fast and very quietly, and to be honest, I half hoped that he wouldn't hear me in all the racket of the cafeteria. But my words wiped the smile off his face.

"You've been reading Secrecy's blog." He let go of me and sighed. "One of these days I'll find out who she is, and then I'll wring her neck with my own hands. Don't you want any lunch?"

Silently, I shook my head. Persephone was sitting at our table now with Arthur, Eric, and Gabriel. You could see her red cheeks all the way from where I was. An hour ago, I'd felt ravenous, what with missing breakfast, but suddenly my stomach was churning. "Can we go somewhere else? Where no one can hear us?"

Henry sighed again. "Listen, about Milo . . . why would I bother you with that?"

"Yes, why would you bother me with things that worry you?" I repeated, putting as much sarcasm as I could manage into my voice. "I'm only your girlfriend. Why would you tell me what goes on at your home, or what really is on your mind? Why would you introduce me to your family?"

"I do tell you what's really on my mind," said Henry. "No one should know me better than you do."

I laughed indignantly. "I suppose that's a joke, is it?" Henry looked hurt, but I couldn't stop for that now. "Even Secrecy knows more about you than I do."

"Heaven only knows where she got that from." Henry ran his hand through his untidy hair. "Anyway, it wasn't even perfume—it was a stupid fragranced candle. Jasmine and vanilla, what a nasty combination. Don't you want to know what I've found out about our friend Senator Tod?"

"No," I said. By now I didn't mind that we were in the

middle of the cafeteria. Anyway, only the students at the table right next to us could hear what we were saying. And they were talking at the tops of their voices about the latest Arsenal football match. "I'd like to know why I've never been to your home. Why I don't know your parents or any of their other kids except for Amy, in her dream. Do you have some kind of problem with me?"

"No, Liv! Of course not." Henry was staring at me, horrified.

"Or do you think none of that is anything to do with me?"

He frowned. "Hey, not everyone has such an uncompli-cated family as yours."

"Uncomplicated?" I couldn't be hearing this properly. "My parents are divorced, my mom is living with the new man in her life, his daughter hates us like poison—"

"You're the Sunshine Family," Henry interrupted me. "Everything about you is warm, clean, and friendly, you're all fond of one another—Florence doesn't count—there's always home baking on the table, even your dog could be straight out of an ad. Whereas we are the Drizzling Rain Family. Or maybe the Hailstorm Family. Milo steals fra-granced candles, my four-year-old sister calls every man who crosses her path Daddy, my mother only ever bakes when she's been swallowing too many antidepressants, even our cat's gone out of her mind. She's stopped being house-trained, so the cleaning lady has given notice. Why would I think it might be a good idea to take you home to our place? So that you can see it all with your own eyes?"

Although he spoke quietly, the intensity of his words took my breath away for a couple of seconds. "Yes," I said then, looking him firmly in the eye. Oh, I loved him so much. And

I felt so, so sorry about his mother having to take antidepressants, not to mention the cat. . . .

For a little while, we just stood facing each other in silence.

"Oh, Livvy . . ." Henry put a strand of hair back from my forehead, very slowly. For the first time since I'd known him, he looked vulnerable, and for the first time, I wished I was the big, broad-shouldered one so that I could simply comfort him by holding him close. I almost started to cry, but I managed to blink back the tears. After all, there was no reason to cry, it was just because I was so tired. And hungry.

"It could be that your cat just feels neglected," I said, talking very fast so that Henry wouldn't notice anything. "My aunt Gertrude had that problem once. With Tipsy. Or maybe it was Patsy. Anyway, she called in an animal psychologist, and now Tabby is just fine again. Or Tibby as the case may be."

This time when Henry smiled, it was that very special smile meant just for me, the smile I liked more than anything else in the world.

"Okay. Then how about meeting at my place this evening?"

Just like that? He was suggesting it himself? I was suspended somewhere between confusion, relief, and distrust, and the mixture unsettled me so much that I just went on babbling. "Oh yes, that would be great," I said breathlessly. "Or no, well, of course I mean yes, but I have kung fu this evening, and after that I was going to the movies with Lottie and Mia, we planned it ages ago—you're welcome to come, too, if you like. Although I bet it'll be another of those tearjerkers with vampires, because Lottie is going to choose the film. That's a good thing for me because at least I can get a bit of sleep—see these rings under my eyes? Another few sleepless nights and I'll look like a panda. Mom must be wondering why her concealer runs out so fast. . . ." Oh heavens, I sounded just like Persephone. It was with some difficulty that I managed to stop my endless nattering by pretending to have a coughing fit.

Henry waited patiently until I'd finished. "Tomorrow evening, then?"

So he really meant it. I took a deep breath and nodded. "Yes. Yes, tomorrow evening will be perfect."

I felt so relieved. My distrust and confusion had gone away, and everything between us was all right. Why hadn't I said all those things earlier? It had been easy, after all.

I took Henry's hand and drew him behind one of the trolleys for dirty dishes, to kiss him. We didn't need to have the whole cafeteria watching. Couples making out in school got on my nerves, but I thought we were pretty well hidden. Henry seemed to think so too and held me close. Only when the Arsenal fans began shouting and clapping and Henry carefully moved away from me did I notice that one of the girls who helped out in the kitchen had wheeled our camouflage away.

Embarrassing.

"Just take no notice," said Henry, smoothing my hair. Unlike me, of course he hadn't gone scarlet in the face.

"So what have you found out about Senator Tod?" I whispered.

Henry gave me a conspiratorial grin. "I did suspect there was method in his madness, remember?"

"Dona denting the tenor . . . oh yes."

"Rotor," Henry corrected me. "It took me a little while to work it out, but then it all came clear. Anagrams."

"Like Anna, level, and madam I'm Adam?"

"Sort of, but those are palindromes: they have to read the same backward as forward. In anagrams, the letters can be all over the place. Senator Tod Nord. Rodents at rondo. Stranded on root! Tornado, nerd, sot." He beamed at me. "I did wonder who he was calling a nerd. But he was just telling us his name, every time!"

His enthusiasm was infectious. "So do we know this character?"

"Not yet," said Henry. "But Google knows him. His name is . . ."

"No! No, don't tell me! I want to work it out myself. I love word puzzles." I tugged him over to our table. "Does anyone have a pen and a piece of paper? A paper napkin will do."

"The lunch break ends in exactly one minute," said Persephone.

Damn it.

16

"AND IF YOU don't eat them all, there won't be any sunshine in the Sunshine Family tomorrow." Mom was looking down on Mia and me with her hands on her hips. I felt afraid of her. Not only because she was covered all over with flour and looked a bit like a zombie, but because her eyes were sparkling in such a nasty, determined way. Muffins towered up all around us, on the working surface, on the shelves, the table, the windowsill, mountains of muffins, and they all looked burned, moldy, and downright unappetizing. When I picked one up, the crust broke open in my hands, and a maggot crawled out.

"I can't eat that, Mom," I said miserably.

"You can and you will. I don't take all those antidepressants for nothing!" My zombie mom grabbed hold of Mia, tried to force her mouth open and stuff a muffin into it, and Mia began screaming. I snatched her away from Mom, stumbled backward over a pile of muffins with her, and looked around in panic for a place to hide or some way to escape. There in front of us—a green door . . . Oh, thank goodness, it was only a dream. I didn't have to be afraid of my zombie mom anymore. With a blink of my eyes, I made her and all those disgusting muffins disappear, then I blinked the screaming Dream-Mia away—I had to go out to protect the real Mia's dream door. I'd borrowed a bracelet of hers on purpose and put it on before I went to sleep. I couldn't forget what Grayson had said last night: suppose someone was really stealing into Mia's dreams by night? Anabel, for instance.

The corridor was empty; everything was calm and peaceful. The sight of Henry's black door opposite mine made me smile—I was so glad that we'd cleared things up between us. I'd visit him tomorrow, and then I'd finally meet his family. And the cat. I felt a bit excited when I thought about it. I hoped they'd like me. Maybe I ought to take something home-baked to make myself popular. It sounded like they weren't used to that sort of thing. And cat treats for the cat. Or simply a bag of cat litter. I'd looked it up on the Internet, and it seemed that many cats stopped being clean around the house because no one cleaned out their litter tray.

But now my priority was Mia. Her door was right beside mine. It was a plain wooden door painted forget-me-not blue with a dull silver doorknob, just right for a natural stone house somewhere in the countryside, like the line of little pennants hanging over the lintel. There was no lock, no peephole, and the flap of the letter box was so wide that a small animal could easily fit through it. Last time I'd been here, Fuzzy-Wuzzy, the big toy rabbit with the fox's tail, had been patrolling up and down outside the door, but there was no sign of him tonight. Experimentally, I tried the door handle. It wasn't locked! How careless of Mia's unconscious—anyone could just go in like . . .

"Hello, hello, hello!" A large head appeared right in front of my nose, and I jumped back in alarm. Fuzzy-Wuzzy, the toy rabbit in the yellow overalls. I'd never before realized how much worse soft cuddly toys look when they're larger than life. Particularly when they've been loved as hard as Fuzzy-Wuzzy. There was nothing cute about his missing eye now—it gave him a malicious look, and that impression was reinforced by the two long buck teeth that showed when he spoke.

"Wanna pome! Wanna nurthewy whyme!" he lisped in a grotesque kind of baby talk that was in total contrast to his monumental appearance. His voice was squeaky and childish, like the voice of a rabbit in an animated cartoon.

"You want a poem? A nursery rhyme?"

"Yeth!" Fuzzy-Wuzzy clapped his forepaws. "Rethite it! Rethite it for Fuzzy!"

"Any old nursery rhyme?"

"A nithe one! One that Fuzzy liketh!"

"Okay. Er . . . *Sing a song of sixpence, a pocket full of rye . . .*"

"Nooo! Fuzzy not like zat whyme. Want uvver pome! Want pwoper pome! Or Fuzzy eat you up!" He opened his mouth wide, baring those enormous teeth.

Hmm—maybe the security precautions here weren't so bad after all. Fuzzy-Wuzzy was a creation of Mia's unconscious, so he presumably had some particular poem in mind. One that Mia had loved when she was little. I could think of about a hundred and twenty of those, some in English, some in German—an intruder would have difficulty getting the right one before being eaten alive by Fuzzy. Always supposing that the intruder went to the trouble of talking to him at all, because in spite of his alarming appearance and his threat to eat me up, I could think of many ways and means of getting past him unnoticed.

"As a breath of air I could have made my way into Mia's dream three times by now," I said regretfully. "Or I could have turned into a squirrel to get in through the letter box."

"Zat'th not a pome! Now Fuzzy mutht eat you." He began making for the doorway. "But Fuzzy not like girlth to eat. Fuzzy only like cawwotth to eat," he added with a triumphant giggle, slamming the door in my face.

I sighed. Great—at least that cleared up one point: any reasonably experienced dreamer, like Anabel, for instance, would easily be able to get into Mia's dreams, holding a carrot. I thought it over. As I could hardly keep watch outside Mia's door myself every night, I must think of something else. I snapped my fingers.

"Miss Olivia!" Mr. Wu was bowing to me in his black fighting gear, as if I'd just plucked him out of a martial-arts film. I nodded, pleased. This was better than a silly toy rabbit.

"I want you to guard this door tonight," I explained. "Don't let anyone in or out. And raise the alarm at once if an intruder tries it. Loud enough for me to hear you, anyway." I imagined a gigantic gong outside the door and handed Mr. Wu the beater that went with it.

Mr. Wu tossed the beater up in the air and skillfully caught it as it came down. "The best-locked door is the door that you can leave open," he lectured me.

"Yes, I'm sure you're right. But this one must stay locked tonight, whatever happens. You mustn't let even a breath of air through. Do you understand, Mr. Wu?"

He performed a couple of kung fu moves against an invisible opponent so fast that my eyes could hardly follow him. "My other name is Lightning—the Tiger's Claw of the sky."

"Terrific," I said, impressed. I'd done well there. (And if I ever met the real Mr. Wu again, I'd apologize for all this.) I just wasn't sure whether this Mr. Wu would function without me there. By way of experiment, I went around the nearest corner and came back as a breath of air. This time it worked even better than at my first attempt. I floated several yards along the corridor, no problem, making straight for Mr. Wu.

"Stop, windy intruder!" A well-aimed blow in the air right in front of me, and I was blown a few yards back. "You shall not pass!" With his other hand, Mr. Wu struck the gong. A deep note, kind of solemn but above all deafeningly loud, sounded all the way down the corridor and was thrown back from the walls again and again as an echo. I floated a little way farther. Yes, that was quite loud enough to put even someone as cool, calm, and collected as Anabel to flight. Mr. Wu—'scuse me, the Tiger's Claw of the sky—was the perfect guard to station at Mia's door. If I hadn't been a breath of air, I'd have rubbed my hands with glee. Mia's door seemed secure enough for now, and I could go back to my own dream—and *sleep*! And woe betide anyone who woke me before lunch tomorrow, which was Saturday.

But I wasn't to get to bed just yet. The sound of the gong hadn't quite died away when Henry's door opened and Henry came out. I stopped right in the air where I was, motionless. The corners of his mouth lifted slightly as he glanced at my door, but he didn't stop outside it; he went on down the corridor.

"He who believes in his dreams will sleep his life away, young man with untidy hair," said Mr. Wu as Henry passed him.

Henry cast him and the enormous gong a surprised glance, but he didn't slow down. He went purposefully around the next corner.

I followed him without a moment's thought, as the best, most invisible, and fastest breath of air the world has ever seen. Or *not* seen, rather. I could even turn somersaults—invisible, inaudible somersaults. How surprised Henry would be when I materialized right in front of his eyes! But first I'd try wafting through his hair and stroking his cheek, as breaths of air do when they're feeling in a good mood.

It had taken me just five minutes to find out what Senator Tod's real name was. Henry had done it faster only because he'd used an anagram generator on the Internet. Senator Tod Nord. Dona dents rotor . . . Tornado, nerd, sot. All of them anagrams of one and the same name. For fun, I'd made up a couple more. Finally I had come to the names we were really concerned with as possibilities, and after some attempts with names like Tad, Ned, Ron, and Don, I was left with only one. It even had the man's title; he was Dr. Otto Anderson.

The search engine had given me two Otto Andersons in the United Kingdom, and one of them was a specialist in psychiatry at a hospital in Surrey. The very one to which Anabel had been sent.

It was a nasty thought, being treated by a crazy psychiatrist when you were crazy yourself. But maybe this Dr. Anderson wasn't as crazy as he seemed. One way or another, I couldn't help admiring Anabel for convincing her psychiatrist that it was possible to meet in dreams. How had she done it without making him think her even nuttier than she was, anyway? Because of the sleepwalking business, I'd thought of taking Mia into my confidence but decided not to, because I could just imagine her reaction—she'd go looking for a hidden camera at once. No one in her right mind would believe what was going on.

But this Dr. Anderson had not only believed Anabel— he'd tried the whole thing out himself, and now he was prowling up and down the corridor making trouble. The question was, what exactly did he want from us? And also, why hadn't we seen anything of Anabel?

So far we had not told Arthur anything about our sensational discovery. I was in favor of letting him in on the secret, but Henry wanted to wait a little longer.

And speaking of Henry—I'd taken my eyes off him (Eyes? Better not think too hard about that, Liv!) and had lost sight of him. Not that that's any problem for a breath of air. I blew around the corner at gale force ten, and there he was again. He was standing outside an elegant door covered with lavishly embroidered brocade, looking all around him. I hovered in the air above him and admired the tendrils, flowers, birds, and butterflies embroidered in pale pastel shades. Rather kitschy, but attractive.

If I'd had to guess, I'd have been one hundred percent sure this was a woman's dream door.

Henry bent down and carefully touched a bird embroidered in pink silk. With a faint creak, the door opened.

Oh no.

Of course this was the moment when I ought to have revealed myself, laughing, and Henry would have explained— also laughing—whose this door was.

But in fact, it was the moment when Henry went through the doorway, and I went through it with him as a breath of air. Into the dream of some female entirely unknown to me.

The door latched quietly behind us.

17

AT FIRST I thought I'd landed inside a blue-and-gold Fabergé egg, because the walls were curved, and a huge, glittering, domed roof rose above us. In fact, there was glittering, shimmering light coming at us from all sides. And splashing, trickling sounds, and the faint hiss of vapor escaping. On closer inspection, I saw that we were in some kind of spa, a very luxurious place with the atmosphere of a Turkish bathhouse. The floors were covered with mosaic tiles, midnight blue sprinkled with gold, while the walls had been plastered and then painted in tones of shining light blue. Gaps in the walls, with elaborately ornamented golden frames around them, led from one room to another, and everywhere there were pools for swimming and relaxation, exotic green plants, huge gilt-framed mirrors, mountains of folded towels, and a great many broad, well-upholstered lounge chairs.

And people. Any number of people. Some were wearing bathing things or a bathrobe, a few had just a towel wrapped around them, but most of them were naked. Like the man just getting out of a sauna who was red as a lobster. If I hadn't been a breath of air, I'd have closed my eyes for a moment.

Who on earth would dream a thing like this? And— eeek!—what had happened to Henry's clothes?

I'd been looking around with such interest that I hadn't noticed how he did it—but anyway, now he was wearing a soft blue bathrobe, obviously just the thing for these surroundings. But he was far from being invisible. Hadn't he recently told me that there wasn't much point in walking around in a dream undisguised if you wanted to spy on someone? Because people can lie about themselves even better in dreams than in real life. *As an invisible observer, you can learn a lot about people in their dreams*, he had said. So what was he doing here if he didn't want to spy on anyone? It looked to me almost as if he had a date to meet someone here.

He strolled slowly past a group of lounge chairs and toward a large whirlpool. I followed him, trying not to pay any attention to the lobster-red man, who had made himself comfortable on one of the chairs. Anyway, I had to concentrate much harder on floating than before, because in all the steamy vapors here, I had mutated from a breath of air to being a small cloud. No more hovering and swirling—and with my ease of movement, my high spirits had also left me. The sound track intensified that effect: whoever was dreaming this dream had ghastly taste in music. The sound of Celine Dion singing "My Heart Will Go On" was coming from hidden loudspeakers. Lottie used to make us watch *Titanic* with her at least four times a year, so I knew the song much better than I liked. Lottie always wept buckets over that film, but she said that kind of crying was very healthy and important for your mental hygiene.

When I saw David Beckham sitting beside the whirlpool, dangling his legs in the water, I was relieved for a second or so. For that tiny second, I thought all this must be David Beckham's dream, and the next moment Henry would out himself as a keen football fan and ask for his autograph, or something like that. Even Celine Dion seemed to fit the context—after all, David Beckham had married a Spice Girl, so anything in the matter of musical taste seemed possible.

But then, even before I could take a closer look at Beckham's tattoos, someone said, in a husky voice, "Henry! Dear boy!" and it wasn't David Beckham, but a naked woman stretching in the whirlpool. That is, I couldn't really see if she was entirely naked—the water was bubbling too much for that—but she had nothing on from the waist up, anyway. With her smooth, slightly tanned skin, her golden-brown shining hair and her huge green eyes framed by long, thick lashes, she could easily have passed for a mermaid. Only her dark-red lipstick added a slightly vulgar touch.

Henry smiled at her. Not just as if he'd expected to find her here, as if he were happy about it. I felt myself getting a little heavier. I was slowly sinking toward the floor.

"Hello, B," said Henry. He didn't have even a brief glance to waste on Beckham. Bee, Bea, or B? Was it a code name? It wouldn't have been her cup size if she'd been wearing a bra, anyway.

B poked one of her long legs out of the whirlpool. I wouldn't have been surprised if she'd had a fish's tail instead.

"Don't you want to come into the water?" She smiled seductively.

"No, he wouldn't," I felt like saying, but clouds can't talk. Henry undid the belt of his bathrobe, let it drop from his shoulders to the ground with a casual gesture, so purposefully that B sighed happily in the whirlpool, and I found I was having problems staying in the air. Without doing anything about it myself, I had dissolved into something between a cloud and condensation, and I knew I couldn't stay in that peculiar state for long. But that was the only thing I knew— what the hell was going on here? Secrecy's snide remarks shot into my head. What was it she'd written? That Henry wasn't exactly known for being backward where women were concerned?

Without really noticing what I was doing, I turned into a dragonfly and settled on the leaf of a spider plant beside the pool. That was better. As a dragonfly, I could at least breathe and cling to whatever was under me with all six legs.

Meanwhile B narrowed her eyes and looked Henry appreciatively up and down. "You have a fantastic body," she purred. She was right too. Even David Beckham paled beside Henry, literally, because he had already disappeared without a trace.

At least Henry was wearing bathing trunks, I saw, not that that really reassured me right now.

"What are you waiting for?" Laughing, B flung her head back. She had beautiful teeth too. "Not afraid of me, are you?"

No, Henry definitely didn't look afraid of her. Far from it. I felt my wings begin to quiver. Was this maybe why Henry was so happy to wait before our relationship got any closer? Because he was seeing other . . .

Don't go into the water, I begged him in my thoughts, all the same. I wished I could have put my front legs over my eyes (why did I always have to turn into creatures with excellent vision?), but I did no such thing. Instead I stared at Henry as he slid into the water, submerging as slowly as a male model in an aftershave ad. When he came up again, tiny drops of water shimmered around him in slow motion with the light breaking on them, and larger beads of moisture stood out on his smooth skin. With a satisfied smile, Henry settled down comfortably in the pool opposite B. They had it all to themselves now. And Celine Dion started up again. *Every night in my dreams, I see you, I feel you, that is how I know you go on. . . .*

Could dragonflies throw up? Because that was what I felt like doing right there and then.

Now an elderly man in a crumpled suit had taken over for David Beckham beside the pool. He was sitting on a shabby plastic chair that didn't suit the grand surroundings in the least, and he was saying something in a foreign language, maybe Russian, but anyway, he sounded gruff and unfriendly.

B was reluctantly listening. She frowned. "Am I leading children astray?" For the first time, I heard the slight accent in her voice. "Well, look at him, Papa. He's more of a man than you ever were. And I have a right to a bit of fun."

The old man answered in his own language, sounding even less friendly than before, and to reinforce whatever he was saying, he spat on the ground.

"That's not true," cried B indignantly. "I don't look a day older than twenty-nine, and this young man has come of age and knows exactly what he's doing."

"Absolutely," said Henry, although that was a lie. He hadn't quite come of age; he wouldn't be eighteen until February, a week later than Florence and Grayson. "And now I'll ask you to go away and leave your daughter in peace, or I'm afraid I'll have to lend you a hand."

B's father didn't look as if he felt like doing as Henry asked. He opened his mouth to reply, but Henry raised a hand, and it was as if he had muted the sound track: B's father was talking volubly, with much gesticulation, but you couldn't hear a word he was saying, even when he shouted harder and harder with his mouth wide open, and the veins on his forehead stood out. At another wave of Henry's hand, two white-clad pool attendants appeared, picked up the old man, chair and all—he was still shouting silently—and carried him away.

"That's that, then," said Henry, turning back to B, who was looking at him admiringly.

"How did you do that?" she asked. "No one else has ever managed to silence him."

"Then it was about time," said Henry, shrugging his shoulders in a way so typical of him that I began trembling again on my spider plant leaf, and this time the leaf trembled too. What was I really doing here? Why had I followed him? I didn't want to watch any of this. All I really wanted was to wake up.

By now the whole plant was shaking, but Henry didn't notice.

"You really don't deserve that kind of thing, B," he went on. "A woman like you shouldn't let anyone treat her so badly."

"Oh, you wonderful, wonderful man!" B was obviously about to swim over to him, and over the next few days, I kept wondering what would have happened next if I hadn't grown larger on the spider plant leaf and then, slowly, slipped backward off it. I landed with a loud splash in the bubbling water between Henry and B. She let out a little shriek and spluttered, while Henry stared at me blankly.

I'd had no control at all over turning back into my own shape, so I wasn't surprised to find that I was naked, too, although my skin shone in metallic green and blue, and there were still four delicate dragonfly wings on my back, drenched with water and hanging uselessly down.

But that made no difference now.

B was the first to recover from the shock. She coughed and spat out some water. "Oh no, no!" she said indignantly. "It was so nice just now. Perfect! We can do without a weird sort of elf, or something out of *Avatar*. What's all this about?"

Yes, what *was* it all about? I didn't know either. I didn't know anything anymore.

The guilty look in Henry's eyes only made everything worse, and it also made me so angry that I entirely forgot to be embarrassed.

"No idea," I snapped as I corrected my skin color and got rid of the wings. "Why don't we ask Henry?"

But Henry wasn't saying anything. The sight of me had obviously deprived him of speech.

I swam to the side of the pool, climbed out, and marched away, dripping water, past all the other naked figures. My feet were still green, and everyone in the place seemed to be staring at me. Well, let them stare—I could guarantee we'd never meet again!

Why couldn't I wake up? Where was the door leading into the corridor? I wanted to go home, that was all—I just wanted to go home.

As if someone had turned on a faucet inside me, I began

shedding tears. They ran down my cheeks, and there wasn't a thing I could do about it. Oh, damn it! This was too much! That stupid door had to be somewhere here. Blinded by tears, I felt my way along the wall.

"Liv!" Henry took my forearm in both hands and turned me around to face him. Without stopping to think, I freed myself with the move I'd practiced with Mr. Wu over and over again, until it was part of my flesh and blood. And when Henry immediately made another grab for me, I drove my fist into his sternum. That was the gua tong choy move.

But instead of bending double under the force of my blow, Henry put out his hands and tried mopping the tears off my cheeks. "Livvy, please! Don't run away."

He was back in jeans and T-shirt again, and perfectly dry, and that made me furious as well. He obviously had the nerve to think of his outward appearance in this situation, while I was wandering around the place on green feet, naked, soaking wet, and in floods of tears.

To make matters worse, he made a bathrobe appear out of nothing and held it out to me. And yes, there was definitely pity in his eyes. "You shouldn't have done that, Liv," he said softly. "Here, put this on."

That was the moment when my tears dried up, and I went rigid with fury. It cost me only a tenth of a second to get myself fully clothed and without a hair out of place. I'd even imagined my glasses on. And now at last I could see clearly again: there was a door covered with fabric right beside me.

"There we are," I replied, and even my voice was rigid—frozen rigid as an icicle. I raised my chin and looked straight into Henry's gray eyes. "Sorry to have disturbed your rendezvous. I had no idea you fancied older women. She's terrific, no doubt about it—except maybe for her musical tastes." Celine Dion was still yowling over the loudspeakers, saying her love was safe in her heart, her heart was still beating, and life went on. How nice for her. "But, hey, you can't have everything."

I tossed my hair back, turned on my heel, and flung the door open. I'd studied the art of making a dramatic exit from watching Florence. Stupidly, I had picked the wrong door. This one led into a cupboard full of towels.

Damn it, damn it, damn it! I couldn't even make a proper exit.

Behind me, Henry said my name again, but before I could turn to face him, I felt heavy pressure on my chest. And then I made a dramatic exit after all, because a gigantic furry ginger paw broke through the domed roof and kicked me out of B's dream.

18

IT WASN'T REALLY a gigantic paw, because Spot's paw was rather small by comparison with the rest of him, and he was patting my cheek with it. The cat was sitting on my chest, purring loudly, and I was so grateful to him for waking me from my dream that I didn't even scold him. In fact, I let him go on sitting there and tickled him under the chin until my pulse had calmed down a little. I'd never before longed so much to be back when a bad dream was nothing but a bad dream. There was a large lump in my throat, because the tears I'd shed in my dream had all gathered there. But I knew that if I gave way to my urge to cry it would be like breaching a dam—there'd be no stopping it. So I tried to concentrate on the soothing sound of the cat's purr and just not think.

However, Spot wasn't there simply to be tickled under the chin. He gave me a gentle reminder in the form of another pat on my cheek.

"How did you get in here, anyway, kitty?" I cautiously put him on the floor, switched on the bedside lamp, and got out of bed. Someone must have opened my door, because I'd definitely closed it before going to sleep.

"Or have you found out how to push door handles down?" Spot was still purring as he rubbed around my legs. I glanced at my alarm clock. Three thirty. Presumably the cat wanted to go out on his usual nocturnal mouse hunt. Normally, Grayson was responsible for letting him out (it was also Grayson who had to remove the dead voles that Spot brought home and left on the doormat), but today Spot seemed to have chosen me to open the door.

"Okay, come on, then," I said, and Spot went out the half-open door ahead of me. He waited at the top of the stairs as I checked that Mia was in bed and sleeping peacefully (she was). Downstairs, I opened the door from the kitchen to the terrace for him, and as usual he suddenly wasn't in any hurry, but sat in the doorway washing himself, while I stepped from foot to foot to keep warm as I slowly froze into an icicle. All the same, I watched Spot regretfully when he finally felt like setting off. There had been something comforting about his presence. Or at least, it had kept my thoughts occupied. When I went back to bed, I felt sure I'd have the images from my dream before my eyes at once: Henry taking off his bathrobe and plunging into the whirlpool; Henry smiling at B; Henry saying, in a deep voice, *A woman like you shouldn't let anyone treat her so badly.*

A woman like you . . . Instead of going back to bed, I went into the bathroom and stared at myself in the mirror. Without glasses or contact lenses, I couldn't see myself very clearly, but even so I knew I couldn't compete with B. I was the opposite of beautiful, grown-up, and sexy. It was pathetic.

As if on cue, I thought of all the nasty things Secrecy had

written and the comments of the other students. Maybe they were right to say that Henry and I hadn't slept with each other yet only because I was too childish and immature for him.

The opposite of desirable.

And then, without further warning, my tears began to flow, and Spot wasn't there to take my mind off them. I was unable to stop crying, although I really did try to. I hung over the basin, bent double as if I had a bad stomach upset, and cried harder than ever before in my life.

When someone knocked on the door, I couldn't have said how much time had passed. I didn't want to know either. I didn't want to know anything anymore. There must be some way of deleting the last few hours from my memory. The only question was, where could I find a hypnotist to do it for me in a hurry? Apparently electric shocks could do it, too, but perhaps the hard bathroom tiles would work if I just banged my head on them hard enough. There was another knock on the door.

"Liv? Are you in there?" That was Grayson, and he sounded tired and irritated.

Couldn't I be left in peace in this house, even at night? I wanted to be alone. Alone with the tiles on the bathroom floor. "Go . . . go and use the guest toilet, Grayson," I said, sounding just as irritated. The worst of my sobbing was over, but it had left me with hiccups.

Grayson muttered something to himself on the other side of the door.

Even without contact lenses, I could tell from the mirror that my face was blotchy and my eyes swollen. I tried cold water, but that did nothing for me, so I took a cotton pad, soaked it in Florence's orange face tonic, and dabbed my face with it. It didn't do anything about the blotchiness either, but at least it smelled delicious. What I needed was soothing face cream. Maybe I'd find some among Florence's expensive little pots and jars, although Mia and I were forbidden to touch them on pain of death. So far I hadn't, but now I felt an urgent need to unscrew the golden lid of one of them. Calendula cream. I couldn't read the small print, but calendula sounded healthy and reassuring, the natural enemy of red blotches. I slapped plenty of it on my face.

"I can hardly break the door down, can I?" Grayson was obviously still leaning on the other side of it.

"No, but you can—hic—just go away," I said.

"I'm not talking to you—and no, I can't, not without rousing the whole house. . . . Liv, what are you doing in there?"

"Have you—hic—lost your marbles?"

I could hear Grayson's sigh through the door. "Not cutting your wrists, are you?"

What? "No, I'm rubbing cream into my face." And now the delicate little golden glass lid slipped out of my hand and fell into the basin. "Oh, damn it! Hic."

"Did you hear me? You're fine, both of you."

Who was he talking to out there? I hoped it wasn't Florence. She'd murder me when she found out that the lid of her calendula cream was cracked. Maybe I could conceal it with a little gold nail polish? I'd seen some on Florence's toenails the other day. I opened the drawer where she kept her bottles of nail polish, about sixty of them.

"No, you idiot, I can't see it with my own eyes," said Grayson outside the door in annoyance. "Because I don't happen to be able to see through walls . . . No, how could I . . .

Liv, please open the door! I have to convince myself that you're all right with my own eyes."

"You're out of your mind," I said. There—gold nail polish, next to a bottle of pale brown! Florence had sorted them out by color.

"Don't say that, Henry, not to me," said Grayson.

The little bottle of nail polish slipped out of my hands, but I just managed to catch it before it hit the tiled floor. Henry! The shock had cured my hiccups as if by magic.

"He couldn't reach you on your cell phone, so he called me," said Grayson. "And now he's driving me insane and keeping me here outside the bathroom door."

Fingers flying, I opened the bathroom door, and Grayson, dazzled by the light, narrowed his eyes. Silently, he held out his iPhone to me. "At last!"

I put my hand out, but then I couldn't bring myself to take the phone. The mere idea of hearing Henry's voice . . .

"Tell him I'm asleep," I whispered.

Grayson rolled his eyes. "It's a bit late for that. Anyway, I was asleep myself, and he couldn't have cared less." He yawned. "Liv, can't you two sort out your problems in the daytime?"

No, I was afraid our problems couldn't be sorted out at all. Either by day or night.

Grayson put the phone to his ear again. "Did you hear that? She doesn't want to talk to you. But like I said, she's fine."

Oh, sure. I was really, really fine. Except for the tears coming to my eyes again.

"What?" Grayson was looking at me rather more

thoroughly now that he was used to the light. He frowned. "Yes, I tell you! Perfectly normal. And now I'm ending this call, okay? It's four thirty, and we're all supposed to be fast asleep right now. If you call again, I'm not answering, is that clear? See you at practice." With a snort, he ended the call. "What have you been doing to him?"

"What have *I* been doing to *him*?" I felt like snorting myself now, which helped a bit to get the tears under control. "I only disturbed him getting up close and personal with someone else, that's all. Do you happen to know a woman called B?"

"Shhh!" Grayson reached past me and switched off the bathroom light. "Don't go waking everyone else too!"

"I haven't finished in here," I said, switching the light on again.

"Oh, yes you have." Grayson switched it off. "You ought to be in bed. Have you seen yourself in the mirror? You look terrible."

"Do you think I don't know that?" I tried to slam the bathroom door in his face, but he got between me and it, took my arm, and hauled me out into the corridor.

"We have an important game this afternoon, and our coach wants us to have extra practice. I've had enough of all this. I need some sleep."

"Then go to bed, why don't you?" I made a halfhearted attempt to shake off his grip, but I was thankful at heart that he had made me leave the bathroom. Otherwise I'd probably have spent days in there, doing stupid things with my head, the tiles, and Florence's nail polish.

But Grayson wasn't to be shaken off just like that. He didn't let go of me until we were in my room and he had closed the door behind us. Then he leaned back on it and took two deep breaths.

So did I. I could see the pity in Grayson's glance even in the poor light of my bedside lamp, and it was hard to take. I narrowed my eyes. I mustn't cry in front of him. I wouldn't either.

"What's that on your face?"

"You mean my nose? Ugly, isn't it? Like everything about me. No wonder Henry doesn't want me."

"I meant that white stuff . . ." Grayson raised his forefinger and ran it over my forehead. I'd forgotten all about Florence's calendula cream. I wiped my face with the back of my hand.

"You're not in the least ugly, Liv, just rather blotchy in the face—and like you'd been crying your eyes out." Grayson looked at me seriously. "As for Henry . . . I've no idea what's been going on between you two, but I've never seen him so distraught."

Distraught? I doubted whether he needed calendula cream himself.

"What are you two getting up to in your dreams?" Grayson suddenly sounded angry. "Why don't you simply stop it and concentrate on real life? Heaven knows that's complicated enough."

"You'll have to ask Henry that question." I let myself drop facedown on my bed. "Anyway, what you feel in dreams is just as real." Unfortunately. And sure enough I started crying again. Oh, shit.

"One more reason to keep away from them."

I'd buried my face in my pillows, but I could hear Grayson coming closer. He hesitantly sat down on the edge of my bed.

"Whatever happened between you is your business," he said, and his tone of voice was considerably gentler now. "But I do know one thing: Henry would never hurt you, Liv."

Oh, wouldn't he? He just did. I stifled a sob in my pillow.

"I promise you that's true," said Grayson, a little more firmly. "I've known him since we first went to school, and since he met you . . . he's been entirely different."

I sat up abruptly. "Oh yes? Different how?"

A shadow fell on Grayson's face. "It's difficult to explain that to you."

I wrinkled my nose angrily. "But an explanation would be really helpful," I said. I'd meant to say that with an under-tone of sarcasm, but it came out as a pathetic plea.

Grayson looked as if he'd rather be somewhere else. "Henry . . ." He hesitated again. "Henry's had . . . quite a few girlfriends before, okay?"

Yes. Well. Good explanation. No doubt preferring older girlfriends who looked fantastic in whirlpools. If that was the best Grayson could do to cheer me up, I ought to have tried the bathroom tiles.

"But none of them ever lasted for long. And it was all superficial," said Grayson hastily. He had guilt all over his face. "Henry never let anyone get really close to him, but it's not like that with you. He's different. He's . . ." Grayson paused for a moment. "He's kind of himself with you. Happy."

This conversation was clearly going in the wrong direction.

I shook my head. "Happy? So what about the—" I stopped short. I couldn't bring myself to tell Grayson about the naked mermaid. Even if he was with me, Henry obviously couldn't leave her alone. That was simply too humiliating. "Yes, sure, and because he's so happy he also tells me *everything* about his life!" I said instead.

"Liv . . ."

"It's true. Even Emily knows more about him than I do."

Grayson stood up and wandered over to the window. Only now did I notice that for a change he was wearing a T-shirt tonight. "Henry's never talked about himself much, not even to Arthur and me. He'd sooner bite his tongue off. It's just that over the years we've inevitably picked up this or that."

"Like what, for instance?" I asked.

Grayson's face was working. He turned back to the window and acted as if he were looking out. "At his eighth birthday party, we all had to leave early when his mother staggered into the living room and started cutting her wrists instead of the birthday cake. Because Henry's father was having a relationship with the Swedish au pair. His thirteenth birthday was a total washout. That was when his mother went missing for a whole week, and Henry was left alone at home with Amy, who was four months old, and little Milo, while his father was sailing around the Mediterranean on a yacht and couldn't be reached. He never could be reached when Henry really needed him. I can't count the times Henry's been late for school or for practice because he had to deal with some crisis at home. . . ."

Grayson had been talking fast and in a strained voice, as if what he was saying hurt him physically, and I felt the same. All this was much, much worse than I'd thought.

And yet, while the ghastly images of Henry's family life that he was revealing made my heart heavy with pity, I knew they didn't alter one fact: Henry had been in the process of deceiving me with someone else, and that hurt as much as ever. Except that to make matters even worse, I also felt I was being coldhearted and selfish because, although poor Henry had enough to put up with, what with his totally screwed-up family, I couldn't forgive him for getting in the whirlpool with a naked woman.

I heard a miserable sound, and for a moment I thought Spot was back. That was before I realized that I'd made the sound myself.

Grayson turned toward me. I was afraid to look at his face, because if he looked at me sympathetically again, I'd have to go and lock myself in the bathroom again. Forever.

But there wasn't any sympathy in Grayson's eyes this time, only something like anger. "I'm an idiot," he said abruptly. "It's up to Henry to explain all this to you, and he ought to have done it long ago. No idea why I'm doing it for him now."

"Because you want to be helpful." I didn't know exactly why, but suddenly I felt just a tiny bit better. Not so miserable.

"But if he's done something that hurts you, then . . . then I guess my help isn't much good." Grayson grinned at me, embarrassed. "Apart from which I was laying it on a bit thick. I mean, back then he wasn't *entirely* on his own with Amy and Milo. The gardener and the housekeeper were there too. And the pets, and the au pair. But he doesn't trust them an inch when it comes to Amy. Au pairs, I mean, not pets."

I tried to laugh, and sure enough, it worked a bit.

Grayson came over to me and looked hard at my face. "How long since you had a good night's sleep?"

I shrugged my shoulders and leaned back on the pillows. Suddenly I was incredibly tired. Tired, exhausted, and overstrained.

He glanced at my alarm clock. "You could get a few hours'

sleep now—I'll tell everyone to be quiet and not wake you. You don't have to worry about Mia. I looked in on her not long ago, and she's sleeping peacefully in her bed."

I couldn't help smiling. "I left a few security precautions in place outside her dream door, just to be on the safe side. Maybe you should do the same with your door."

"You think so?" He had already turned to go, but then he turned back and looked suspiciously at me. "Who'd be interested in my dreams? I'm not involved in any of this. And I very much hope you're not thinking of taking advantage of my trust and visiting me in my dreams."

"Never! Except in an emergency," I assured him, and quickly switched off the bedside lamp. It was easier to go on talking in the dark. "Grayson?"

"Yes?"

"Thanks. Sometimes I don't know what I'd do without you." Hesitantly, I added, "And I'm sorry. I mean, sorry you aren't getting enough sleep because of me. That you feel you have to worry about me. And that we destroyed that horrible bush."

I heard Grayson sigh. "That's all right."

"No, it isn't. You really are the best, nicest"—and best-looking!—"big brother anyone could wish for."

He laughed quietly. "And you're the most annoying . . . and blotchiest little sister I've ever had. Sleep well, Liv. Everything will look better in the morning."

TITTLE-TATTLE BLOG

The Frognal Academy Tittle-Tattle Blog, with all the latest gossip, the best rumors, and the hottest scandals from our school.

ABOUT ME:

My name is Secrecy—I'm right here among you, and I know *all* your secrets.

13 January

So there was I thinking that without Jasper to call the referee animal names, start fights, or strip off his jersey in the middle of a game, watching the Frognal Flames would be boring, but guess what? I was dead wrong. Okay, so it might have been better if we'd won, but apart from that I can't complain. It was a great show.

And am I ever glad not to be a boy—all that testosterone can't be much fun. Seems like it's even more unpredictable than PMS. Arthur has just set a new record. With two obvious fouls just eight minutes into the game, wow, Gabriel didn't really have to call the ref a blind, beer-bellied sad sack. And as for Henry—terrific to see the elegance with which he missed the basket on all of his free throws, without reacting at all.

A word in the ear of Eric Sarstedt: We like you fine, we really do, and you're trying hard to stand in for Jasper. But never mind that, just keep your jersey on, okay? If we want to see hairy backs, we can simply go to the zoo.

After the game, Grayson, as captain of our team and deputy chief editor of *reflexx* magazine, gave his co-editor and girlfriend, Emily Clark, an interview. I'm glad to say we can let you read it—an exclusive, just for you.

Emily: "I need a statement for *reflexx*. A word or so explaining why you lost. The extra practice doesn't seem to have done your team much good."

Grayson: "They just need a good night's sleep. Right, I'm off."

Emily: "Do I put that in?"

Grayson: "No, of course not. We'll do it later, okay? I have to join the others."

Emily: "Later's no good. You know our deadline. Just a sentence."

Grayson: "My God, Emily, think something up yourself."

Emily: "Grayson Spencer is disappointed in his team members. Their adolescent behavior has foiled his best efforts yet again. One really wonders why he invests so much time and energy in this silly sport and his team, when he could be concentrating on more important things in his last year at school."

Grayson: "Silly sport? Basketball? Because it doesn't entail tormenting horses by plaiting their manes into little braids?"

Emily: "Because it means practicing three times a week with a bunch of weak-minded idiots and the effect is catching."

Short pause.

Grayson: "Okay, that sounds super. Put it in the magazine."

Emily: "Grayson. I didn't mean it like that. Wait . . ."

Grayson: (has gone already).

As I always say, couples shouldn't work together. It's bound to end in tears.

Can't wait to see the report that will appear in *reflexx* on Wednesday. Or maybe it won't appear at all. ☺

See you later!

Secrecy

PS—Liv and Mia Silver, a.k.a. the ax murderesses, a.k.a. the spectacled snakes who go around chopping down trees, weren't there to watch the game—and I for one didn't miss them. My heart still bleeds when I think of that beautiful topiary peacock. How about all of you?

19

MR. WU WAS STANDING in his fighting gear outside Mia's door like a soldier of the Royal Guard, except that instead of a gun he had the gong beater over his shoulder. However, I wasn't sure whether he had been on duty while I was awake as well. After all, he was my dream creation, and if I was not asleep, then how could he exist here?

"No intruder has ventured to come to blows with the Tiger's Claw of the sky," he informed me.

"Did anyone try it, then?" I asked intently, although at the same moment I thought that a figure whom I had only imagined could hardly have seen anything that I hadn't seen. (Yes, I know, a rather complicated thought. The kind to be avoided if you don't want to get your brain tied in knots.)

"All crows under the sun are black." Mr. Wu nodded his head back and forth. "There was that stranger with the hat. . . ."

Hat? The stranger could only have been Senator Tod. Or rather, Dr. Anderson, Anabel's psychiatrist. And did that mean that he had really been here, or just that Mr. Wu, as part of myself, was only saying what I was afraid of? But what could Senator Tod want from Mia? Maybe he had just passed by in search of someone else—me, for instance.

"This really is complicated," I murmured, casting a quick look at Henry's black door. When I had stepped into the corridor and saw that it was still right opposite mine, my stomach had contracted painfully. Although I told myself I was here only for Mia, I mustn't pretend—secretly, I'd hoped to meet Henry.

I'd refused to speak to him all Saturday. After sleeping in until eleven, I ought to have jumped out of bed fresh as a daisy, but you don't jump out of bed fresh as a daisy when you've caught your own boyfriend in a whirlpool with a naked woman and cried half the night. I for one had the feeling that there was lead in my veins instead of blood. Or poison.

In spite of the extra practice and the basketball game, Henry had left me seven voice mails and tried the landline three times, but in the evening, when the game was over and I finally felt strong enough to face him without instantly bursting into tears, or screaming, or doing both at once, radio silence suddenly set in. No more calls, no texts.

And when someone rang the doorbell, it was only Emily, wanting to see Florence and discuss plans for the twins' birthday party, of course without Grayson. They were taking over the living room for that, so Mia and I had to leave it ourselves. Although I didn't really mind, because all I wanted to do this evening was lie in bed, staring at the ceiling and feeling terrible. First I took a bath, staring at the bathroom ceiling, and likewise feeling terrible. Maybe it was the effect of the hot water, or maybe it was also because I still had to catch up on sleep, or it was a kind of protective function of the body simply to switch off in stressful situations, but anyway, my eyes closed as soon as I was in bed. My last thought was for the dream corridor. In no circumstances did I want to go into it today. For one thing, I didn't know whether Henry would be waiting for me there, and for another, I wanted him to wait in vain. If he was waiting.

Yes, well. Here I was, in spite of my good intentions—and here Henry wasn't.

"First words get confused, then ideas get confused, and finally so do the facts," said Mr. Wu.

"I guess you're right about that." I sighed and patted his shoulder. "Go on guarding this door, please. You're doing fine."

So now what? I turned on my own axis. My eyes focused on Henry's door again. The brass lion's head and the fittings of the three locks, one above another, shone as if freshly polished in the dim light of the corridor. For a few seconds, I stared at the words DREAM ON, carved into the wood in playfully curving characters, then I just walked away. *I must get out of here.* I ran down the corridor, turned the corner to the left, and didn't stop until I saw the next door that I knew. It was Arthur's, and for a split second I actually thought of knocking at it. Arthur might know the answers to my questions.

I quickly let my hand drop again. Had I really come to this—looking for Arthur's company out of sheer desperation? I could have kicked myself, but I never got around to it, because suddenly I felt sure that I wasn't alone. It wasn't the first time that the corridor had been lying there perfectly calm and peaceful, yet I could sense someone else's presence.

And I wasn't wrong. Senator Tod came out of the shadows

where the corridor next branched. Along with his cloak and the slouch hat pulled right down over his forehead.

"Well, well, if it isn't the leopard girl," he said, and he sounded positively glad to see me.

I was neither particularly shocked nor especially afraid, which surprised me a little.

"If it isn't the Senator," I replied. "Dressed to the nines as usual. Although that leather cloak reminds me a bit of the costumes in cheap B movies."

Senator Tod put back his head and let his laughter ring out. By now this gruesome sound, however, had lost a good deal of its effect on me. I didn't even get goose bumps. He fell silent and came a step closer. Now I could see the watery blue eyes under the brim of his hat.

"Is that by any chance a spider on your arm?"

It was. A large, hairy tarantula was slowly climbing up my sleeve. It was only with difficulty that I suppressed a shriek. If this hadn't been a dream, I'd have hopped around, screaming at the top of my voice. To be honest, I'd have done that even with a spider only half the size of this one. I wasn't very keen on animals with more than four legs, so I had spent quite a lot of time screaming while we were in India. But I wasn't going to give Senator Tod the satisfaction. And this wasn't real life. In real life, I was lying safe and sound in my bed, in a house that was a total no-go area for tarantulas.

"You know, I've never met a girl who wasn't afraid of spiders," said Senator Tod, gloating. As he saw it, I was rigid with terror. "Psychologically, there's a simple explanation. The living creatures we fear most are those whose physical appearance is least like that of human beings."

It took me a bit of an effort, but I put out a hand and stroked the tarantula's hairy back.

"So nice and fluffy," I said. "Have a feel of it yourself. I think it's called confrontation therapy, isn't it?"

I was expecting him either to pounce on the tarantula or turn it into an even bigger spider (which is what I'd have done in his place), and I was preparing to turn myself into a brimstone yellow butterfly. But Senator Tod just gave me a crafty smile.

"Oh, very brave, little one," he said. "But you can't fool me. I see just what's going on inside you: dilated pupils, pulse beating faster, higher frequency of breathing. . . . Oh, look at that, here come some more. . . ."

Two more tarantulas had appeared between us and were making for my legs. And yes, my breathing really was a little irregular.

"I count on subtle effects, you see," Senator Tod went on, sadistically clicking his tongue, and two more spiders turned up. This time they came scrambling down from the walls.

This was getting to be more than I could take.

"You can keep your eye on one spider—but two?" The watery blue eyes were watching me intently. "It's the unpredictably quick movements that make them so frightening. Did you know that they can jump a long way?"

"Is that so?" As the spiders came closer, I grew two extra arms. And two extra legs. All of them very hairy. As Senator Tod watched, I turned myself into an enormous tarantula, and it wasn't even difficult—I had the little brutes right there before my eyes to be copied. Before my eight eyes, to be precise, two large and six small eyes, all of them staring at Senator Tod.

Taken completely by surprise, he staggered back, and suddenly held up a little bottle filled with some kind of bright, shining liquid. He seemed surprised by it himself, but he held it out in my direction and shouted, "Don't come any closer!" I wasn't going to, but I burst out laughing. Someone had been watching *The Lord of the Rings* once too often. "The light of Eärendil? I'm afraid that won't work here." I was laughing so hard that I could hardly keep my balance on my thin spidery legs, while my huge body swayed back and forth, but I managed to exchange the little bottle in Senator Tod's hand for one of the tarantulas on the floor. I moved the other three to his slouch hat. And then, because my peals of laughter seemed to have detracted a bit from my terrifying appearance, I changed back to my own shape and smoothed down my T-shirt.

That had done me good. I ran through Mr. Wu's large selection of wise sayings for one to suit the situation, but I could think of only one in a hurry, and it wasn't really appropriate. All the same, on principle, I came out with it: "When the wind of change blows, some build walls, some build windmills."

However, Senator Tod wasn't interested in wise sayings. He was having difficulty shaking off the spiders he had imagined into being himself, as I noticed with satisfaction. When he had finally done it, Arthur's door opened, and Arthur came out.

"Am I in the way?" he inquired, looking from me to Senator Tod and back again.

"Not at all," I said as Arthur's door closed behind him. "Frodo here and I are just having a shot at applied psychology. Did you know that . . ." But I got no further, because Senator Tod had straightened up, raised his arm, and thrown something that looked like a bolt of lightning at me. It would have hit me, too, if a kind of energy field hadn't formed in the corridor right in front of me like a wall. The bolt of lightning bounced off it and shattered into a thousand tiny sparks.

Arthur looked surprised, and only now did I realize that he wasn't the one who had come to my rescue.

I spun around. Henry. He was standing a little way behind me in the corridor, holding the palm of his hand up in front of Senator Tod. At the sight of him, my heart started racing the way it ought really to have raced when I saw the spiders just now. Where had he come from all of a sudden? Had he been here all the time? Had he perhaps been watching me and following me all along?

He was looking good, better than ever, pale, with bright-gray eyes and a slight smile on his lips. With a casual movement, he dug his hands into the pockets of his jeans. Arthur applauded.

Senator Tod seemed to be temporarily speechless. He was staring at all three of us with hostility.

"Who are you supposed to be impersonating now, Senator? Thor, the god of thunder? Or Zeus?" Henry shook his head pityingly. "Delusions of grandeur, black leather, lightning—a clear case of megalomania. But I'm sure you made the same diagnosis yourself long ago, didn't you, Dr. Anderson?"

Senator Tod looked as if he'd been caught in the act of wrongdoing. He straightened his hat.

"Dr. Anderson?" Arthur repeated.

Henry nodded. "Dr. Otto Anderson. Anabel's psychiatrist in the hospital. He's a bit fatter and shorter in real life, and he wears glasses, but, hey, who wants to look the same in dreams as in real life?"

It was obvious that this news took Arthur completely by surprise. His face expressed a whole range of emotions in turn. Astonishment. Understanding. And finally anger. His jaw muscles were working.

"Did Anabel send you? Are you letting a girl of eighteen exploit you?"

Dr. Anderson had recovered a little, and seemed to be gradually getting his usual self-confidence back. "Your girlfriend, Anabel, is right—you three really are still children," he said with a brief, scornful laugh. "I don't let anyone exploit me, certainly not a schizoid girl like her. However, I'm grateful to her for showing me the way into this dream world. Because unlike her, I soon realized that you can do more here than play games."

"So what can you do instead? Rule the world or something?" inquired Henry. "I'm not trying to probe your mind too far, but you still have a lot to learn if that's what you want."

"Where's Anabel? And what does she have to do with you?" asked Arthur.

Senator Tod made a throwaway gesture. "The poor child thought that maybe she could get out of the hospital by manipulating me in dreams. But I'm afraid her plan didn't work—I don't let anyone manipulate me. However, I must say that I find the possibilities of this place fascinating. Just for a moment I thought I had lost my own mind. . . ."

"How about Anabel?" I asked. My heart was still racing, but I'd stopped looking at Henry. It seemed a better idea to concentrate on Senator Tod.

"Anabel . . . yes. I'd have shown myself very appreciative, but unfortunately the girl didn't want to cooperate. And I could really have done with her help—all this is still entirely new to me. But characters like Anabel don't appreciate it when their plans don't work. You young people will know that better than anyone." He laughed again. He was regaining his self-confidence with every passing second. Oddly enough, he no longer seemed to me quite so ridiculous, but very dangerous instead. "And because I'm afraid she didn't want to play by my rules, I had to . . . Well, let's just say she's taking a little rest."

I was coming out in goose bumps all over now.

"With young women patients of her sort, one always has to go carefully—highly intelligent, an influential father, I didn't want to take any risks," Senator Tod went on calmly. He seemed to relish our shocked silence. "But luckily, as the psychiatrist treating her case, I had all sorts of ways and means at my disposal."

"What did you do to her?" I whispered. Images of the whole arsenal of depressing movie clichés about psychiatric treatment were unreeling before my mind's eye: electric shocks, straitjackets, lobotomies, and I saw Anabel tied down to a bed, staring into space with empty eyes.

Dr. Anderson came a step closer. "There are some very acceptable soporifics that prevent REM sleep," he said, sounding pleased with himself. "That's why you haven't seen Anabel here for so long. Maybe you'll come to visit her sometime? She'll be staying in my department for a long time yet, and she's so lonely." Then he struck his forehead. "Oh no, that won't do—I put her on a no-visiting regime. All for her own good."

"You . . ." All the color had drained away from Arthur's angelic face. "You're lying! Anabel is far too clever to let . . . Oh God!"

Dr. Anderson smiled triumphantly. "You're still in love with her, aren't you, my young angel? I'll admit that she's an extremely pretty girl—those incredible turquoise eyes!" He paused for a moment and winked at Arthur. "Yes, I can understand you. But believe me, she's bad news for you."

"You monster," said Arthur with difficulty.

"If Anabel hasn't sent you here, then why are you trying to get close to us?" asked Henry, frowning. "What do you expect us to do for you?"

The self-satisfied smile gave way to an expression of annoyance. "I don't expect you to do anything for me. But you're the only ones roaming around these corridors, myself excluded. And I have to practice on someone!" His chin jutted, and I could see the deranged light in his eyes. "Anabel talked so much about you all in her therapy sessions, and I must say she has a good understanding of human nature. When I first set eyes on you, it was like meeting old friends."

Arthur's jawbones were still working. He was probably imagining all the things about him that Anabel had told her psychiatrist.

"You're still better at this than I am, but that will soon change." Dr. Anderson had raised his voice now. "And then, my dear children, you'd better be careful!"

Henry was right. The man really did suffer from megalomania. I felt like throwing a bolt of lightning back at him.

But nothing came of that idea. An electronic beep sounded, and as we were looking around for the source of it, Senator Tod disappeared without a trace.

"His duty beeper in the hospital," said Henry. "He's awake again. All the same, we know a little more now. I thought he was delightfully free with his information."

Arthur was still looking baffled. "I just can't believe any of this," he murmured. Then he pointed to his door, right behind him. "Why don't we go in here and discuss it further?" He tapped in a numerical code—making sure we couldn't see it, of course—and the door opened. "I'd like to know how you two found out who he is. And think what we should do next."

I was about to follow him, but Henry grasped my wrist and held it firmly.

"*We* aren't about to do anything, Arthur," he said. "We're not a team any longer, remember? Even Dr. Anderson doesn't change that."

"Henry . . ." Arthur's expression might have melted a heart of stone, but Henry was already turning to walk away. And taking me with him, my wrist still in his steely grasp.

I felt Arthur's eyes on our backs, and then I heard his door latch shut.

20

"WHY EXACTLY WERE you going to see Arthur?" Henry asked in his usual light, conversational tone. But his body language was saying something else entirely. He was still holding my wrist tightly, and I had difficulty keeping up with him.

I didn't reply, if only because I didn't know why I was going to see Arthur myself. It probably wouldn't have been difficult to break free, but I let Henry lead me to his door. Meanwhile I was feverishly checking my appearance—you never knew in dreams. Hair—check. Clothes—check. Blotches gone—check. Glasses gone—check. You didn't need those in a dream, anyway; in dreams my eyes worked perfectly without any help.

I couldn't manage to slow my pulse down; that was all. I was almost certain that Henry could hear my wildly beating heart.

He let go of me and took out three keys to open his door. The sight of them reminded me that he'd given me a replica of one of them. Along with a string so that I could hang the key around my neck. At the time, that had felt romantic. Now it seemed to me pure mockery. What use was one key when you needed three to get into his dreams?

"Coming?" He was through the doorway already. I followed him—and was blinking at bright sunlight. We were in some kind of park with flowering shrubs and tall trees. No, wait a moment, not a park . . .

"A *cemetery*? How appropriate." I slipped my hands into the pockets of my jeans. My heart was still doing its own thing, but I had the rest of myself under control. No tearful lump in my throat, preventing my voice from sounding the way it ought to sound. "On the other hand, it's a pity, because I was looking forward to a dip in that whirlpool."

"That wasn't my dream," said Henry.

"No, right—it was your girlfriend B's dream."

"She isn't my girlfriend."

"No? So she's your lesbian cousin and unfortunately you can meet her only in dreams because in real life she was kidnapped by the Taliban and has been kept prisoner for years in a cave in Afghanistan, right?"

A smile flitted over Henry's face, but next moment he was serious again. "I'm sorry, Liv. I know what it must have looked like to you. But I had my reasons. . . ."

"You know what it looked like to me? Well, it looked like my boyfriend was getting into a pool with a naked woman." I brushed away the hand he had obviously put out to stroke my cheek.

Henry frowned. "You do realize that it was only a dream, don't you?"

"For that mermaid slut, maybe, but not for you."

He said nothing for a second. Then he said, "If you visit

someone in a dream, you have to adapt to it. That was all I did. And you shouldn't have . . . What the hell did you think you were doing? Why did you follow me in secret?"

For a moment I couldn't breathe, I was so annoyed by the way he was suddenly turning things upside down. "The question is how far you'd have adapted to the dream."

"No, the question was why you followed me in secret."

"I just happened to be invisible in the shape of a—" I stopped short. No way was I going to justify myself at this point. I stared intently at my feet. Stupidly, I had a tearful lump in my throat again after all. It was only with difficulty, and in a very low voice, that I managed to ask the only question that really mattered. "What were you doing in that woman's dream, Henry?"

He didn't reply at once, and I raised my head to look straight at him, although it cost me an effort. I was so afraid of seeing that guilty expression on his face again.

But what I saw was more like helplessness. "It's complicated," he said.

"Explain it, then."

"There are things you couldn't understand even if you wanted to."

"Try, anyway."

Henry compressed his lips.

"Is it because I'm inexperienced in some things?" The question burst out of me, and I was annoyed with myself, because it sounded so inhibited and Victorian that next thing I knew I'd probably have a little lace cap on my head. I couldn't even *talk* about sex. But it was no good—I had to go through with this now. "Or is it to do with masculine needs that I don't know anything about?" Oh God, this was getting worse and worse. I began to hate myself. I also thought I saw slight confusion in Henry's eyes.

"What . . . ? No." He came a step closer, and this time I did let him touch my cheek. Carefully, his hand moved up to my forehead. "None of this has anything at all to do with you."

"What is it to do with, then?" It was as much as I could do not to rub my head against his hand the way Spot always did when you stroked him. But nor could I manage to push his hand away, which would certainly have been the most sensible thing to do.

He sighed. "I did tell you it was complicated. My life is complicated. There are things I have to do because no one else is going to do them." His fingers wandered down again and very gently stroked my cheekbone, going down to my chin. "You won't be able to understand. In your family, you're always there for one another, and everyone wants nothing but the best for everyone else. It's not like that with us. My father has . . . Well, let's say he's kind of lost sight of what fathers are supposed to do. I wouldn't mind that if it only affected the weekends when he visits to see Amy and Milo, although he regularly breaks their hearts. But I can't let him risk their future. He calls it doing business, but in reality he's just squandering an enormous amount of money. Money that doesn't belong to him: it belongs to Milo, Amy, and me. My grandfather left it to him in trust until we come of age. I'd be okay without the money, but I don't think anyone will be offering Milo scholarships later, and he's going to need them."

I was listening intently, hardly daring to breathe, let alone interrupt him or say that I still didn't entirely understand the connection.

"My grandfather died four years ago. He knew what would happen if he simply left the money to my father." He indicated a gravestone beside us, and I jumped. Bizarrely, it had Henry's name carved on it. HENRY HARPER—BELOVED HUSBAND AND FATHER. Only when I saw the date of birth did I realize that Henry had been named after his grandfather. "That's why he decided to set up a trust. The idea was to secure our future. And it was also because my mother . . . Well, she's not in any shape to . . . to look after those things." He was floundering more and more, and now he stopped talking entirely.

"I know," I whispered. That was a mistake. Henry stopped caressing me and frowned.

"What do you know?"

"That your mother has problems," I said.

"Yes, that's one way to put it." He took a step backward. "Read about it in Secrecy's blog, did you?"

"No, I just kind of picked it up, that's all. And Grayson said . . ." Oh no! I was telling tales. "Grayson indicated . . . ," I finished lamely.

"Did he indeed?" Henry folded his arms, leaning back against the gravestone of someone called Alfonse G. Oppenheimer.

"He only wanted to help. To make me understand," I said quickly.

"So did it help? Are you feeling sorry for me?" Beneath the light tone of Henry's voice, there was something else, something that I found difficult to interpret. Injured feelings? Rage?

"Yes, I am," I said, although I guessed that was exactly what he didn't want to hear.

Sure enough, he uttered a small, joyless laugh and vaulted

over the gravestone of Alfonse G. Oppenheimer to come down one grave farther on, a large marble slab. "I ought to be grateful to Grayson. Pity is a wonderful basis for a relationship."

I hesitated for a moment, but then I followed him. I didn't walk over the graves themselves, although there was no need to avoid them. After all, this was a dream, so it made no difference at all what happened to the pansies on Alfonse G. Oppenheimer's grave.

Henry didn't look up when I reached him. Okay, so he was angry, obviously because I felt sorry for him. Although there probably wasn't anyone in the world who wouldn't have felt the same under the circumstances. How could he blame me for it?

"You've never told me anything so personal before," I said slowly. "Do you realize that? This is the first time."

No answer. Okay, so he didn't want me feeling sorry for him. I changed tack. "I really didn't mean to sound ungrateful—but you'll have to explain the connection between your story and the woman in the whirlpool a little more closely."

Henry's mouth twisted in a sarcastic smile. "Well, yes. I did say you wouldn't understand." He had folded his arms again, and this time so did I.

"I keep thinking and thinking, but I just don't see why family circumstances mean you have to . . . er . . . flirt with a naked woman. And of course I wonder what else you'd have done if I hadn't splashed into the water between the two of you."

Henry's eyes narrowed slightly. "Anything necessary," he said quietly but very firmly. "I'm sorry if that hurts you. But

I'm very good at telling the difference between dreams and reality, and you don't seem to be."

I stared at him, baffled. "What? Henry, seriously, what would you do if you saw me carrying on with someone else in a dream?"

Henry shrugged his shoulders. Whereas a little while ago his expression had reflected all kinds of emotions, it was absolutely impenetrable now. As if he'd put on a mask. "Well, first, I wouldn't know about it, because I don't go spying on you like a jealous dragon, and second, I think it's perfectly okay to have a few secrets from each other in a relationship. Anything else is so . . . boring."

I bit my lip. "Yes, I see." What I saw most of all was that he was being like this on purpose. I just didn't see why. A few minutes ago I'd felt that he wanted very much to make up our quarrel. Now he seemed to be doing his level best to antagonize me. It wasn't like Henry—there was something very wrong here. "Then I suppose we have different ideas of what a good relationship is like," I said quietly.

He nodded. "That's what I'm afraid of too." For a while, we looked at each other in silence, and then he said, "I really am so very fond of you, Liv, but there are things in my life that are simply nothing to do with you."

"B in the whirlpool, for instance."

"For instance."

I was perfectly calm now. Pity, anxiety, rage—I didn't feel any of that. It was as if someone had blown out all the candles inside me.

"Well, it's a good thing we talked about it," I said. I almost quoted one of Mr. Wu's sayings: "When there is no agreement on basic principles, it is pointless to make plans together."

That one would fit the situation perfectly. However, I didn't say it out loud.

"Is that it?" asked Henry.

I nodded. "Yes, I suppose it is. If that's what you want."

Even now, nothing in Henry's face moved. He just looked at me, and I turned away to locate the door in the corridor. It was right there in front of us, next to an ornamental cherry tree in blossom. Nice of Henry to have created such a spring-like atmosphere for dumping me. Or rather, getting me to the point where I dumped him. All we needed was the right musical accompaniment. As I made for the door, I almost expected my knees to give way under me halfway there, leaving me to collapse on the ground in floods of tears, but nothing of the kind happened. My tears had gone away as well. Everything inside me felt like a big black hole.

In the doorway, I couldn't resist the temptation of turning back once more. Henry hadn't moved from the spot. He was sitting on the slab of marble, as motionless as if he were made of marble himself.

21

MIA HAD FORESEEN it in her dream: no one would notice if a clone replaced me, not even Mia herself. Although she was the only one who gave me a searching look now and then, as if she guessed that there was something wrong with me. So far, however, she hadn't looked as if she was planning to smother me with a cushion again.

It had been a strange week. The strangest part was that I'd survived it. And no one had noticed that it wasn't the real Liv but a horrible clone getting up as usual every morning, drinking Lottie's grapefruit juice, going to school on the bus, having lunch with Persephone, doing her homework in the evening. I had locked the real Liv and her broken heart up in a dark place where she could feel as miserable as she liked about Henry, and her lost love, and cry her eyes out to her heart's content. I didn't care.

Clone-Liv did me good service that week. She even got an A on the French test. Clone-Liv's great advantage was that she felt almost nothing. For instance, she couldn't care less about Florence's withering glances. And when the Boker called and Clone-Liv happened to answer the phone, where-upon the Boker simply rang off, she just smiled and dismissed it with a shrug of her shoulders. She even stood up well to the piercing detective look in Mia's eyes.

Every day, I expected Secrecy to announce in her blog that Henry and I weren't together anymore, but the revelation never came. Maybe that was because the students in their last year at school (including Secrecy?) had been doing exams all week and didn't have lunch in the cafeteria, where it might have been obvious that we weren't still a couple. Or maybe it was because my clone hadn't yet thought it necessary to tell anyone, so no one could pass the gossip on to Secrecy. Although mind you, no one had asked, not even Grayson, who had heard our quarrel. However, since I wasn't crying all the time and staggering around like a blotchy-faced zombie (that part was reserved for the real Liv in her dark hole), he presumably thought that everything was all right again. Which meant that Henry hadn't said anything either.

He and I had seen each other only once, at school by our lockers in the middle of the week. At the very moment when I was confronted with him, Clone-Liv failed me and the real Liv took over. Apart from a hoarse "Hi!" I hadn't uttered a word, because everything I'd successfully suppressed over the last few days came right back at the sight of him. My sense of overwhelming grief simply deprived me of speech.

Henry didn't seem to have any such problems. Probably because I wasn't his first ex-girlfriend. He even smiled at me.

"You look as if you've been sleeping better," he said. "It suits you."

"Thanks," I wanted to murmur, but I couldn't get even that out. In fact, I had the general impression than I'd never be able to speak again. Clone-Liv was trying with all her might to push real Liv aside and keep her from bursting into tears, while Henry got his things out of his locker and went on talking cheerfully.

"Biology exam coming up—cross your fingers for me," he said, winking as if we were good friends.

And then, at last, after a hefty nudge in the ribs, real Liv slunk away and Clone-Liv was back in charge. "Sure, I'll do that, and good luck," she said just in time, before Henry disappeared around the corner.

Like I said, it was a strange week. I'd really thought I would never be able to close my eyes again, but in fact, I slept almost as if I were in a coma. Every evening, I was just waiting to go to bed as early as possible without anyone noticing. But only to sleep. I kept strictly away from my dream door. Senator Tod could practice on someone else—I was no longer available.

I did have a guilty conscience about Anabel, though. Sure, she was a lunatic who had tried to murder me, but she still didn't deserve to be sedated and isolated by her own psychiatrist, using heaven knows what methods. So last Sunday I had looked up Anabel's father's number in the phone book and made out that I was Anabel's friend Florence Spencer calling to find out how she was. When Mr. Scott said I was the third person today to ask after her, Anabel's friends Henry and Arthur had called, too, and he was just off to the hospital himself to see with his own eyes that his daughter was all right, I felt relieved.

As for Mia—like me, she was sleeping all night again, and I was beginning to wonder whether someone else really was responsible for her sleepwalking. Couldn't there have been some natural cause for it? If not, the person to blame seemed to have given up trying to get into my little sister's dreams.

Mia herself had taken the precaution of installing a complicated anti-sleepwalking system in her room, a clever construction made of wires, string, saucepan lids, and a Swiss cowbell that would set off an earsplitting alarm if she got out of bed without first removing the string around her ankle. I almost stumbled over this device when I went into Mia's room on Saturday evening, only to find Lottie turning critically back and forth in front of the mirror.

It was just before six, and the whole house was buzzing with activity because this was Ernest's fifty-third birthday, and he wanted to celebrate it at a restaurant with a small family party, as he put it (he wasn't to know that the family party had been infiltrated by a clone). It was nice that the family party included Lottie, not so good that the Boker and Emily were in it. And naturally Charles would be there as well, which had Lottie in a state of great agitation. I mustn't forget to tell her that she'd recently had a boyfriend called Jonathan—just in case Charles mentioned it to her.

"No, this one's no good either!" Lottie was grimly inspecting her reflection in the mirror. "I look like my aunt Friederike in the dress she wears for housework. Like a country bumpkin."

I exchanged glances with Mia. "That's the eleventh dress she's tried on," Mia whispered, and then her piercing detective look was back. "Are you okay?"

It wasn't the first time Mia had asked me that question this week. To be precise, it was the twenty-sixth time. I'd kept count. And when she looked at me through her glasses, like now, wrinkling her nose, the real Liv was very close to surfacing again. I couldn't let that happen. It was just too dangerous.

So Clone-Liv replied nonchalantly, "Of course. Thanks for asking." Then I turned to Lottie. "You look great!"

"No, I don't," she wailed.

"I'd wear the green dress if I were you. That's the one that suits you best," said Mia.

"But Ch—er, but everyone will have seen it so often before," said Lottie, sighing deeply.

"You don't want Ch—er, everyone thinking you've dolled yourself up specially for them, do you?" replied Mia.

"That's true." Lottie took off Aunt Friederike's housework dress, picked up the green dress lying on Mia's bed with a whole heap of others, and slipped into it. I helped her to do up the zip fastener and looked at her admiringly.

"Perfect," said Mia. "Now you just have to do something to your hair to make it look as if you hadn't done anything to it."

If it wasn't too late for that, because Lottie had used the curling iron on it, which had much the same effect on her natural curls as pouring water on burning oil.

"Maybe I could dampen it down a bit," said Lottie, making for the bathroom.

"Yes, or get it wet right through," I murmured, wondering how and when I could broach the subject of Jonathan.

Mia pushed the sleeping Buttercup aside and dropped on her beanbag. "Are you really all right, Liv? You look kind of funny."

"If you ask me that once more, I'll ask Lottie to do you one of those elaborate braided hairstyles, like that fruit basket the other day."

Normally Mia would have put out her tongue at me, but not today. Was it my imagination, or did she squint at one of her decorative cushions in passing?

I went out of her room, to be on the safe side.

Ernest's invitation for this evening had taken us all by surprise. Or more precisely, the reason for it. Not even Mom had known it was his birthday. Incredible. Even if she'd met him only in February last year, you'd think she'd at least have checked the key data before moving in with him, and his birthday was part of that.

We'd baked a cake in honor of the day, with 53 picked out on it in mandarin segments, and Florence had departed from her principle of not being in the same room as tree murderesses. Ernest had been moved to tears that his daughter could actually bring herself to have breakfast at the same table as us and the cake.

On the other hand, I didn't get a chance to tell Lottie about Jonathan before we set off for the restaurant. It was only a couple of streets away, but Ernest drove there with Lottie, Mom, and Florence, because their shoes weren't suitable for a walk. Mia and I set out on foot. Grayson was coming straight from basketball, and Charles, Emily, and the Boker were meeting us at the restaurant. After a few rainy days, it was bright and cold again, and ice had formed on the puddles. Mia enthusiastically broke it to splinters by jumping on every puddle with both feet at once.

"No one would think you're going to be fourteen in March," I said.

"Oh, come on, it's fun," said Mia, hopping to another puddle. "And it helps you to work off your aggression."

She looked challengingly at me, and for a moment I

wondered whether it might be a test. By way of an experiment, I crunched the layer of ice under my feet to pieces, and I had to admit that Mia was right. This was as satisfying an activity as bursting the blisters of Bubble Wrap. And who was going to tell me what I was too old to do and what I wasn't? For a while we hopped from puddle to puddle like girls possessed, and for the first time that week, I could really laugh again. Not the pretend, Clone-Liv laughter that I'd been practicing, but a genuine Liv laugh.

Only when we realized that someone was watching us did we stop. But it was only Grayson on his bike, staring at us in a slightly disconcerted way and looking as if he could do with a bit of therapy to work off his own aggression.

"Did the team lose?" asked Mia, not very sympathetically.

"Don't ask," he growled, getting off his bicycle and pushing it across the road.

The restaurant was directly opposite. It was a very classy joint, with a red-and-gold awning and a doorman, and although the best icy puddle of all lay between the sidewalk and the road, Mia and I managed to walk to the entrance in a very grown-up manner.

In fact, we were the last to arrive, and unfortunately everyone else was already sitting down. Mom waved. She had the Boker sitting next to her, so not surprisingly she looked nervous.

"I can see three empty chairs at the end of the table," remarked Mia, razor-sharp as usual, while she slipped out of her coat and gave it to the waiter. "One next to Emily, one opposite Emily, and one beside the empty chair opposite Emily. I'll have that one." With a gloating giggle, she left us standing there.

Grayson was helping me out of my own coat. "Now we can argue over the other two places," he said.

"Hmm. Cholera or the plague?" Clone-Liv didn't bother to conceal her dislike of Emily. The real Liv wouldn't have been so forthright. But Grayson just gave me a good-humored smile. "Well, since it wasn't me who gave Emily a genuine sterling silver sign of infinity, I'd rather sit beside her than opposite her." I added, "Then I won't have to look at her all the time." And I could also sit next to Lottie. I still had to speak to her, and it was urgent—unless it was too late for an explanation, because Charles was already deep in conversation with her. I hoped the name Jonathan hadn't cropped up yet.

Grayson had given my coat to the waiter, and now his eyes wandered from my hair down to my boots, inspecting the effect. "Wow! You look terrific."

"I know," I said, for once sharing his opinion. I'd finally found the right things to wear with the short, cream-colored layered tulle skirt that Mom had given me for Christmas; I needed a style that wouldn't make me look like a confused ballerina or a would-be bride. Worn with black lace-up boots, thick gray tights, and Mom's gray cashmere pullover, the skirt suddenly looked cool.

"The later the evening, the lovelier the guests," agreed Charles as we went over to the table. I gave him my best Clone-Liv smile, which even extended to the Boker. It didn't matter that she wasn't about to smile back; the main thing was that she was sitting at the other end of the table. Although I did feel a little sorry for Mom. Grayson had sat down in front of Emily. He had given the Boker a peck on the cheek and Emily no kiss at all, which lowered the warmth of her expression to zero on the sourpuss scale.

"Suckling pig in plum sauce." Mia was deep in the menu. "With cavolo nero and *orchids*? Genuine orchids?"

"This restaurant has two Michelin stars," said Emily cuttingly. "I'm afraid you won't find hamburgers on the menu." At the other end of the table, the Boker smiled approvingly.

"Could you keep your voice down a bit?" asked Grayson, sounding annoyed.

One place farther on, Charles was looking inquiringly at Lottie. "Have you been to the cinema recently? Any films that you'd recommend?"

Only now did I begin to appreciate the full extent of Ernest's courage in getting all these people whom he called his family together around the same table. It was as if he'd seated barrels of gunpowder next to burning fuses. The Boker despised Mom, Mia, and me. Mia and I couldn't stand the Boker, any more than we could stand Emily, who thought even worse of us than we did of her. Obviously she was also at odds with Grayson. In his own turn, Grayson had quarreled with Florence. Florence would happily have had Mia and me publicly whipped. Mom feared the Boker even more than earthquakes and tax returns. Charles hated his mother for treating him like a child. And so on and so forth. While Ernest sat in the middle of the party, feeling fond of us all. For the first time, as he raised his glass, looked around the company, beaming, and thanked us for coming, I felt deep admiration for him, and I could understand why Mom had fallen so much in love with him, never mind his Dumbo ears and bald patch. That is to say, the real Liv could understand it, and even Clone-Liv felt emotional enough to take herself off to the parallel universe where she belonged.

A kind of solemn feeling spread through me, and at the same time, I didn't feel well. I'd functioned like a machine all this week, I just had to get through it, not feel, not think, not remember anything. But now, in view of Ernest's generosity and optimism, I suddenly couldn't keep all my suppressed feelings from sweeping toward me like a tidal wave and closing over my head. Along with my memory. It was all back again, and it hurt horribly. In my mind's eye, I saw Henry sitting on that marble slab, pale and calm, looking at me.

"Is that it?" I heard him say.

Was that it? It was too much for my self-control, anyway. I tried desperately to breathe calmly, but found that I was doing the exact opposite. I met Mia's inquiring eyes. This time I wouldn't be able to avoid her question, and everyone at the table would see me collapse. . . .

Emily, of all people, rescued me.

"Oh, yuck, Liv!" She flapped her hand in the air in front of her nose. "What's that disgusting old-lady perfume you're wearing? It takes my appetite right away."

My breathing returned to normal. No, I wasn't going to collapse. I'd hold out for Ernest's sake. "What a shame, you'll miss eating the two Michelin stars," I said. "And how did your exams go?"

"Just fine." Emily was ostentatiously speaking through her nose. "It's all a matter of organization and discipline. Unfortunately there are always people in our year who think they can take it casually, between parties and basketball games."

"Why don't we change places?" Grayson suggested, looking at her and obviously ready to pick a quarrel. "I like Liv's perfume."

I was about to explain that I wasn't wearing any perfume at all, when trouble started up two places away.

"I can recommend *About Time*—that's a really good film," Lottie was telling Charles, and Charles asked, "Did Jonathan like it too?"

I swiftly interrupted. "Have you all decided what you're going to order? I think I fancy . . . er . . ." I opened the menu. Duck liver marinated in bitter chocolate and creamed beet-root, for fifty pounds? Calf's head with radish and mint vinaigrette and aioli with capers, seventy-five pounds? Heavens, this wasn't a menu: it was a horror story. But at least I'd averted the escalating argument for now; everyone was busy studying the dishes on offer, and I'll say one thing for them, there wasn't a wide choice so you could see the whole range easily.

Just then the waiter arrived to take our orders.

Determined not to spoil Ernest's evening, I opted for tor-tellini stuffed with mascarpone, flavored with Périgord truffles. I hoped there couldn't be much wrong with that.

Mia said she'd like spaghetti carbonara with Aquitaine caviar, but without the caviar, please.

The waiter didn't bat an eyelid, but Emily said, "In this case, the caviar is the main ingredient, Mia."

"Leave her alone," said Grayson.

"It will cost your father seventy-five pounds, and she'll only push it about on the plate looking desperately for the pasta," said Emily, and she turned to the waiter. "Maybe you can simply bring her a children's dish, pasta with some kind of neutral sauce. And I'll have the lobster velouté with arti-chokes and coriander."

"You are—" Grayson began, but I interrupted him. "That

sounds delicious, Emily. I was thinking of it myself." Well, thinking of it so far as wondering what *velouté* meant.

Grayson shot me a rather irritated glance, but for now he kept his mouth shut.

Lottie and Charles ordered monkfish à l'Armoricaine. That's to say, Lottie ordered it, and Charles just said, "The same for me, please," and leaned toward Lottie. "About this man Jonathan . . . ," he began.

"Yes, the monkfish does sound delicious too," I cried. If you ignored the oysters and curried apple and cucumber salad that came with it. I was getting rather agitated. This was like watching Wimbledon—no way could I keep an eye on all the doubles players at once.

"Sure, delicious," muttered Mia, drawing my attention to the table next to ours, where the waiter had just served up a fish. A whole fish, glazed eyes and all.

Now it was Grayson's turn. "I'd like the turbot, please, without the palourde clam compote," he told the waiter.

"But that's the best part of the dish," said Emily when the waiter had gone away. Grayson seemed to have been just waiting for that.

"And I'm sure you're about to tell me why, teacher."

Oh God, I couldn't take much more of this. We hadn't even reached the starters yet. I looked helplessly from one barrel of gunpowder to the next. And those were only the people I could hear. Who knew what was going on at the other end of the table?

"Palourde clams are the only Venus clams that can be eaten raw, and they . . ."

"Who is this Jonathan you keep talking about?"

"What makes you think anyone's interested in that?"

"But you told me you didn't like action films!"

Maybe I ought to reconsider and stage a collapse after all—at least that would take their minds off their own problems, and later they could say I had spoiled the evening and it was all my fault.

"Is that it?" I heard Henry's voice at the back of my mind again.

At this moment Ernest struck his wine glass with a fork, and silence fell.

"While we're waiting for our orders to arrive, I'd just like to say a few words, if you will allow me. It won't take long." He smiled at all the guests. "When I celebrated my birthday this time last year, I would never have thought that a year later I'd be standing here"—rather clumsily, he pushed back his chair and got to his feet—"as the happiest man on earth. Because of meeting you, Ann."

Mom blushed.

"I had come to terms with my life—I'd never have expected to fall deeply in love again." Ernest's voice was so solemn that it gave me goose bumps. Not just our table but the whole restaurant seemed to be listening, because although Ernest was speaking softly you could hear every word he said.

The Boker pretended to have a fit of coughing.

But Ernest went on, entirely undeterred. "I didn't realize what I was missing, but now I know that I never want to let you go again. Ann?" He reached into his jacket pocket and brought out a little box. When he opened it to reveal a ring with a shining stone in it, Mom let out a small, stifled sound. So did the Boker.

Tears came to my eyes. I couldn't do anything about it.

And I wasn't the only one with moist eyes sitting there. Lottie even gave a quiet sob.

"Ann, will you be my wife?" asked Ernest.

Mom was fighting tears back too. "Yes," she whispered. "Oh yes, I will."

22

YOU HAD TO say one thing for Mia's anti-sleepwalking device: it definitely did what it was meant to do. When the saucepan lids began clattering, I woke at once. By the time the cowbell joined in, I was sitting upright in bed. And I was on my feet long before the last lid stopped clattering.

I wasn't the only one. Everyone else in the house, even Lottie on the top floor, had been woken, and within a few minutes, we were all in Mia's room. Mom and I were the first. As we came through the doorway, we immediately saw that Mia was the only one still asleep. It was icy cold in her room, the window was wide open, and Mia was sitting on the windowsill with her back to us. To be precise, sitting on the very edge of the windowsill, with her legs dangling in the air outside.

Mom gasped and clapped her hand over her mouth. I only just managed to suppress a loud groan. One false move, and Mia would fall out of the window. Yes, we were only on the second floor of the house, but falling twelve feet to a paved path would be dangerous enough. The question was, what could we do now? If we spoke to her, or actually touched her, she might wake at just the wrong moment.

While various horror scenarios shot through my mind within the fraction of a second, all featuring a lifeless Mia in a pool of blood among the frozen flower beds, Ernest shot past us, simply picked Mia up in both his arms, and pulled her back into the room. I'd never have expected him to act so fast and so energetically.

I breathed out. And then in, and then out again. Suddenly everything in the room seemed to me brighter and warmer, although of course nothing had changed. The only real light came from the streetlamp outside the house.

Ernest, who must surely have been a firefighter in an earlier life, carried Mia to her bed and laid her carefully down on it. Mom was with her in a moment, clinging to her like a sumo wrestler. Unmoved, her eyes completely empty, Mia stared past her and up at the ceiling.

"What's going on?" Florence, who had been the last to arrive, was standing in the doorway behind Lottie, Buttercup, and Grayson, rubbing her eyes. "It sounded like the house was falling down." Intrigued, she looked at all the saucepan lids scattered around the room, and the string still tied to Mia's ankle. Buttercup began barking excitedly—thank goodness she'd left it until now—and Lottie asked, "Should I fetch the thermometer and take her temperature?"

Grayson cast me a long and very eloquent glance, to which I replied only with a shrug of my shoulders. He went over to the window and closed it firmly.

In Mom's convulsive embrace, Mia was fighting for air. At last her eyelids began opening and closing again. Then she shook her head, obviously confused. "Mom?"

"It's all right, darling, we're here with you," said Mom, loosening her clasp slightly.

"Did I . . . did I walk in my sleep again?" Mia sat up. "I can't even remember my dream."

"Never mind, your alarm system worked brilliantly," I said, switching on her bedside lamp.

"Try to remember your dream," said Grayson, urgently and without a lot of sympathy.

Mia still looked as if she were only half awake. "There . . . there was the sea," she murmured. "And a landing. I sat on it and dangled my legs in the water. . . ." She inspected her saucepan lids. "Was it really loud enough?"

"Oh yes." Lottie was rubbing her arms. "I thought a garbage truck had rammed the house."

"But it didn't wake me. There's something wrong with me." Mia sank back on her pillows.

"It's been a day full of surprises." Mom stroked Mia's forehead, looking at Ernest. "When a child's mother plans to remarry, it can come as rather a shock," she whispered to him, although at room-filling volume. Then she turned back to Mia. "I'm going to sleep here with you tonight, mousie, okay?"

Mia looked at me. I knew what she was thinking. We hadn't had a shock this evening—all that was way behind us, months ago, when Mom and Ernest had told us they were moving in together. At the time, yes, that had in fact been a shock—but while the proposal of marriage could be called a surprise, it was a nice one.

All the same, it was fine by me if Mom slept with Mia tonight. She was already snuggling down under the quilt with her, one arm around her waist.

"Mom, it's all right," said Mia. "I'm glad you and Ernest are getting married. The wedding will be sensational! Just think of the meeting between Great-Aunt Gertrude and Mrs. Spencer . . ."

"Not forgetting your great-aunt Virginia," added Lottie.

"I have a kind of gloomy foreboding," murmured Florence, and Mom and Mia both chuckled.

"Sleep well, then, both of you." Ernest looked very relieved when he left the room with us, closing the door behind him. "It's all right," he added, repeating Mia's own words.

But of course it wasn't. Nothing was all right. But for her alarm system, my little sister might well have jumped out of the window tonight.

I sensed Grayson's eyes resting on me, but I didn't respond. Instead I went straight back into my room with a murmured, "Good night."

To my surprise, I dropped off to sleep again easily, and when I went through my dream door into the corridor, it was as if I'd never been away, although it baffled me to find that Henry's door was still right opposite it and hadn't changed at all. Elegant, black, and forbidding, with a fierce lion's head as a door knocker.

I quickly looked away, and instead examined my own door—I'd really expected it to be rather run-down, like me, paint peeling off, a few notches in it, maybe a different color, one that matched my state of mind better than its cheerful mint green. But my door was in excellent condition. The lizard winked at me before coiling up again into a shining doorknob.

Mia's door was on the right of mine, and there was no sign

of Mr. Wu anywhere. Instead, as I was about to take hold of the handle, someone else came out of the doorway.

"Mom?"

Mom put her forefinger to her lips. "Shh! Mia needs to rest," she whispered.

I looked at her with mixed feelings. How sweet of Mia to show her confidence in Mom by posting her to protect her dreams—and how useless. I realized that when she opened the door a little wider and beckoned me in. "But of course you're welcome, Liv darling. If you keep quiet and lie down with us. We were just counting sheep."

"No, no, that's not the way to do it. How do you know that I'm the real Liv?"

Dream-Mom shook her head with an indulgent smile. "The real Liv? What nonsense you're talking, darling! As if I wouldn't know my own daughter. Oh, there's Grayson."

I turned around. Sure enough, Grayson was standing in the corridor behind me. His door latched quietly behind him.

"Grayson dear," said Mom with a touch of reproof in her voice. "This is January. We don't want you catching a chill, going about bare-chested like that."

Grayson was staring at me suspiciously. "Is that Mia's door?" he asked.

I nodded. What was he doing here? Hadn't he said he was never going into this corridor again?

"Grayson, have you—?"

He interrupted me. "I know what you're thinking. And I'm still sure we ought to leave all this alone. But your sister very nearly jumped out of the window just now, and I wanted to . . ." He shook his head, and suddenly looked embarrassed.

"You wanted to do what?"

"I think I wanted to stand guard. Somehow or other."

A warm feeling spread through me. Touched, I grinned at him.

"It's so drafty here!" Mom clicked her tongue impatiently. "How about it, Liv? In or out? It's Herdwicks we're counting, very cute little sheep. . . ."

"Maybe later," I said. "You can shut the door—that's okay."

And Mom did shut it, although not without advising Grayson once again to put on something warm, with the result that he was now wearing his quilted anorak.

"That was neat," I said appreciatively. "Particularly as you're right out of practice."

However, when Grayson looked down at himself, shaking his head, I assumed that he had really been trying to imagine something different.

"Didn't you say you'd installed a security system outside her door?" he said with a look of disapproval. "It doesn't look very secure to me."

Oh, the Mr. Wu system had been very secure indeed, but obviously I couldn't rely on it indefinitely.

"This way anyone can just walk into Mia's dreams," Grayson went on. He peered down the corridor in the dim light, clearly feeling uncomfortable.

I sighed. Unfortunately he was right. On the other hand, while I respected his idea of standing guard outside Mia's door, it couldn't be done in practice. So there was only one thing for it.

"I'm afraid there's no alternative to telling Mia about all this," I said.

"No, Liv! You can't drag her into it too."

"She may know about it already by now. And she'll have to protect her own door. That's the only way she can prevent anyone from getting into her dreams and making her walk in her sleep and do terrible things."

"If we only knew—" But Grayson never finished his sentence, because at that moment we heard a man's voice.

"Stop right there, you stupid brat, or you'll be sorry!" it thundered around the next bend in the corridor. "Stop this minute!"

That voice was not unknown to me. Unfortunately.

A figure turned the corner and came toward us at break-neck speed. A slender, graceful figure moving with great elegance in spite of her obvious haste.

It was Anabel.

I didn't have much time to stare at her and overcome my surprise, because she was making straight for us. Senator Tod was close behind her in his flowing cloak and his slouch hat, calling her names nonstop.

By this time, Anabel had reached us, and I acted instinctively. I let her go by and then barred Senator Tod's way, standing protectively between the two of them.

He stopped, gasping for breath.

"You again!" he growled. "I've had about enough of you kids!"

"The feeling's mutual," I assured him. Only now did I realize that I had raised my hand, like a traffic cop. No idea what I thought I was doing. Unobtrusively, I lowered it again, but without taking my eyes off Senator Tod.

Anabel was standing behind me, and when she suddenly

began to laugh, I realized, all at once, how ridiculous my attempted rescue had been. Anabel was the last person to need support in a dream. At the same time, I felt a little relieved to see her here. The idea of her in that hospital, helpless in the hands of Senator Tod with his medical methods, had troubled me in spite of myself, as I'd been ready to admit.

"Laugh all you like, you . . . you little devil," said Senator Tod. "I'll soon find out which door is yours. And then . . ." Narrowing his eyes, he looked at Grayson. "Who's this newcomer?"

"Oh, do give up, Doctor dear." Anabel moved to my side. Her voice sounded as sweet and innocent as ever, and it sent a shiver down my spine. Should I really be relieved to see her? Anabel Scott was far and away the craziest, most dangerous person who had ever crossed my path—how could I have forgotten that? She hadn't changed her appearance; she still looked like a reincarnation of Botticelli's Venus, even in plain jeans and a T-shirt. Her golden blond hair fell over her shoulders in soft waves, going all the way down to her waist, and her huge turquoise-green eyes could cast a spell over you at once. She was so beautiful that it almost hurt to look at her. In that respect, she'd really been a perfect match for Arthur.

"How are you, Liv?" she said in friendly tones, and then beamed at Grayson. "Hi, Grayson. To be honest, I'm surprised to see you here. I thought you'd given up all this."

"Aha. Aha." Senator Tod nodded. "Grayson Spencer, is it? The stupid, vain, naïve, good-natured member of the group."

"No, you genius. That one is Jasper Grant," Anabel set him right. "Grayson is the cautious, sensible, responsible, unimaginative one. Henry is the one with the authority problem, and Arthur is the good-looking guy with the giant ego." She cast Grayson a glance, with her eyes twinkling. "Sorry, he's not so good at remembering names."

So far Grayson hadn't said a word. He was just looking from Anabel to me and then to Senator Tod, with a baffled expression on his face.

Anabel's smile widened. "As usual, your face tells me exactly what you're feeling, Grayson. It's a while since you came here—maybe we ought to update you. Okay, so while you stayed in your own dreams like a good boy, trying to forget about setting a demon free, Liv, Arthur, and Henry got to know my psychiatrist out here. Let me introduce Dr. Otto Anderson. Not the brightest spark in his field, I'm afraid, but just the man for my purposes."

"This is . . ." Senator Tod looked as if he'd explode with fury any moment now. Before too long, he'd be hurling thunderbolts. "I've never for a second let you manipulate me! I saw through you right away!"

Anabel tilted her head on one side. "Just the man!" she repeated gently.

"I don't understand a word of this," said Grayson. "What does it have to do with Mia? Why are you doing this to her? To revenge yourself on Liv?"

"Mia?" Anabel raised an eyebrow. "Liv's little sister?"

"Yes, damn it, Liv's little sister," said Grayson. "And I want you to leave her alone. My God, Anabel, you've done enough harm already."

Anabel looked genuinely confused. "Can someone tell me what he's talking about? Maybe you, Henry?"

I was about to spin around, but managed to turn and look without haste. Sure enough, there was Henry leaning against his door, arms folded and one knee slightly bent, as if he'd been standing there all the time.

He was the only one of us who managed to return Anabel's smile.

"Good to see you," he said. "We were anxious about you."

Anabel nodded. "I know. My father told me you'd phoned. So sweet of you. Did you really think the good doctor here had put me out of action with sleeping tablets?" She uttered a tinkling laugh.

Senator Tod looked as if he were grinding his teeth.

"Well, you haven't been here for some time," I pointed out.

"Are you so sure of that?"

Oh, damn it. Of course not. Arthur had been right: Anabel was too clever for Senator Tod. And for me, too, I'm afraid. She was the best of us all at managing her dreams. Nothing was easier for her than to roam around the corridors without any of us noticing. And she wasn't to be underestimated in the real world either. Idiot that I was, I'd phoned her father because I felt sorry for her, while she'd presumably been tricking the entire hospital.

Although I really didn't want to, I glanced at Henry, only to find that his eyes were resting on me. That in itself was enough to make my heart contract painfully again.

"How nice it is to see you all!" Anabel went on in a conversational tone. "All we need is Arthur, and it would be like the old days." With a contented sigh, she leaned back on the wall beside Henry's door. "You learn an amazing amount when you're invisible, but it's kind of boring." She grinned at me. "Sorry if I scared you, Liv, but I really couldn't resist! A little rustling, and you felt sure the devil was after you."

"And so he was." Only now did I notice that the pupils of

Anabel's eyes were tiny, as if she were looking at a bright light. Even though it had turned quite dark around us. And colder. I felt fairly sure that she'd soon be conjuring up her demon.

But for now Anabel was aiming at subtler effects. "You've no idea how boring it is in the hospital—without the dreams I'd probably be dead of sheer tedium. No, I wasn't about to give them up. I just wanted the good doctor to think so while I was studying his weaknesses at my leisure. You have a good many weaknesses, don't you, Otto?"

"If you think you can blackmail me, you greatly over-estimate the credibility of a mentally ill patient," said Senator Tod. "No one would believe someone like you. And what's more, I've never broken any laws. . . ."

Anabel laughed again. "Blackmail! I'm far beyond such childish, laborious methods now. No—I have something special in mind for you. Don't worry, you'll like it."

At that moment the electronic alarm that we'd heard before went off. "The beeper," said Anabel, while Senator Tod turned pale, and the next second disappeared entirely. "The patient in room 207 is a friend of mine—I give her my dessert, and in return she rings for the doctor every night he's on emergency duty and gets him out of bed. I bet he goes racing straight to my room." She yawned. "A shame. It's so nice here with you, I could stand around chatting for hours, particularly as the story of your little sister sounds really interesting, Liv."

"What's happened to Mia?" Henry looked inquiringly at me.

I was intently studying my feet.

"Hasn't Liv told you?" asked Grayson. "Mia has been sleepwalking."

"No, Liv hasn't told me anything about it," said Henry. He sounded annoyed.

I raised my head to give him a look of even more annoyance. If anyone had no right to complain that I wasn't telling him enough, then it was Henry.

"I've no idea how she fixes it," said Grayson, stationing himself in front of Anabel, "but Anabel is making Mia do dangerous things in her sleep. A few days ago, she was trying to smother Liv with a cushion, and tonight she almost jumped out of her bedroom window."

Henry looked dismayed. "When did this start?"

"A couple of weeks ago. I can't think why Liv didn't tell you."

"Nor can I," said Henry. "But now I understand what Mr. Wu was doing."

"You can't think why I didn't tell you?" I tried my best not to sound shrill, but I wasn't sure whether I really succeeded. "Probably because you always tell me everything, don't you? So I'm sure you automatically expect other people to do the same. Apart from the fact that we're not a couple anymore, and I don't have to tell you anything."

"What?" cried Grayson. "You're not a couple now? Since when?"

"Oh, didn't Henry tell you?" I asked sarcastically. "I expect that was because he didn't think it was very important."

"Those things have nothing to do with each other." Henry moved away from his door. The casual expression had entirely disappeared from his face. "If Anabel is manipulating Mia's dreams, you ought to have told me."

"Now, now, my dears." Anabel, of all people, was intervening. "I for one have nothing to do with it."

"Who does, then?" asked Grayson angrily.

Anabel smiled gently. "To be honest, Grayson, I won't claim I didn't have plans for you all, but . . . no, I really never thought of making Liv's sister go sleepwalking."

It was crazy, but I believed her, in spite of the mad gleam in her eyes and the expression of gleeful triumph on her face. And before she could suddenly disappear, no doubt because a furious Senator Tod came storming into her room at the hospital, she added, "Well, think it over. Couldn't there be someone else who has a score to settle with Liv?"

HENRY LIVED IN a detached redbrick house with several bay
windows, lots of white-painted lattice windows, and a green
front door with a semicircular fanlight. It was hidden behind
brick walls to shoulder height, and didn't look at all like the
gloomy, neglected, depressing house of horrors I'd imagined.
The front garden was well tended; the garden gate was obviously well oiled. I did have to skirt around a child's play car
and a basketball on the way to the front door, but that made
the house seem homey, like the tabby cat asleep on the doormat next to a pair of brightly colored rubber boots. What
surprised me even more was the fact that it had taken me
exactly twelve and a half minutes to get there. On foot.
Without running. Imagine it: I'd been in a relationship with
this guy for months, and I'd had no idea that he lived only a
twelve-and-a-half-minute walk away from me. One more
reason to feel annoyed with him.

All the same, I hesitated for a moment before ringing the
bell—I mean, I could always just pet the cat and go away
again without losing face. Then I pulled myself together.

After all, he was the one who had sent me a text thirteen and a half minutes ago, not vice versa. It had made me forget all about last night and my worries over Mia and Anabel. All it had said was: *We must talk*. I'd asked Grayson for Henry's address the next minute.

And I guessed he was only too right about that.

"Okay, so we'll talk," I said out loud just as Henry opened the door and stared at me in astonishment. I tried to make sure I had a neutral expression on my face, which was terribly difficult, because my heart had sunk what felt like a good couple of inches. Would just seeing him ever stop hurting? Would I be able to be in the same room as him someday without feeling I was about to die of longing?

But at least no other member of his family had opened the door to me. Secretly, I was extremely relieved about that. And it helped me to stay in control of myself a bit when I saw that Henry was having difficulty doing exactly the same thing.

"I . . . what . . . ?" he stammered. As usual, there were deep shadows under his eyes, and his skin was almost transparent, which would have looked unhealthy in anyone else, but not Henry.

"This text came from you, didn't it?" I held my cell phone out to him. "So what did you want to talk to me about?" Up to this point I'd kept really cool. Unfortunately I had to go on chattering and spoil the effect. "Lovely house, by the way. Lovely windows. Lovely . . . er . . . green bush. Lovely door. Lovely cat. And lovely rubber boots and . . ."

"Yes, all of it is just lovely," agreed Henry, and a tiny grin lifted the corners of his mouth before he frowned again. "Listen, Liv, this isn't a good moment."

"You sent the text," I reminded him, with a lot of emphasis on the word *you*.

"Yes, I did. But I didn't expect to see you here a minute later. We do have to talk, but not now."

"Because?"

"Because . . ." He looked anxiously down the road, which seemed very peaceful in the light of the setting sun. There was almost no traffic here on a Sunday afternoon. "Because it doesn't happen to be a good moment."

I bent down to pet the cat. "Well, since I'm here, can't you at least take the opportunity of telling me what it's about?"

Henry hesitated briefly. "It's only . . . I was thinking about what Anabel said."

I abruptly raised my head. Anabel? He wanted to talk to me about Anabel?

"I know she tells lies right, left, and center, but in this case I'm more or less sure that—" He stopped short. A swanky cross-country vehicle turned the corner at high speed. The engine roared in the afternoon silence, and as it screeched to a halt outside the garden gate, Henry rolled his eyes. "It would be a really good idea if you left now, Liv. If possible before anyone sees you who . . . oh, shit."

Apart from the fact that I had no idea how to disappear through the garden gate without being seen by whoever had just parked right in front of it, it was too late, anyway. A tall man got out of the passenger side, a man in his late fifties, maybe older, even though he still seemed to have all his hair. He was suntanned, his eyes were hidden behind dark glasses, and when he opened his mouth and began talking, I saw a flash of snow-white teeth.

"Find your mother," he told Henry without any other greeting. "I must have a serious word with her. Milo's been stealing again. He denies it, but Biljana saw him." He opened the back door of the car and helped a little girl out of her child seat and down to the sidewalk. She was wearing thick striped tights, a short red skirt, and a flower-patterned quilted jacket, and she beamed, wide-eyed, at Henry. It was his four-year-old sister, Amy. I already knew her from her dreams, where Henry and I had sometimes met. They were colorful and sweet as sugar. A boy climbed out of the car after her. I'd have known him anywhere as Henry's little brother—he was kind of the narrow-shouldered mini-edition of Henry himself. He had the same double cowlick on his head that made the hair stand out in all directions, and the same intensely bright gray eyes. However, he didn't seem as self-possessed as his brother; in fact, he looked miserable.

"I didn't steal anything," he told Henry with his lower lip jutting. "She's lying just to make me seem bad. She probably took it herself. Ouch!"

His father (at least, I supposed it was his father) had grabbed him by the back of the neck and was holding him tightly, like a naughty kitten. Amy opened the garden gate and skipped over to me.

"I don't steal things," she said, looking curiously at me. "Milo doesn't steal things either. How about you?"

Well, maybe a stupid trapper's cap, but that was all.

Henry groaned. "What's been st . . . er . . . what's gone missing?"

"Grandpa Henry's rococo snuffbox," said Henry's father, pushing Milo through the garden gate ahead of him. "The one from the J. P. Morgan collection. It's no joke, and no silly boy's prank. Go on, call your mother, will you?"

"She's . . . she's not in," said Henry. "Let go of Milo."

Only now did the driver's door of the car open, and a woman got out. "That rococo snuffbox is very valuable," she said in an Eastern European accent, rolling the letter *r*.

Up to now I'd been standing perfectly still on the steps up to the house, wishing I could make myself invisible. It seemed to have worked, too, because apart from Amy, no one had taken any notice of me. But the sight of the woman put an end to my invisibility. A gasp escaped me. Or a groan. Or a mixture of both.

It was B! The mermaid from the whirlpool. She looked staggeringly lovely, just like in the dream, although she was wearing a fur coat that, if it was genuine and I was not much mistaken, had cost several jaguars their lives, making it an offense against the protection of endangered species agreement. And against my dignity as well—I felt almost personally insulted. A jaguar coat? Seriously? How symbolic could you get?

My gasp had attracted the attention of Henry's father. "And who have we here? Is this your little girlfriend, Henry?"

"Little ex-girlfriend," I corrected him.

"I said let go of Milo." Henry was frowning angrily. With three strides, he was beside Milo, freeing him from his father's grasp, only to grab him by the nape of the neck himself next minute.

"Ow," said Milo. "I really didn't do anything."

"No, he didn't," Amy piped up. She was sitting in her play car now, looking around at us all, wide-eyed. "But I did a wee in my pants, and Biljana was cross."

With a deep sigh, Henry let go of his brother, and the relieved Milo rubbed the back of his neck.

Their father smiled at me with his dazzling white teeth, offered me his hand, and said, "Ron Harper."

"Er, Liv Silver," I muttered in confusion as he shook my hand vigorously.

"Pleased to meet you, little ex-girlfriend." Ron Harper's eyes twinkled as he looked at me. Oh my God! Was he actually flirting with me?

I let go of his hand as if I'd burned myself.

"Ronald! The snuffbox!" B reminded him. She was standing there stretching the way she'd stretched in the whirlpool.

"Yes, of course." Henry's father looked back at Milo, who was already halfway to the door. "This time there will be serious consequences. Apart from which, I am deeply disappointed in you."

"Same to you," said Henry's brother, taking another couple of steps back and almost colliding with me.

"We could call the police," said B, taking out her cell phone. "Or simply search his things."

I noticed Milo's hand moving toward his anorak pocket, and felt almost sure that he'd put the snuffbox in there. Because although I could see his face only from the side, it looked as guilty as if he had a confession hanging around his neck. I felt terribly sorry for him.

"Milo, whatever you've taken, just give it back," said Henry, suddenly sounding incredibly tired.

"But I don't have that silly box," said Milo, taking his hand out of his pocket again and putting it behind his back, clenched into a fist. It couldn't have been clearer.

In his place, I'd probably have tried to get rid of the thing much sooner, maybe by just dropping it unobtrusively into a flower bed. But it was too late for that now.

"Oh dear, it's nearly dark," I said, making up my mind. "I'll have to get home, or there'll be trouble with my—oh, look there! A squirrel!"

And as they all looked the way I had pointed, and Amy said, "Where? Where?" I reached for Milo's fist and let the thing he was hiding there slip into my hand.

I was astonished that the cheap squirrel trick had worked so well.

With great presence of mind, Milo kept his hand behind his back and didn't bat an eyelash.

"I can't see any squirrel," said Amy.

"I'm afraid it ran away," I said regretfully.

"I hate squirrels," said B.

Yes, very likely, because it would take hundreds of them to make a whole fur coat.

"See you later, Henry." I strolled to the garden gate deliberately slowly, digging my hand into my coat pocket, and turning back once more.

Henry's father was sighing. "Milo, let's have that snuffbox."

"Why do you always have to believe her?" Milo said accusingly. "I didn't steal anything, I swear it. It was her! She's probably planning to sell the box on the sly. . . ."

"You brat!" B tapped her long fingernails on the roof of the car. "I saw it with my own eyes!"

"Come along, Milo." Henry rubbed his forehead. "Give him the snuffbox, and let's get it over and done with."

"I haven't . . ."

"That will do!" His father took Milo's arm, dragged him over, and forcibly bent his fingers back. When he saw that Milo's hand was empty, he looked surprised. "Okay," he said through gritted teeth. "You wanted it this way. We'll just have to search you from head to foot."

By this time, I'd reached the garden gate and was out on the sidewalk. At close quarters, I was sorry to see that B still looked amazing. Except maybe for her lipstick, and surely her forehead could only be that smooth if she was injecting Botox into it.

"Is your coat real jaguar?" I asked.

B raised her perfectly plucked eyebrows in surprise. "Why, yes! Most people confuse it with leopard."

"I know." I couldn't resist turning back once more to look at Henry. He hadn't condescended to favor me with a glance since his family arrived. But now he was smiling at me—a sad, resigned smile. I couldn't possibly return it.

His father was busy with Milo's body search. He was already pulling off the child's anorak, swearing quietly. Milo himself, however, no longer looked such a picture of misery. He glanced at me over the brick wall—and winked!

High time I got out of there.

"What I really need is a snow leopard coat," B was saying behind me, and I turned one last time to look at her.

"Don't be ridiculous," I said. "The only one who really needs a snow leopard coat is the snow leopard itself."

TITTLE-TATTLE BLOG

The Frognal Academy Tittle-Tattle Blog, with all the latest gossip, the best rumors, and the hottest scandals from our school.

ABOUT ME:
My name is Secrecy—I'm right here among you, and I know *all* your secrets.

21 January

This isn't exactly breaking news, but still, you could say it was news about breaking, ha ha ha. ☺

Emily Clark and Grayson Spencer have broken up.

Liv Silver and Henry Harper have also broken up.

Hands up, everyone who suspects a connection between those two events. ☺

But to be honest, the end of the relationship could be foreseen in both cases, and it won't surprise anyone, will it? Emily says she had to make a break because Grayson was too immature for her, on account of being short of ambition, vision, and masculine self-assertion.

Grayson isn't saying anything. But if you ask me, he doesn't look like someone with a broken heart. And Grayson got the highest score on the English exam last week, finishing just above Emily—maybe if you're a genius the ambition isn't so important.

As for the reasons why Henry and Liv split up, I can only make my own assumptions, but I guess sex is top of the list. Also the fact that outside school, Liv is under the same roof as a very attractive new singleton by the name of Grayson. . . .

And now to the real breaking news of the day: Jasper Grant has changed his relationship status on Facebook from "It's complicated" to "In a relationship." Unfortunately he forgot to give a link to the girl concerned, but it's my bet that I wouldn't be wrong to say she's one of his forty-four new Facebook friends, or more precisely one of the twenty-eight new female friends. Anyone fancy a guessing game? Just click your way through the profile and add your comments, so I'll know which of those French girls you think Jasper fancies. I'll give a prize to whoever is the first to guess right. Oh yes, and while you're at it, you can tell me why they all look like film stars. And why all their names begin with *L*. Lola, Lilou, Lucy, Louise, Louanne, Lilly, Léa, Lina—there's something not quite right about all those French girls.

See you soon!

Love from Secrecy

WHEN I ARRIVED at school the next morning, everyone but me—as usual—had read the Tittle-Tattle blog, and they were all staring at me. However, there was sympathy in their eyes for a change. Too bad. So the news about the end of my relationship with Henry had finally filtered through to Secrecy.

"Oh, Liv, how mean of Henry! But never mind, now we can console each other!" Persephone flung her arms around me and drenched my school uniform with tears. As far as I could gather from the remarks she sobbed into my shoulder, Jasper had found a new girlfriend over in France.

"But I thought you and Gabriel . . . ?" and/or Eric—Persephone spent the lunch break flirting with both of them for all she was worth.

She took her head off my blazer and sniffed. "Gabriel? He's only to take my mind off things! So that I can survive Jasper's absence! Jasper was, is, and will always be my one great love!" With a sweeping gesture, she mopped her tears away, and I surreptitiously examined my blazer for traces of snot. "Like Henry is yours!"

I really did wish she'd keep her voice down a bit, but she wasn't about to oblige me by lowering it. On the contrary: she grabbed hold of my hand and announced, as if she were declaiming something on stage, "Let's found a Broken Hearts Club!"

Sure, why not? But only over my dead body.

Feeling rather melancholy, I thought back to the time before Henry. When I'd still been like Mia and immune to boys. What had happened to me? It was pathetic, the way I'd spent last night staring at my cell phone and biting my nails, hoping that Henry would call me. Which he hadn't.

He didn't call even though I was in possession of a snuff-box worth $25,000. I'd had quite a shock when I Googled "rococo," "snuffbox," and "Morgan Collection." Milo had stolen a little treasure. A tiny little treasure, now lying in the top drawer of my bedside table along with Charles's trapper's cap. I really didn't want to give Milo away, but I could hardly keep the snuffbox. For that reason alone, I'd have been glad if Henry had phoned.

And I'd have liked him to explain about B. Although what was there to explain? It made things no better that the woman he fooled around with in that whirlpool by night was his father's girlfriend. If you stopped to think about it, that made things worse.

Why did he send me a text if he didn't want to talk to me? I had reached for my cell phone about seventy times to ask him that very question, but then I didn't call him after all. It was bad enough that he'd opened his front door to find me standing outside. I wasn't the sort of girl to stalk her ex-boyfriend, to keep on phoning him, and refuse to accept that it was all over. . . . No, I was only the sort to stare at her cell phone and cry nonstop.

Oh God, and that made me perfect for Persephone's Broken Hearts Club.

"Maybe Grayson will join too," said Persephone.

"Grayson?"

"Yes, boys can have broken hearts as well!"

"But . . ." Oh, nothing was going to come of all this. I snatched Persephone's phone from her hand and looked for Secrecy's blog. And when I'd read it, I felt, if anything, worse. "See you in chemistry," I whispered to Persephone, and made for the lockers to find Grayson.

He was just taking out his books when I arrived, out of breath.

"Grayson, honestly! You acted injured all day because I hadn't told you about Henry and me, but you didn't feel you ought to tell me that it's over between you and Emily as well, right?" I asked. Or rather I gasped, but it made no difference. Grayson understood me, all the same.

"Henry and you kept it from me for over a week," he retorted. "Emily and I didn't break up until Saturday evening. After dinner."

"Then you had the whole of Sunday to tell me about it, instead of just looking at me in that injured way."

"I was looking worried, not injured. Anyway, I was hardly at home. I didn't have time to tell you."

"It wouldn't have taken long. A sentence would have done it. *Oh, and by the way, Emily has dumped me.* Or you could have told me last night. . . ."

I closed my mouth.

Could I seriously be cross with Grayson? The way he looked after Mia was so sweet. When I'd looked to the right in the dream corridor last night, I'd seen him sitting outside Mia's dream door. I was so touched, I almost went over to hug him. Not that he could really have done anything about an intruder, but it's the thought that counts. And he'd been so nice, sitting there trying to look dangerous.

I was still hesitating over telling Mia the whole story, because fundamentally there was no real proof that her sleep-walking didn't have a natural cause. Particularly as I was still inclined to believe Anabel when she'd said she had nothing to do with it. Which was probably stupid of me, because Anabel must be involved all the same.

But however that might be, this time I'd slept in Mia's bed with her, if only so that she wouldn't have to activate the alarm device again. Surprisingly, she'd been perfectly happy about that idea; she thought walking in her sleep was creepy, and her bed was broad enough for two. She had insisted on tying our ankles together with her jump rope, so that if she got out of bed I'd be sure to be woken. Or dragged along after her. But nothing had happened. Mia had slept well and deeply, no one suspicious had come to her door, and I was feeling much better today because of that. Back when I walked in my sleep myself, it had stopped just as suddenly as it began, and with luck it would be the same for Mia. Until then we'd just have to make sure she was tied to something and couldn't harm herself. . . .

"Why have you stopped telling me off?" Grayson was still looking down at me with a frown. "Should I be worried? Anyway, Emily didn't dump me; it was the other way around. Just saying."

"Oh yes?" Now I couldn't help laughing. "That's not the way Secrecy describes it. And how about the sign for infinity you gave Emily, anyway?"

"It's only a figure eight lying on its side," said Grayson drily.

"I see. All the same, Persephone would welcome you to our Broken Hearts Club." I went over to my own locker to get out my chemistry textbook.

"Such an honor," said Grayson. "But you'd better ask Henry."

And with that he disappeared around the nearest corner.

"You'd better ask Henry what?" Someone beside me put an arm around my shoulders. It was Arthur. Oh, great. I really hadn't missed him these last few days! Although— did he know that we'd seen Anabel, and she was far from being Senator Tod's unfortunate victim, but rather the other way around?

I freed myself from his grasp. "Nothing that's any of your business," I said quickly.

He smiled and strolled on to his locker. "I'm sorry about what's happened, by the way, Liv. I could have sworn you and Henry were head over heels in love. When I heard last night that you'd split up, I couldn't believe it at first."

"You sit up at night to read Secrecy's blog, do you?" I asked, horrified. Okay, I could believe almost anything of Arthur—but I'd really never have thought of that.

Arthur laughed. "Of course not," he said. "No, I heard about it from Henry and Grayson."

Oh, of course, because the three of them had been close friends since sharing their buckets and shovels in the nursery school sandpit, and told one another everything.

Arthur ignored my skeptical expression. "I saw them in the corridor last night. They were sitting outside your little sister's door, so I joined them for a while."

I didn't believe a word of it. "And then, over a dream beer, Henry told you he and I had split up? While Grayson poured out his heart to you about Emily?"

"Well, not directly," said Arthur. "Grayson and Henry were talking about it and I came along. . . ." At least he was being honest. "In the past they'd certainly have asked my advice. You may not believe it, but I was always the expert on girls in our little circle."

"Before you lost your heart to that nutcase who thinks she has to let a demon loose on the world," I couldn't help saying.

Arthur's right eyelid twitched. "You know, I miss the old days when I hung out with the others and we talked." He stroked his chin, thus reminding me how I'd broken his jaw. Had he done that on purpose? "About girls, and how complicated life is, and basketball, of course. Boy stuff, that's all. I miss them."

The school corridors were emptying. Soon the bell would go. "You expect me to feel sorry for you?" I asked, annoyed. Annoyed mainly because I did feel sorry for him. It must be hard to lose such good friends. Still, that had nothing to do with it. "You ought to have thought about that before you lied to them and got drawn into such a bad business," I said.

Arthur looked as if he really would think about it. "Yes, I guess I ought," he said. "I kind of naturally assumed we'd all stay friends until we were old and gray. But maybe last night was at least a beginning. . . ."

A beginning of what? Did he really think that Grayson and Henry would make things up with this character who'd been happy to have me killed in his family vault? Never! On the other hand, they'd known one another all their lives and had been through thick and thin together. While I was still new here—and a girl.

The bell woke me from these gloomy thoughts, and for once I was even glad of it. "Well," I said, relieved, "never mind that, I'm off. Maybe I can read about the boy stuff you go on about in the Tittle-Tattle—"

I stopped short. An idea that seemed both totally absurd and absolutely logical had occurred to me.

"Wait a second," I said slowly as a great many little cog-wheels began interlocking with each other in my mind. "So in the corridor last night Grayson and Henry told you that they'd ended their relationships?"

Arthur nodded. "I just told you so." Suddenly he looked like the old, self-satisfied Arthur I'd known before.

"What an amazing coincidence that Secrecy writes about that very thing in her blog today!"

Arthur shrugged his shoulders. "I'd say I agree with Nietzsche: no winner believes in coincidence."

He wasn't a winner. He was a nasty little fraud. He was . . .

"Arthur, are you Secrecy?" It burst out of me.

Arthur began to laugh. "My God, no! What funny ideas you get, Liv. I'm not Secrecy. To be honest, I haven't the faintest idea who Secrecy is. I had a suspicion a couple of times, but it always turned out to be wrong. That really is a weird notion."

"But . . ."

"But of course we all have Secrecy's e-mail address." He smiled at me, and I had a feeling that he was enjoying the horrified look I'd given him.

"Meaning that you supply Secrecy with information?"

"Yup." Arthur pushed an angelic lock of hair back from his angel-face. "Now and then. From a fake account. What Secrecy can do, I can do better. I'm the perfect informant, you see. One learns so much in dreams. Things that no one else knows. Oh, don't look so morally offended. Don't forget that if you get up on your high horse it's a long way to fall." He looked at his watch. "Do you know how late it is? Time for your next class."

I lifted my chin. "You're right there," I said, trying to sound as icily scornful as possible. "My high horse and I must just go and find a toilet to throw up in first, because this conversation makes us sick to our stomachs."

Arthur was still smiling, but it wasn't a casual smile, more of an artificial one. And underneath it I could clearly sense hurt feelings, but that didn't bother me.

I set off for the chemistry lab. And on the way I'd have to send a couple of texts.

25

"COME INTO THE water, dear boy." B was stretching seductively in her whirlpool, and this time she had a fish tail shimmering in all the colors of the rainbow. She was stirring the water up into waves with it.

Henry hesitated, looking at me.

"Don't do it," I wanted to say, but I couldn't utter a word. I was a tree, with my roots going down through the mosaic tiles and into the earth below. I had to watch, helplessly, as Henry undressed and slid into the water to join B.

"Too bad, too bad," whispered a voice beside me. It was Anabel's. She patted my bark sympathetically. "Fancy having to watch this. But that's just like Henry. It's his own fault if he loses his heart to her, of all people."

In the whirlpool, B swam over to Henry and flung her slender arms around his neck.

"I'm sure you wish you could close your eyes," whispered Anabel. "What a shame that you're a tree."

Yes, what a shame. Henry and B were beginning to kiss, and there wasn't a thing I could do about it.

"There's only one solution, Liv," said Anabel. "You'll have to wake from this dream." She pointed to the golden decoration of the opposite wall, where there was a splash shower, and a mint-green door next to it. My door.

Thank goodness. It was only a dream. *My* dream. Which wasn't going to prevent Henry and B from kissing. They were holding each other close, and Henry had one hand in B's hair, while the other . . .

"Just wake from the dream," said Anabel gently, and I did. Why don't you realize immediately in a dream that it *is* a dream, even when you've just been a tree? It was crazy. My heart was thudding unnaturally fast, anyway, and in my relief I nestled closer to Mia. Her alarm clock said 5:30, so there was another hour to go before it went off. Mia was breathing peacefully and regularly. She'd tied our ankles together with her jump rope again, and that wasn't the only reason I hadn't been afraid to go to sleep. Out in the corridor, Grayson would be on guard, maybe even with Henry again. After all, he'd kept Grayson company last night.

I'd sent a text saying: *A admits sent info to Secr. L.* (It was a short text because of the difficulty of typing on the old-fashioned cell phone.) At least he'd replied: *Can't say I'm surprised. After all, he's an A.* And a smiley after it. I'd considered texting back to say I had the rococo snuffbox and ask what I should do with it, but then I didn't. For one thing, it would take ages to type that message, and for another, if he'd wanted me to text back he'd have asked a question. But he hadn't. Apart from which I also had other worries on my mind. Thanks to Secrecy, the whole family now knew that Grayson and I belonged to the Broken Hearts Club. Florence had been kind enough to enlighten them.

Mom had been rather hurt that she hadn't heard it from me first, but she'd tried not to let that show. "I remember just what it's like to be unhappy in love for the first time, mousie," she had said, stroking my head. "But believe me, it won't be for the last time by a long chalk."

What a great prospect. If that wasn't a huge comfort, I didn't know what would be. However, she had said the very same thing to Grayson, stroking his head too. His expression had been priceless. I could have had a fit of the giggles all over again when I thought of it.

"I liked that boy." Lottie had set to work at once baking comfort muffins for Grayson and me, while Mom was still at the head-stroking stage. Lottie herself was a bit cross with me for not saying anything to her, because now she was a week late with the baking. For me, anyway. For Grayson the experience was still new. "And I'm sure . . . er . . . Emily is very nice too. Even if she doesn't let it show."

"Yes, she's very good at hiding that," said Grayson, who looked as if the mere smell of hot chocolate was a comfort to him.

The muffins were a sign that Lottie didn't take any of it too seriously. If she had been really worried, she'd have baked her all-the-year-round vanilla crescents, for when extreme comfort was called.

"I did like Henry, though," she said, stirring the large pan of chocolate that she was melting on the stove. "But maybe it's better this way. Men just make life so much more complicated. And they're so odd. Take Charles, for instance. After weeks of indifference, he's suddenly mad keen to go out with me again."

Which of course was because of his jealousy of the

nonexistent Jonathan. For some reason that, plus the fact that Lottie staunchly denied ever knowing anyone called Jonathan, seemed to egg him on. Men really were odd.

Mia moved slightly in her sleep. She had been the only one who really understood how I felt. "Honestly, you go and fall in love just once and something like this has to happen," she had said. "I think Henry is really cool, but he must be an idiot if he wants to break up with you."

That was the end of the subject so far as she was concerned. Before going to sleep, she'd switched the conversation to Secrecy. I had told her that Arthur had admitted to supplying the blog with information. Very confidential information, like the fact that Henry and I weren't together anymore. That hadn't surprised Mia.

"After all, that's what keeps Secrecy's blog going. All the scandalmongers who read it write to her whenever they find out something," she said. "Maybe they hope that then they won't be the focus of her attention themselves. Have you noticed, by the way, that it's a long time since she wrote anything nasty about Hazel Pritchard?"

"Yes, and I realize that she must get sent tons of information. But . . . how does Secrecy decide who's telling the truth and who isn't?" I stared thoughtfully at the ceiling. "Think about it. Her rate of hits is always surprisingly high, at least as far as I can judge. So since she must have lots of informants, how does she know which of them she can trust? Particularly as I'm sure she must be told stories that aren't true all the time."

"Hmm." Mia had also been staring at the ceiling. "Good question. Maybe she works only with informants that she knows—and knows she can rely on."

"Then Arthur would be lying when he says he doesn't know who she is?"

"Possibly. If you didn't guess right after all, and he's behind it himself." Mia had propped herself up on her elbows. "Although it occurred to me the other day that Secrecy could be more than one person."

Another good idea.

"Well, Watson, looks as if this case has been beyond you," I said all the same, just to annoy Mia a bit. "Didn't you say you'd have the whole thing cleared up by Christmas?"

"Oh no, Sherlock! Don't take that attitude. Admittedly, Secrecy is a tough nut to crack, but not hard enough to foil Mia Silver."

Unfortunately I wasn't so sure of that. Of course I hadn't told Mia how Arthur came by the information that he'd passed on to Secrecy.

"Don't look so doubtful." Mia nudged me. "Go to sleep instead! You look worn out. . . . Sorry, I guess it's the whole love business. I hope and pray it never happens to me." And with that, she turned on her other side and fell asleep at once.

She was lying on her back now. In the sparse light from the streetlamp outside, she looked much younger than usual. Her long fair hair was spread out on the pillow, where it mingled with mine; you couldn't tell where hers ended and mine began. I knew it was impossible that she'd avoid falling in love, but I hoped for her sake that it wouldn't happen for a few years yet. And that it would be even longer before love could make her unhappy.

It was beginning to get light outside; a bird started to sing, then two, and then the rising sun cast the delicate shadows of branches and leaves on the wall, a copy of the magnolia in the front garden. It looked beautiful, like a Chinese ink drawing. The room slowly filled with golden morning light, more and more birds began singing, and now and then I heard the shrill, striking cry of the gibbons. . . . Wait a moment! Abruptly, I sat up in bed. Monkeys? Golden morning sunlight? We were in London in the depths of winter. It was still pitch dark at this hour; there were no birds singing, and definitely no gibbons uttering their cries! My eyes wandered around the room. Mia was fast asleep, everything looked the same as usual—apart from the mint-green door in the wall.

This was all wrong.

I hadn't woken at all. I'd only dreamed of waking, but in reality I was still asleep.

26

I QUICKLY BEGAN undoing the jump rope around my ankle, but then I realized that wasn't necessary. After all, this was only a dream, so I could just make the rope disintegrate and turn to dust. However, I couldn't bring myself to dispose of Mia like that. She looked so peaceful lying there in the golden morning sunlight. When I closed the door behind me, the gibbons were still calling.

Everything was the same as usual out in the corridor. Whenever I came here, I briefly held my breath as I looked to see if Henry's door was still in the same place. Yet again it was right opposite mine. In spite of all that had happened, that was a comforting feeling, I couldn't deny it.

Grayson was on guard, just as I'd expected. He was sitting outside Mia's door in jeans and T-shirt, reading a book that he hastily tried to hide behind his back when he saw me coming.

"You really are a genius if you can read a book in your dreams," I said. "What's it about?"

"The principles of genetics," said Grayson awkwardly. "I thought I could use the time to study."

"Genetics?"

"I know it's only a book I dreamed up, but maybe you can trick your brain in this place. . . ." He rubbed his forehead. "Or maybe not," he added.

"You look tired. Like me to take over here for a bit?"

"Definitely not! I haven't been here long, and I don't want to go back into my dreams. I was dreaming of Emily and Emily's horse, she was comparing me with . . . Well, anyway, Granny was there, too, and she was in a filthy temper again. . . ."

"Like this afternoon?" I asked sympathetically.

"Worse," said Grayson, but with all due respect to him, I didn't think that was possible. The muffins had just gone into the oven when the door opened and the Boker came in, dressed from head to foot in discreet shades of beige and ocher. And with her nostrils distended in rage.

"Please leave the kitchen, Miss Whistlehooper," she had said to Lottie without ceremony or even a greeting, ignoring me entirely as usual. "And take that delinquent girl with you. I have something serious to say to my grandson."

But Lottie and I couldn't leave the kitchen because we had to time the baking muffins, so Grayson and his grandmother went next door into the living room, which she called the salon. That suited her rank better, anyway. Luckily she uttered her serious remarks loud enough for us to hear them easily in the kitchen. At least, if we kept perfectly quiet and put our ears as close to the door as possible.

The Boker was furious with Grayson for "committing the unforgivable folly" of breaking so suddenly with "a wonderful girl like Emily." As if she (the Boker) didn't have enough on her mind with Ernest's stupid midlife crisis, now Grayson had to behave childishly too. "Dear boy, you must consider my heart," she complained. "God knows I'm not as young as I was, and since Saturday and that . . . that . . . engagement," she said, almost spitting out the word, "I haven't had a wink of sleep."

Which seemed to me a remarkable achievement, considering that Saturday was days ago. And the Boker didn't seem particularly tired, in fact the opposite. She continued her lamentation with much vigor. Emily was all that a young man like Grayson could wish for: clever, pretty, from a good family, and above all very ambitious. "With a girl like Emily beside you, you're sure to succeed in life," she cried. "She'll always make sure that you stay on the right track." She dismissed Grayson's objections that he was only seventeen and was planning to decide on his own life, by pointing out that his grandfather had been eighteen when he met her, and it had been the making of him, so he, Grayson, had better stop making trouble. Grayson had no answer to that, and a little later the Boker marched out of the house in high dudgeon.

"Granny can really be rather . . . interfering sometimes," said Grayson unhappily, stretching his legs out in front of him.

"Well, I think it was mean of Florence to tell tales." I sat down on the floor beside Grayson and leaned back against Mia's door.

"She didn't," replied Grayson. Only now did he make his book on genetics disappear. "That's the creepiest thing of all: Granny reads Secrecy's blog. And in my dream she spat at me for failing the biology test."

"Oh. That sounds really bad. But not as bad as my dream," I said, looking down the corridor. The milky white light in it seemed brighter than usual. "Guess what: I woke from a horrible nightmare, and I was so relieved that I was lying in my bed safe and sound. Or rather, Mia's bed. Then, after a while, I realized that I wasn't awake at all. I'd only been dreaming that I woke from my dream, if you see what I mean."

Grayson slowly shook his head. "Er . . . no, not entirely."

"It was a dream about dreaming a dream, so to speak." I pulled my nightgown down over my knees and admired the lace at the hem. This was the first time I'd worn it, and it wasn't really my style, but when I saw it in December while I was out shopping with Mom in those little vintage boutiques near Covent Garden, it had been love at first sight. Sleeping Beauty must have been kissed awake in a gown like that: creamy white with lace, and a border of little embroidered roses. I wondered whether I ought to imagine something more practical, but it was simply too pretty for me to do that.

Grayson ran his hand through his hair. "A dream of a dream in a dream? Sounds complicated."

"It is. But doesn't it show how versatile this dream business is? We can never really know whether we're awake or asleep. Maybe we're not real at all; we just exist in a dream."

"Stop that at once," said Grayson. "You're making my flesh creep. Oh, hi, Henry. Have you ever dreamed of a dream in a dream?"

As usual, Henry had approached without a sound. I'd have liked a little longer to prepare myself to look at him casually. All things considered, my effort might not be entirely perfect, but it was a good shot. Anyway, I was glad that the new nightgown looked so good. Even if I felt a little overdressed in it.

"Everything okay here?" asked Henry.

"We've only just arrived," Grayson told him.

Henry got down on the floor with us. "Have you checked that the air's clear in Mia's dream?"

"Er . . . no. What do you mean?" Grayson looked at him in confusion.

Henry sighed and stood up again. "I mean, someone could have walked into the dream before you arrived." He was making for the door. "I'll take a quick look."

"Wait!" I cried, jumping up myself. "You can't just walk in like that. It's Mia's dream—and you don't have anything of hers. Besides, I'm sure she wouldn't want you to."

Henry let go of the door handle. "But how else are we to find out if there's anyone in there?"

"We could simply wait," suggested Grayson. "An intruder would have to come out again sometime, and then we'd catch him."

Henry frowned. "Anyone in there is probably too clever to be caught in the doorway like that. And it could be too late by then."

Deep down inside, I felt that he was right, but an obstinate part of me wouldn't admit it. "I mean, seriously, she could simply be having vivid dreams, and if she were sleepwalking, I'd be awake by now. We've been tying our ankles together with a jump rope."

Henry, who had been avoiding my gaze, suddenly looked at me. The corners of his mouth turned up, and a very familiar glint came into his eyes. "With a jump rope?" he asked, amused. "You know, Liv, sometimes I really miss—" He broke off and bit his lower lip. "Maybe it would be best if you go in on your own and make sure she's all right." He cleared his throat. "If she is, you can come and tell us. If not—"

"Then I'll come and tell you too," I said. My heart was beating a little faster, not so much because of Mia's dream as because I would have loved to know what exactly Henry sometimes missed. But I could hardly ask him that. Not in front of Grayson.

I turned to the door and cautiously pushed the handle down. It wasn't locked. And there was no one guarding it, not even Mom. I didn't understand Mia's unconscious mind— surely she must sense danger looming ahead.

"See you soon," said Henry. "And, Liv . . ."

I looked over my shoulder.

"Be careful. If only because of the new nightgown. Which really suits you."

I managed not to smile, closed the door from inside, and looked around me. I was in a cottage garden, and it was summer. Mia's door fitted perfectly into the cottage itself. The picket fence had blue sweet peas climbing over it, while marigolds and herbs bordered a little garden path that led to a large orchard of fruit trees. Beyond the fence, sheep were grazing in the sun. It was an idyllic scene. I was glad to think that Mia had such lovely dreams. I heard her laughing some-where, and I was about to run over and reassure myself that all was well, but for safety's sake, I turned into a dragonfly in case some intruder really had slipped in. Although the dragon-fly reminded me painfully of B's dream, it made me small enough not to attract attention, but large enough to avoid being snapped up and eaten by one of the many birds twit-tering for all they were worth in this garden. I flew cautiously along a washing line with picturesque white laundry pegged out to dry, and came to an apple tree with a large swing hanging from it. The kind of swing we'd always dreamed of having.

Mia was sitting on its wide seat. And beside her—so was I.

For some reason, I was wearing the smoky blue ball gown I'd worn to the Frognal Academy Autumn Ball, and I must say it really suited me. In fact, Mia and I made a pleasant sight, sitting side by side on the swing, laughing. I settled on a leaf and watched us, feeling touched.

"If you had to make a list of the most embarrassing moments in my life, what would you put first?" asked Dream-Liv.

"That's difficult," said Mia. "There are so many of them."

That made us both giggle, and I tossed my hair back over my shoulders. Feeling slightly ashamed of myself, I noticed—or the dragonfly-me noticed—how silly that looked.

"Well, I guess top of the list would be that time in Hyderabad when you suddenly wet yourself on the bus." Mia dangled her legs. "You wrapped a beach towel around you so that no one would notice. . . ."

"Oh yes, that was really embarrassing," said Liv-on-the-swing, and a diabolical grin flashed over her face.

A sparrow flew up from somewhere and looked at me with its head on one side, as if wondering whether I'd fit into its beak, but I took no notice. It could have been a dangerous bird of prey for all I cared; I didn't mind. Because something had just become clear to me—something that altered the situation considerably.

That grin—it wasn't my grin. Any more than those were my eyes looking all around the garden and coming back to Mia.

The person on the swing beside her wasn't someone she had dreamed up.

She was just someone making herself out to be me.

I realized I was having difficulty in keeping my balance. The longer my dragonfly eyes stared at the Liv in the ball gown, the less like me she looked. What I'd been most afraid of had actually happened. But who on earth was she? Who was sitting there beside my little sister, asking her questions?

The false Liv bent over to Mia, giggling. "And the second-most embarrassing moment?"

The silly giggle was too much for me. With a single furious beat of my wings, I shot past the hungry sparrow and stopped behind the nearest apple tree. There, in the shelter of its sturdy trunk, I changed shape again.

When I stepped out of the shadows and went over to the swing, Mia and the fake Liv looked at me in surprise.

"Sherlock Holmes!" cried Mia, and Liv said, "Benedict Cumberbatch."

They were both right. I was Benedict Cumberbatch as Sherlock Holmes. "Hey, Watson," I said.

"Hey," Mia whispered back, delighted. The false Liv must think that Mia had dreamed Sherlock here because she'd been feeling a little bored. Fake-Liv smiled, obviously amused.

I looked her up and down. "And who's this supposed to be?" I asked. Normally I'd have been enjoying this, particularly since I was doing very well with Benedict Cumberbatch's deep voice, but right now I was too angry. Who the hell was this in front of me?

"This is my sister, Liv." Mia beamed at me.

I gave her a typical Sherlock look. "She does look like your sister—almost enough like her to take people in." Wow, my voice was so sexy.

"What's all this?" asked Dream-Liv, flabbergasted.

"Oh, come on!" I was getting more and more sure of myself. "I saw it a mile off. The artificial tilt of your head, that stupid giggle, the affected way you toss your hair back—the real Liv is light-years cooler than you."

"And you're nothing but a totally overestimated late starter of an actor with no noticeable talent," said Dream-Liv, annoyed. "I'll never understand what women see in you. You look like a fish. If it wasn't for that voice, not a soul would think anything of you."

"But, Liv!" Mia was staring at her pretended dream-sister in horror. "You're his greatest fan."

"Very true," I said, returning to my own form.

Dream-Liv and Mia were both left gasping for air.

"Take a good look and then tell me which of us is the real Liv," I said. In my own voice again, unfortunately.

"Well, I've been sitting here all this time," said Dream-Liv with a confused smile. "Whereas you were Benedict Cumberbatch just now."

"That's true," murmured Mia.

"Okay," I said. "Then let's settle it once and for all. Show us what your poor bruised bum looked like after the skiing trip in Switzerland, Liv!"

The false Liv began to laugh. It wasn't my laugh, and while she was laughing, she changed shape. Her hair grew longer and wavier, and took on a darker golden shade of blond, her complexion was pure alabaster, and her eye color mutated from an ordinary blue to a definitely extraordinary turquoise.

I could hardly take in what I was seeing. Would we never learn to see through her mask of innocence? At least Henry hadn't done any better at it than me. He had believed her.

"Anabel," I said, hoping my voice sounded as acid as I felt. "What was it you said? *I for one have nothing to do with it?*"

Anabel slid off the swing and stationed herself in front of me. She was still wearing my ball gown. I'm sorry to say that she looked even better in it than I did.

"Of course I have something to do with it," she said, and as usual, her gentle voice made me shiver. "Who else?"

Yes, who else? Mia seemed only mildly surprised by what was going on in her dream. She looked interested rather than shocked.

"But . . ." I stared at Anabel. How had she done it? How had she made her way into Mia's dream? "You're locked up in that hospital. Miles from London. How did you get your hands on something belonging to Mia?"

Anabel's right eyelid twitched. "I have ways and means that you don't know anything about," she said.

Had she always been so tall?

"In fact, you know remarkably little for someone who changes shape so perfectly." She smiled her honey-sweet smile. "My compliments on your Benedict Cumberbatch impersonation. I couldn't have done it better myself."

No, no, no.

This was all wrong.

Her height. And something else, a tiny detail, I'd seen it only very recently, it was . . .

"You're not Anabel," I said slowly. An icy certainty rose in me, almost choking me. "Your eyelid. When we were talking beside my locker yesterday, it twitched just like that." For a moment even the twittering of the birds seemed to stop.

"Arthur!" I whispered, and his name echoed almost like a scream in the silence.

"Oh, damn it," said Anabel in Arthur's voice. "You really are good."

27

AND NOW IT was Arthur standing in front of me, beautiful as an angel, and all at once the whole thing seemed to me so logical that I could only wonder how I hadn't seen through him at once.

"Oh, come on, Liv, you didn't really think we were friends again, did you?" he asked.

Yes. No. Not directly, but I'd believed there was a truce between us.

"So it was you all the time." I realized myself how resentful that sounded, and I was annoyed. I quickly added, "By the way, you've forgotten to take my ball gown off."

The fact that for half a second Arthur looked down at himself, taken aback, gave me a brief moment of satisfaction. Of course he wasn't wearing my dress anymore, but black jeans and a long-sleeved black T-shirt that made him look perfect. I wouldn't have been surprised if a pair of huge black angel's wings had spread wide on his back.

"Ha-ha, very funny," he said. "And yes, it was me all the time. It wasn't particularly difficult to trick your little sister. She's not a complicated character—the opposite, if anything."

"Hey!" said Mia indignantly.

"That was a compliment," Arthur told her. "You're darned straightforward for a girl. Nice to find there are still some like that."

Failing to take this as flattery, Mia wrinkled her nose.

"So you've been spying on her to provide Secrecy with information?" I was trying hard to sound superior, but not succeeding very well. Especially as I realized that that certainly hadn't been his only reason.

Arthur smiled at the way my voice shook. "Of course I knew you wouldn't like the whole school to know your secrets, but that was just a side effect, for fun."

"The sleepwalking . . ."

"The sleepwalking," Arthur imitated me. "Yes, the sleepwalking—brilliant, don't you agree? It took me weeks to find out how to get someone to walk in her sleep, and I have to admit that it doesn't work with everyone. Obviously you need a basic tendency to do it. Luckily your sister has that." He paused for a moment. The birds were still silent, and a misty veil had come over the sun. "Isn't it weird to think that she could simply get up one night and hang herself in your garden shed?" said Arthur.

My fingers clenched convulsively. "Arthur, Mia has never harmed you."

"That's true, poor thing. She has to suffer just because it's her bad luck to be your sister." He looked at me attentively, and now his tone of voice was spiteful. "Smart, brave little Liv who's wound Grayson and Henry around her little finger. And who's so good at kung fu . . ."

"You're still annoyed with me."

"Annoyed?" he interrupted. He wasn't looking amused now, on the contrary. His eyes were sparkling with pure rage. I instinctively took a step back.

"Annoyed?" he repeated. "I might be annoyed if you'd left a scratch on my car. Or if I'd lent you my iPad and you wrecked it. No, I'm not annoyed with you; I never was. I *hate* you."

Okay. So now we knew.

"You've destroyed my life, Liv Silver. You've ruined all my plans. It's your fault that Anabel and I aren't together anymore. It's your fault I've lost all my friends. And it's your fault that chewing still hurts me."

Arthur almost shouted that last bit. All his self-confidence seemed to have left him, and Mia was so startled that she slipped off the swing and came over to me.

"You—broke—my—damn—jawbone," Arthur went on a little more quietly, as if he still couldn't grasp that.

"Really? That was you?" asked Mia. "Secrecy wrote that it was an accident."

"Yes, an accident called Liv Silver," said Arthur bitterly.

I supposed it wouldn't be any use reminding him of the circumstances leading up to that. A dark cloud came in front of the sun. More clouds were towering up above the meadow where the sheep were grazing. A summer storm was brewing. Uneasily, I looked around at the cottage. This was probably the time to go out into the corridor and tell Grayson and Henry what had happened.

But there was one thing that I wanted to know first.

"Why—" I began, but Arthur didn't let me finish.

"I hope you're not going to ask why I'm doing all this, are

you, Liv? It's simple: I'm not stopping until you feel worse than I do. Why should you keep your friends when I've lost mine? Why should you have a happy relationship when I can't?"

A flash of lightning shot out of the storm clouds on the horizon, and soon after that there was a loud rumble of thunder. Leaves whirled through the air. The sheep had disappeared, and the birds seemed to have gone into hiding somewhere as well. I'd heard enough, and I turned to go.

But I didn't get far, because the ground broke apart in front of me, and within seconds I was facing a broad, deep pit.

"An earthquake!" cried Mia, reaching for my hand.

Hot vapors rose from the pit. By now the sky had clouded over entirely.

"It's not an earthquake," I said, looking furiously at Arthur. "Oh, really, Arthur! The apocalypse? Couldn't you think of anything better?"

"I like it." Arthur laughed. "Particularly because it's a lot of fun for me to watch you fail. And this is only a dream. Think how helpless you'll feel if you lose your sister in real life. If she gets up one night to throw herself in front of a moving car. Or . . ."

The pit was getting broader and broader. An apple tree crashed down into the chasm, taking with it the washing line complete with the picturesque white garments drying there.

"Oh, wait a minute. You want it apocalyptic, right?" Arthur snapped his fingers, and a huge yellow snake crawled out of the pit. Mia screeched.

"Stop it," I said to Arthur, and concentrating as hard as I

could, I turned the snake into a brimstone yellow butterfly.
It flew away, lurching through the air.

Arthur laughed briefly and made two more snakes crawl
out of the pit. This time I didn't manage to turn them into
something else. Mia was clinging to me in terror. By now
there were more cracks in the ground, too wide for us to
jump over them.

"You needed something personal, though, didn't you,
Arthur?" If I couldn't control Arthur's imagination, at least
I could distract his mind. I tried to breathe calmly, which
wasn't so easy, because snakes came right after spiders on my
personal horror scale, and they were winding their way
straight toward us, even if slowly.

Arthur's eyes lit up. "That was simple!" He raised his hand
and showed us a glove with a pattern of gray spots.

"Oh!" said Mia, her mind taken off the scene for a moment.
"My favorite gloves! I wondered where I'd lost one." But
that was as far as taking her mind off it went. She pointed
frantically to the snakes. "I think those are yellow tiger
pythons. Why don't we climb a tree? Or could they climb
up after us?"

"Lost it? I took it out of her coat pocket." Arthur smiled
at us. "And I've been wearing it almost every night since then
in my sleep."

"Yuck!" said Mia. "That's kind of . . . perverse, if you
ask me."

Another fruit tree sank into the depths of the pit, with loud
creaking and groaning and splintering noises, and sparks flew
over the meadow where we were standing.

"You're welcome to wake up," I told Mia, while I feverishly

wondered what I could do. Maybe make a bridge grow over the pit so that we could run to safety in the cottage? Or even better, turn myself into a huge bird of prey so that I could pick up Mia and . . .

"You're not so good under pressure, Liv," said Arthur, making another crack in the ground appear, this time running right between my legs. "I'm almost disappointed in you."

I jumped aside, but it was no use. With a growl like thunder, the crack was growing all the time, and the place where we stood was getting smaller. Any moment I would be bound to fall into the abyss, dragging Mia down with me.

And then the light was brighter. The storm clouds had gone away as quickly as they came, and the sun was shining down from the sky again.

The cracks in the ground slowly began closing, one by one.

A muscle in Arthur's face twitched; I saw him concentrating, and for a moment everything seemed to stand still. Nothing moved. Even the snakes froze where they were.

Then they weren't snakes any longer, but fluffy yellow baby chicks cheeping as they ran over the meadow, while the sides of the pit came closer together again, and the grassy ground closed over them as if they had never existed.

"Oh, how cute!" squealed Mia as I looked around with a sigh of relief.

"Henry!" growled Arthur.

"Henry!" I repeated. I couldn't help it, I had to say his name, and that in itself made me feel much better. I could have hugged him as he stood there on the path bordered by flowers with his hands in his pockets, as if he'd had nothing to do with it. He smiled at me. I really could have kissed him for those baby chicks. Which of course would not have been a good idea.

"It was Arthur. The whole time it was Arthur," I said instead, and Arthur imitated my accusing tone of voice at once.

"Yes, it was Arthur the whole time. And it'll be Arthur who makes sure that Liv's smile is wiped off her face forever."

Henry took a step closer. His casual expression gave way to genuine tension. "I regret every minute I have to spend with you, Arthur," he said slowly. "And don't imagine that I trusted you for a single second. What's the point of all this?"

"There isn't necessarily a point to everything." Arthur was giving him a nasty look. "It's enough for me to feel satisfaction. For Liv to suffer the way I've suffered. For her to lose everything she loves." He gave a breathless laugh. "Although you two managed there without my help. Nice of you to dump her, Henry. I think that hit her hard, didn't it, Liv?"

Yes. Unfortunately he was right.

Henry glanced at me briefly, then turned back to Arthur. "Natural catastrophes . . . snakes . . . Your repertoire hasn't changed much, anyway," he said. "And I can dream rings around you any day."

That was true too. Anyway, conjuring up a white horse at this point would have been very suitable (and it would have harmonized so well with my nightgown).

Arthur nodded slightly. "Maybe," he said. "But, Henry, believe me, I'm going to see this through. One way or another. No one will keep me from getting my revenge." He pointed to Mia, who had picked up one of the baby chicks and was stroking it, enchanted. I didn't want him to go on, but I didn't know how to stop him. Now he was smiling again, and it was the most unpleasant smile I'd ever seen.

"Look at my little puppet there," he said. "You do realize that you won't be able to guard her around the clock every night, don't you? I can do anything I like with her. Anything! At any time!" He looked around for Mia's door. "And I can end it soon, but I can just as easily wait." His eyes wandered carelessly over me. "Waiting can sometimes really wear you down, Liv. Yes, I think I'm going to enjoy that." He laughed again. "To be honest, I'm quite enjoying it now. I wish you could see your faces. See it dawning on you slowly but surely that there's nothing, absolutely nothing, you can do to stop me."

I bit my lip. He was right—I felt totally helpless, and I had no plans. There was nothing to be done about so much hostility.

"It will give me pleasure to watch you suffering, Liv," said Arthur solemnly.

"And it will give me pleasure to thwart every last one of your projects," said Henry.

"You may be overestimating yourself, my old friend," said Arthur. With a huge leap, he crossed the meadow and landed right outside Mia's door. "Now, excuse me. I have to go and tell Secrecy how Liv once wet herself in a bus in Hyderabad."

We waited until the door had latched behind him and then looked at each other.

"He's out of his mind," I said. "Just like Anabel."

"No, he isn't," Henry contradicted me, coming closer. For a moment I thought he was going to take me in his arms, but luckily I noticed just in time that he was only going to take a leaf out of my hair. "He's just a vengeful egomaniac who hasn't learned from his mistakes, and so vain that he can't bear to have been knocked out by a girl."

"Kicked," I corrected him.

Henry smiled slightly. "Whatever you say." He was still taking leaves out of my hair, although there weren't any left now.

"I'm scared," I whispered. "He wants Mia to harm herself. And I've seen that it works. She very nearly jumped out of that window."

"It won't happen, Liv, I promise you. I . . . we . . ." He took my hand and pressed it. "We'll think of something."

I've no idea what would have happened if the ground hadn't suddenly disappeared from under us at that moment. Everything went dark. For a fraction of a second, I could still feel Henry's hand in mine, and then I fell alone into a bottomless abyss.

28

THIS WAS AT least the tenth door I was opening, and the tenth room I was crossing. There were doors in all four of its walls, just as there had been in all the other rooms before it, and I had no idea where I was really going.

I stopped, out of breath. My heart was in my mouth, the palms of my hands were sweating, my leg muscles ached. All that even though I knew for sure that this was only a dream. Although not my dream; I was in Mia's dream.

"Mia?" I called, and my voice echoed back from the walls. "Where are you?"

No answer. Instead I heard a soft laugh somewhere. Arthur's laugh.

I pulled myself together and moved on. The door opposite would do as well—or as badly—as any other. It led into another empty room with doors, all of them in their own turn leading into more rooms with more doors. I knew this would never end. I felt that I had been wandering in this labyrinth forever, while valuable minutes passed, and all I wanted was to wake at long last. But I simply couldn't do it, never mind how desperately I tried.

How had I come to fall asleep in the first place? I hadn't meant to. I had been going to stay awake all night, guarding Mia.

Yesterday, after her dream collapsed and I woke with a start, gasping for air, Mia had looked at me indignantly, with her nose only a few inches from mine.

"You woke me," she complained. "Since when have you been tossing and turning so wildly in your sleep?"

I sat up. The faint light of the streetlamp fell into the room, and everything looked as it ought to look.

All the same, I demanded, "Pinch me!"

"What?"

"I want you to pinch me!" I held my arm out to Mia.

"My pleasure," she said.

"Ow! Not so hard!" I'd have a big blue bruise there. But thank goodness, I really was awake, and this was real life in Mia's real room. No tropical sunlight outside, no monkeys screeching.

"Ouch! That's enough." Mia had pinched me again.

"That one's for waking me." She looked at her alarm clock. "Oh no, we'll have to get up in half an hour."

"Do you remember what you were dreaming?"

"Before you woke me thrashing around like that, you mean?" Mia plumped her pillow up again and made herself comfortable. "No, not really. It was all confused stuff, with snakes in it . . . and you were in it, too, I think. . . ."

"And Arthur, right?"

"Arthur Hamilton," repeated Mia, sounding cross. "The

guy who has all the girls in my class sighing in chorus at the sight of him? Why would I dream about him? He looks like someone whose baby picture is used to sell diapers. Can we please get a few minutes' sleep now?"

"Don't you really remember your dream? The earthquake? Benedict Cumberbatch?"

Mia had closed her eyes again. "I'm sorry if you dreamed of an earthquake. If it happens again, try to keep your elbows under control, okay? And not so much wriggling . . ." The rest of what she was saying was lost in an indistinct murmur.

"Mia . . ."

"I want some sleep. You're getting on my nerves."

I sighed. "Sorry. But if you dream of Arthur again, then . . . then you must wake at once, understand?"

Mia just growled. A second later she began snoring quietly.

Henry had said we mustn't let it prey on our minds, but that was easier said than done. Even if, considered in the light of day, Arthur's threats were very slightly less terrifying, I knew that he meant them in deadly earnest. And we could do little or nothing to prevent him from carrying them out.

Henry might think differently, but as I saw it, Arthur should be in a psychiatric hospital along with Anabel. Only, how were we to get him sent to one? If we said he'd stolen one of Mia's gloves and could now control her in her dreams like a puppet, we'd be the ones taken into psychiatric care, not him. The only person who'd believe us would be Dr. Otto Anderson, alias Senator Tod, and he was a psychopath himself.

There was another thing that hadn't occurred to me until now: even if something happened to Mia, Arthur couldn't be prosecuted for it. He'd have been lying in bed asleep half a mile away at the time. No one would think he had anything to do with the case.

On the other hand, if Mia did have a terrible accident, that wouldn't matter much, anyway.

In the morning, Grayson had turned pale with fury when Henry and I told him what had happened in Mia's dream. His first reaction was a strong wish to charge straight off and knock Arthur down. It took quite a while to make him see how useless that would be—Arthur could still go on sleeping and dreaming, and he'd be even more vengeful.

Apart from which, since last night Arthur seemed to have disappeared from the face of the earth, anyway. He didn't turn up at school, no one had seen him anywhere else, and if you rang his cell phone, you only got his voice mail. That scared me even more.

"Nothing's going to happen to Mia," Henry had repeated about a hundred times. He meant it to be reassuring, but it wasn't. Everything Arthur had said last night kept going around and around in my head, like a tune that you can't forget. *I can do anything I like with her. Anything! At any time! . . . Isn't it weird to think that she could simply get up one night and hang herself in your garden shed?*

And I couldn't think of any solution. Mia and I couldn't sleep roped together like those poor working elephants in India forever. And how was I to be sure that Mia wouldn't undo the rope while I was asleep?

The best thing would be if I stayed permanently awake to keep watch over Mia. But putting that idea into practice was just as impossible as getting Arthur committed to a psychiatric hospital. No one could live forever without sleep.

I for one obviously couldn't manage to stay awake even for a single night, in spite of the three double espressos I'd drunk just before ten, and even though I wasn't lying down in bed, but leaning back against Mia's headboard. I had borrowed a book from Ernest, a thriller, but that wasn't a good move. It just confirmed the dim view I took of the world. When the serial murderer's third victim was buried alive, and I was feeling as baffled and helpless as the woman detective inspector investigating the case, Mia complained of the bright light. Reluctantly, but slightly relieved, I closed the book and switched off the bedside lamp. I could work out the rest of the plot, anyway. In the end, the young detective inspector would be buried alive herself in the same kind of casket, and of course she'd be rescued just in time, but she'd be afraid of the dark for the rest of her life.

I looked in turn at the sleeping Mia and the dial of her alarm clock. At some time between 2:20 and 2:21, I must have dropped off to sleep. Because otherwise I wouldn't now be wandering helplessly in this labyrinth of rooms, feeling desperate. The rooms all looked the same, or at least that's how they seemed to me. Once, examining the way the doors were arranged, I thought I'd been in a room before, but as this was a dream labyrinth, there was presumably no point in trying to find my way by logic.

Why didn't I please, please just wake up? If only Spot would come and jump on the bed. And why didn't Mia's alarm clock ring? I'd set it to go off every hour, just in case I did go to sleep.

I didn't know exactly when I'd begun to dream—at first it was a relatively peaceful dream, with elephants and monkeys in it—but when I saw my green door and suddenly realized that the caffeine hadn't worked, I had rushed out into the corridor, panic-stricken.

Grayson, who was standing outside Mia's door with a shotgun, had jumped in alarm when my door banged shut behind me.

"Weren't you going to stay awake?"

"Yes," I cried in despair, "but it didn't work, and now I can't wake up. You'd better slap my face. As hard as you can."

"I don't think that would do any good. Anyway, I don't hit girls." Grayson scrutinized me, frowning. "Calm down, Liv. Everything's all right here. I went to bed long before Mia—and believe me, Arthur hasn't shown up. But Henry will be here any moment. We agreed to meet outside Mia's door. He said there was a way of stopping Arthur once and for all."

I took a deep breath.

"If I could, I'd imagine you a nice soothing herbal tea," said Grayson.

"Why doesn't that silly alarm clock go off?" I tried to remember what time I'd last set it for. Was it three? Or three thirty? "I should have told Mia everything so that she could protect herself," I said.

"No, you shouldn't. You wouldn't have helped her that way; you might even have put her in worse danger. Don't you remember what it was like for you? How long it took you to get used to the idea of this place existing? And how much longer it was before you could manipulate dreams to go the way you wanted?" Grayson sighed. "I don't quite have the hang of that yet myself." He showed me the shotgun. "This was meant to be a really cool machine gun, but instead it's the old thing that Grandpa and I used to take duck hunting when I was nine."

I had to smile, although only briefly. "Does Henry really have a plan?"

"He said so, and he sounds determined. Where can he be?"

"Yes, where?" With a groan, I looked down the corridor.

Arthur had been right. Waiting was the worst thing. Waiting and uncertainty.

They really wore you down.

"If I were Arthur, I wouldn't strike tonight," I said, more to myself than to Grayson. "And not tomorrow, or next week. Why be in any hurry? He can wait until we're all out of our minds with anxiety."

"You don't know Arthur well enough. Patience isn't his strong point. And he certainly won't risk waiting until Henry's found a way to put him out of action."

"How right you are," said Arthur's voice, and his figure materialized out of nothing right in front of us. In my fright I didn't even have time to gasp for air. "And what's more, who says I'm not going to strike every night from now on?"

"Over my dead body," said Grayson, taking aim with the shotgun.

Arthur laughed. "Those were the days, remember, Grayson? When we went duck hunting with your grandpa. I remember the check caps we all had to wear. Although I also remember how difficult you found it to pull the trigger because you felt so sorry for the ducks. And I'm not a sitting duck."

"Exactly," said Grayson, pulling the trigger, but the pellets from the shotgun didn't travel far. They left the barrel in very slow motion, hung in the air in front of Arthur, and then dropped to the ground. Grayson and I exchanged horrified glances.

I went frantically through our options in my mind. I could imagine Mr. Wu. Or I could try attacking Arthur myself. But what use would breaking his jawbone again in a dream be? I could play for time until . . .

"Where's Henry when he's needed?" asked Arthur, obviously enjoying himself. He was all in black, like the night before, and it seemed almost as if he were shining from inside. If you could have a dark light shining.

I could . . . surrender.

"Arthur, please," I said, putting as much genuine feeling as possible into my voice. "I'm sorry that I . . . hurt you. I'm sorry you've had pain and . . . and grief because of me. I'm terribly sorry for all that."

"No, you're not," said Arthur, putting out his hand. Suddenly it was icy cold in the corridor. Within a split second, the walls, the floor, and the doors were covered with hoarfrost—ice crystals even formed on my T-shirt, and Grayson's hair was white as snow with the frost on it. "All the same, it's fun to hear you say so. I like it when you whimper like that. Maybe you should fall on your knees to me?"

How did Arthur do that? He wasn't even moving his hands. He was incredibly good at this.

The floor was like a skating rink now. My teeth began to chatter. My breath formed little white clouds in the air.

I must . . . warmth . . . fire . . . Oh God, it was so cold!

"You're such a . . . ," Grayson began, but he couldn't finish his sentence. The ice was climbing up from his feet at high speed, covering him with a thick, glassy layer that left him rigid as a statue, entirely motionless, an expression of sheer horror frozen on his features.

Arthur laughed, satisfied. "And now for you," he said, turning his angelic face to me. Had I really thought that demons didn't exist? Arthur might not be of ancient Babylonian origin, but he was demonic, no doubt about that.

How could I have let myself think of surrendering? I should have fought back—that was the only answer to someone as vicious as Arthur. But it was too late for that now. My feet were already encased in ice up to the ankles. And the cold had sunk deep into my bones, so deep that I couldn't even think of fire anymore.

All that I could do was stare at Arthur.

"Arthur, please," I whispered through numb lips that were blue with cold. "Don't do anything to my sister. Don't hurt her."

Arthur just laughed. "Make yourself a few nice, warm thoughts while I'm gone," he said, opening Mia's door and disappearing into her dream without another glance at me.

Beside me, Grayson's statue, with a dreadful cracking sound, broke apart into a thousand tiny splinters of ice. They slid all over the floor, glittering in the milky light. There was no sign of Grayson himself.

Oh God—I must do something! Every second counted now. I tried to pull myself together and concentrate. I told myself that what Arthur imagined couldn't have any power over me while he was gone, but at least thirty seconds passed before I finally managed to melt the ice and get my normal body temperature back. Precious seconds during which Mia was in danger, and I hadn't the faintest idea what to do next. At last I felt that I could move my little finger, then my hand, finally my whole body. There was still no sign of Henry when I followed Arthur and slipped into Mia's dream.

And here I was now. I'd gone from room to room, through countless doors, with time running out like water draining away.

Why couldn't I just wake from this dream?

29

DESPONDENTLY, I OPENED the next door. I'd stopped running. It made no difference how fast I raced through Mia's dream; it was never going to end, whichever way I went.

This time, however, I found myself not in another empty room, but in Mia's bedroom.

For a wonderful, exhausted second, I thought I had finally awoken, but then I realized that in that case I'd hardly be seeing a second Liv half sitting, half lying in Mia's bed.

Mia was sitting beside this Dream-Liv and talking to someone standing by the window.

Grayson. He had dug his hands in his pockets and was smiling warmly at Mia. Even before he turned his head to me, I knew it wasn't really Grayson. Of course not.

"You've arrived at just the right time, Liv," said Arthur in Grayson's voice. Obviously he'd been just waiting for me. "What a shame that you're only a painting on the wall, so you can't do anything but watch."

"That's not true," I wanted to say, but I couldn't get the words out. Bewildered, I looked down at myself. My hands consisted of many tiny little brushstrokes in skin tones, everything about me was painted, and as I raised my head again, my figure froze, in exactly the same position as when I was caught in the ice just now, only this time it was in oil paint.

"Tut, tut, tut!" Arthur-Grayson shook his head disapprovingly. "Pictures can't speak. But it's always nice to work with someone whose imagination is even livelier than mine."

He put a broad gilt frame around me and hung me on the wall beside the door, all without leaving his station by the window. The whole thing had happened very quickly, and Mia hadn't even glanced at me. In fact, she didn't seem to have noticed me coming in.

"Hmm." Arthur looked at me through Grayson's caramel-colored eyes. "Very pretty. What shall we call it? *Girl in Fear*? Or no, I know: *Girl, Defeated. Oil on canvas.* Terrific."

I am not a picture. Blood flows through my veins. This is only a dream, and I can be whatever I like. I am not *a picture.*

But I *was* a picture, defeated and unable to move, condemned to listen as Arthur turned back to Mia.

"Did you know that one floor higher in this house there's a secret room?" he asked in flattering tones. "The previous owners of the house left some really strange things there. I can't make heads or tails of them."

Mia immediately looked fascinated. "Can I have a look?" she asked, moving as if to get out of bed.

"Careful," said Grayson, pointing to her leg. "You'll have to undo that first, or you'll wake Liv. . . ."

"Oh yes, so I will." Mia looked doubtfully at the sleeping Liv. "But I'm sure she'd really like to see that room as well. Why don't we tell her about it?"

"We could," said Arthur-Grayson, casting a brief,

mocking glance at me. "But she looks exhausted. Maybe we'd better let her sleep and show her later. Then you'll be the first to see all the clues. . . ."

Oh heavens. He'd really gotten to know Mia in her dreams.

"That's true." Mia began undoing the knots in the rope around her ankle, and I didn't for a moment doubt that she was doing the same in reality, only with her blank, sleep-walking look, so that in effect she was blind. I had tied two reef knots, one above the other, but it took Mia only a couple of seconds to free herself.

Which meant that in real life we were no longer tied together, and I wouldn't be woken by a rope pulling at my leg. Arthur could easily entice Mia upstairs.

Why in hell didn't that alarm clock go off? My sense of time told me that far more than an hour had passed, but maybe I was wrong about that too?

I tried hypnotizing the clock face with my painted eyes, but that was a bad mistake, because Arthur noticed me looking at it. "Wait a minute, Mia," he said. "You'd better turn the alarm off, or it will rouse the whole household."

"Oh, okay." Mia made her way back to the bed and picked up the alarm clock. Arthur gave me a mocking smile. He really had thought of everything.

"Come along," Mia said impatiently to Arthur-Grayson. He stood there enjoying the expression on my face for a moment longer, then winked at me and followed Mia through the door and out into the corridor.

As I tried to free myself from his spell—*I'm the only one with control over myself*, I thought, *I'm the only one who decides what I am, and I am not some damn oil painting*—I was doing my utmost to persuade myself that they wouldn't get far. After all, there were other people in the house, and surely one of them would hear if Mia, walking in her sleep, trod on the loose floorboard that sounded like Aunt Getrude after eating bean soup? Or Spot would get in her way. Or Florence would be going to the bathroom and see her. . . .

I was still trying with all my might to wake from the dream, and a wave of self-hatred broke over me. What kind of a sister was I? I'd gone far too long without taking this situation seriously. Grayson had warned me, but I hadn't listened to him. Instead I'd wandered around the dream corridors, deciphering Senator Tod's silly anagrams and practicing being a breath of air. I ought to have used my time more sensibly, damn it all, I ought to have practiced waking from a dream anytime I liked, I ought to have found out how to defend myself if someone tried turning me into an icicle or an oil painting.

I ought to have been prepared for Arthur.

Girl, Defeated. Oil on canvas, I heard him saying.

And then I suddenly realized that he had said that to me on purpose. He didn't merely want to hurt me, no, his words had another purpose. The more I doubted myself, the safer it all was for him. He'd almost done it, at that. I was wasting my energy, wallowing in self-pity as I hung here helpless on the wall. But it all depended on me.

I had to concentrate on my anger—my incredible anger with Arthur and what he was planning to do to my little sister. It felt like a glowing red ball inside me, getting larger and larger the more I focused on Arthur and my own fury, and at almost the same moment, the gilt peeled away from the picture frame as it broke in two. I was free again.

I ran into the corridor, only to collide with Arthur standing at the foot of the stairs in the form of Grayson. It looked very much as if he was waiting for me there.

Mia was nowhere to be seen. I called her name, but there was no reply.

"Where is she, Arthur?"

"Shhh!" Arthur put a finger to Grayson's lips. With his other hand, he pointed to the ceiling. "Not so loud, she's up there with Lottie. I can only hope your au pair really does spend every night with earplugs in her ears and a sleep mask on her face."

"What have you—" I broke off. It was useless to ask him questions. I knew better than that.

A deep, angry growl escaped my throat. I was a jaguar, and I crouched to spring, ready to tear Arthur to pieces with my sharp claws and my huge fangs. Even as I leaped, I saw the surprise in his eyes. He hadn't expected that, but he reacted at lightning speed. I bounced off an invisible wall that he had set up at the entrance to the staircase with a blink of his eyes. It was like the energy field that Henry had placed between us and Senator Tod the other day.

As I ran into it again, some kind of electric shock threw me a few yards back.

Arthur laughed, and for a moment he was no longer Grayson but entirely himself. "Give up, Liv," he said as he ran upstairs. "You're not good enough to outwit me."

I hissed.

No, no, and no again. I wouldn't allow myself even to think of failing. I mustn't let his imagination determine what I did. He had only as much power over me as I would grant him. As long as I believed that his energy fields were impenetrable, they would be. And he'd already disappeared at the top of the stairs. Who was to say whether he could set up another energy field there?

I didn't stop to try out the invisible wall in front of me. I strained all my muscles and sprang. This time it felt as if I were running into rubber, and for a moment I thought I would be thrown back again, but then it was like plunging into a thick, viscous mass that took my breath away. Half jaguar, half human, I struck out with my arms. My lungs were burning, but I wouldn't stop—I must do it, I must save Mia! With a slight *plop* like suction, the wall let me through, and I landed on the first step of the stairs. Gasping, I filled my lungs with air before scrambling to my feet and running on up the stairs as fast as I could go.

Lottie's bedroom door was open, and Lottie herself was lying in bed, wearing her flowered sleep mask. Her arm was dangling over the side of the bed and down to the floor, where Buttercup was sleeping curled up on a blanket. The scene would look something like this in reality, too, but I hoped that in real life Buttercup would wake and rouse the whole house.

In Mia's dream, Lottie and the dog were both snoring peacefully, while Mia made her way past them, not exactly quietly, and Arthur—back in the form of Grayson—almost trod on Buttercup's tail.

I was about to follow them, but once again I came up against an invisible wall.

"Sorry, no cats allowed in," said Arthur, although I wasn't a jaguar now, I was myself again. Obviously he had just been waiting for me to appear. "However, you're welcome to watch what happens to your sister. We've nearly reached that part of the show."

"Mia!" I shouted—no, I screeched it, for Mia was walking purposefully toward the window. "Don't listen to him. He's lying to you. You mustn't do as he says. You must wake up! It's a trap!"

Arthur cupped a hand behind his ear. "Sorry, Liv, I'm afraid no one can hear you. And I've never learned to lip-read, but I assume you're shouting 'Don't do it, Mia,' or something like that." He laughed again, and in defiance of all reason, I threw myself against the invisible wall that seemed to swallow up my voice, only to fail once more. Maybe I'd wake from the dream when the pain was bad enough.

"Look, there it is. The secret room." Arthur went over to Mia. His voice was gentle again. "You only have to climb through the window and you'll be in it."

Sure enough, if you looked through the window you didn't see the night sky above the roof of the house next door, but another dimly lit room with unplastered brick walls, containing old chests of drawers that looked as if they had all kinds of secret compartments in them.

"Wow, crazy!" said Mia, and she couldn't disguise the enthusiasm in her voice. "To think I never noticed it before!"

Arthur-Grayson shrugged his shoulders and cast me a mischievous look over his shoulder. "I expect the blinds were always down."

"Hmm, yes," said Mia, who obviously didn't take logic seriously in her dreams. Although I knew it was no use, I shouted her name again.

Arthur shook his head. "Liv, lots of people have survived jumping out of third-floor windows," he said gently. "Well, maybe not lots, but I'm sure that one or two have. . . ."

Meanwhile, Mia had opened the window.

Without a doubt, she was doing exactly the same thing in reality too. But maybe the real window would jam. Or maybe Lottie had a vase of flowers standing on the sill, and Mia would knock it over by accident. Maybe the real Buttercup was awake by now and scurrying around her legs, barking. Mia would be woken by the noise, or at least Lottie would, and then . . .

Mia sat on the windowsill and swung her legs over it. It looked as if she would simply climb over into the new room, but I knew that her legs were really hanging in the air many yards above the drop to the paved garden path that ran all around the house.

Think, Liv! Think of a way to beat Arthur with his own weapons.

Something collided with the energy field.

"Bloody hell," said someone behind me. It was Henry. "What's going on here?"

I had no time for explanations. It was too late for that.

Arthur turned around once more, probably to enjoy the moment to the fullest. When he saw Henry, he briefly compressed his lips. I used the moment when his attention was distracted.

"What are you waiting for?" growled Arthur, looking at my little sister again. He seemed to be in a hurry now. "Go on!"

But suddenly Mia hesitated. The room with the brick walls beyond the window had disappeared, and instead you could see the sky. I quickly imagined a large yellow full moon and any number of stars, so that Mia could see as much as possible.

Arthur shot me a hate-filled, furious glance, but I was light-years away from feeling even a glimmer of triumph.

"Mia! No!" I shouted again, and this time, somehow or

other, I seemed to be getting through to her. At least, she looked around at us in surprise, as if she had heard something that puzzled her.

Meanwhile, Henry had obviously dealt with the energy field. He took a step forward. "Come away from there," he told Mia quietly.

She looked at him, wide-eyed. "Away?" she asked.

I leaped forward, but at almost the same time, Arthur made an angry gesture. This time I hit the invisible wall when I was level with Lottie's bed, while Henry, behind me, let out a groan.

Arthur had the upper hand again. "Don't let anything take your mind off it," he told Mia in that flattering voice of his, and she turned away from us and looked back at him. My sky and moon had disappeared; the room with the unplastered brick walls was back right in front of Mia, looking even more tempting than before. "It's your very own mystery, and it's up to you—"

To solve, he had probably been going to say, but he never did. Because suddenly, right before our eyes, Arthur disappeared.

Just like that, without warning and without a sound. One moment he was there, the next he wasn't.

"What on earth . . . ?" whispered Henry, coming up beside me.

Bewildered, I raised my head and looked around the room. Still there was no sign of Arthur. Was this some new kind of mischief, or was the danger really over?

"He must have woken from the dream," said Henry, pulling me to my feet. I hadn't even noticed that I was still crouching on the floor where the impact of the wall had sent me flying. Nor had I felt the tears running down my cheeks.

Arthur's energy field had disappeared with him, and so had the illusion of the room beyond the window.

Mia was still sitting on the windowsill. Ready to jump down. Confused. And I realized that it wasn't over yet.

"You must wake from the dream and get her down from there," said Henry urgently. "Now. At once."

"I can't." I hardly knew my own voice, it sounded so hysterical. "I've been trying to do that all this time." A huge sob escaped me. "I must wake, I must . . ."

"Then do it," said Henry. "Liv, *wake up!*" He took me in both his arms, turned me to face him, and kissed me hard on the mouth.

30

WHEN I WOKE in Mia's bed, still half sitting, my face wet with tears, and gasping for air, I didn't waste any time checking whether I was really awake or not, but jumped out and ran. Only to stumble and fall after five steps, because I'd forgotten the rope tied around my ankle. At least I was sure now that I wasn't dreaming. My knee hurt too much for that.

Without a thought for the others in the house, I raced out of the room, along the corridor, over the creaking floorboard, up the stairs, and into Lottie's bedroom. I felt for the switch, my hands flying nervously, and turned on the ceiling light. Mia was standing in the corner of the room beside the open window, staring wide-eyed into nothing. Buttercup sat beside her, panting, but when she saw me, she came over, wagging her tail.

The window was wide open, and icy air came streaming in. Lottie was lying in bed wearing her sleep mask, just as she had been in Mia's dream, snoring softly.

I felt weak at the knees with sheer relief that Mia wasn't perched on the windowsill anymore.

I tried to say "Mia!" but all that came out was a hoarse croak.

She didn't hear me, anyway. She only went on staring into the void. I hoped she was talking to Henry there. I simply wasn't going to contemplate the possibility that Arthur had come back from wherever he'd gone. At least my legs would still carry me as far as the window. I closed it with a loud bang. Buttercup twitched and pricked up her ears, but Mia was still staring at nothing.

And Lottie was quietly snoring.

On the spur of the moment, I reached for the glass on her bedside table, swung my arm back, and threw the contents into Mia's face. Then, at last, she stopped staring at the void and screeched out loud.

Her screech, which probably loosened a few tiles on the roof above us, also woke Lottie. She snatched off her sleep mask and blinked at the light, scared to death.

Buttercup barked. (Now she barked? Now! What had she been doing earlier? Had she accompanied Mia to the window, wagging her tail and panting anxiously? So much for the theory that the blood of gallant rescue dogs flowed in Buttercup's veins.)

And I rushed over to Mia, who was dripping wet and looked bewildered, hugged her as tight as I could, and sobbed incoherent remarks into her hair.

I've no idea how long I stood there in tears, clinging to Mia, but after a while she pushed me away.

"You're squashing me, Livvy," she said. Her teeth were chattering. "And something in here smells."

Lottie sniffed. "That's only my valerian tea," she said, looking at the bedside table. "It was standing . . . oh!"

"I had to wake Mia somehow." I sniffed hard.

Lottie put her arm around me and looked at Mia and me sternly. "Okay," she said. "Whatever just happened, the first thing you need now is Lottie's hot chocolate."

"Oh wow, if you're talking about yourself in the third person, things must be really dramatic," said Mia in a subdued voice. "I mean, I was only . . . sleepwalking a bit. Wasn't I?" She nudged me. "You should have tied those knots tighter."

"I did tie the knots tightly! You . . ."

"Hush," said Lottie. "No quarreling now. Now is chocolate time, and then we'll see." She turned to her wardrobe and handed Mia a flowered nightdress. "Put this on, or you'll catch your death in those wet things. And the two of you could do with these as well." A pair of thick socks knitted by Lottie herself and a woolen blanket came flying our way.

Five minutes later, Mia and I, wrapped in the blanket, were sitting on the upholstered bench under the kitchen window. The kitchen clock told me that it wasn't nearly morning yet, and I was far too tired to work out how long the whole nightmare had lasted. In any event, much less time than it had felt like while it was going on.

Lottie switched on the coffee machine to froth milk for the hot chocolate. Although Mia's scream a little while ago had been bloodcurdling, no other member of the family had shown up, and I was glad of that, because I wouldn't have known how to face them. I still felt absolutely shattered (and I looked it, too, as a glance at the hall mirror in passing had shown me). I didn't know whether I would ever be able to give anyone a sensible account of what had happened.

I couldn't even explain it to Mia. When she heard that

she'd been about to jump out of the window yet again, she went what for her was unusually quiet.

"How stupid can a person be?" she murmured, obviously cross with herself. "And from the third floor this time!"

Lottie quickly put the hot chocolate down in front of her, and then, in spite of the early hour, she got butter out of the fridge, and then found flour and sugar. Her expression was very anxious, and her hands were shaking slightly.

"I'm going to bake vanilla crescents," she muttered. "And then everything will be all right, my little elf-girls. Then everything will be all right again."

"From the third floor!" Mia was still shaking her head.

"You couldn't help it," I assured her, but I was glad she didn't ask any more questions.

She said she couldn't remember much of her dream, only that it had been very odd, and for the moment I was happy with that. It was bad enough for one of us to have been sent almost insane with terror.

Lottie began weighing out the ingredients for vanilla crescents, humming German Christmas carols—to calm herself down, or so it seemed to me, anyway. As she reached "Silent Night" and slit the vanilla pod open, her hands stopped trembling. It had a good effect on us too. Mia moved a little closer to me on the bench and nestled against my shoulder. "This is comfy, isn't it?"

I had to get myself under control so as not to hug her again. Even though her hair still smelled strongly of valerian tea. Only now, sometime after I'd finished my mug of hot chocolate, was I able to grasp the full extent of what had happened. And I realized that, in spite of everything, Mia would probably be lying on the garden path with several bones broken if Arthur hadn't woken from his dream at the crucial moment. Who was to say that he wouldn't try again the next night? This time with an even more horrible plan.

I groaned quietly. I didn't think I'd survive another night like that.

"The dough ought really to rest for an hour." Lottie was looking undecidedly from her mixing bowl to us. Her brown curls were standing out all around her head. She looked like a Hobbit woman from the Shire, and I loved her so much at that moment that it almost hurt. "But considering the situation, let's miss that bit out for once."

I was all in favor of that. The situation really did call for exceptional measures.

At that moment someone knocked on the kitchen door that opened onto the terrace, and I jumped so violently that Mia almost fell off the bench.

"Don't worry. It's only He . . . Henry?" Lottie raised her eyebrows in surprise and stared incredulously at Henry, who was standing on the other side of the window looking out on the breakfast terrace, waving. "At this time of . . . What is the time, anyway?" She snorted. "Men! There's no understanding them! Do I let him in, Liv? He obviously has something on his mind, and I strongly suspect it's to do with you."

I didn't say a word. How could I? Any answer would have made Mia and Lottie doubt my sanity.

"Never mind, Liv!" Mia wriggled out of the blanket and went to open the door to the terrace. "Can't you see that he's freezing out there? He doesn't even have a jacket on. Come on in, Henry. There's hot chocolate, and in ten minutes' time, there'll be Lottie's comfort vanilla crescents."

"For all the year round," Lottie added.

Mia nodded. "You look as if you needed them. You'd better sit down on this bench with your ex-girlfriend." She turned to me, with an eloquent grin. Then she slipped past Henry and went over to Lottie to taste some of the dough.

Lottie slapped down her fingers. "Hands off. You can help me to shape the crescents."

Henry sat down beside me with a deep sigh. "Thank goodness," he whispered. "She's herself again. I came as soon as I could after her dream collapsed."

Yes, that was obvious. He hadn't even taken the time to put on a jacket. He was wearing only a T-shirt and jeans, and I pushed the blanket over to him in silence.

Mia was looking at us with her head on one side. "Now I remember," she said. "You two were kissing in my dream."

"Really?" Henry looked at me seriously.

I swallowed. "It was only a dream," I said. "That doesn't count, Mia."

"What a shame." Mia turned back to the dough that Lottie had now rolled into a long sausage shape on the work surface.

"Oh, so it doesn't count?" asked Henry quietly. "I had the impression that—"

"I don't want to talk about that kiss right now," I whispered. "Goodness knows we have plenty of other problems! I can't stand it, Henry. He'll try again. . . . By the way, what kept you so long?"

"I . . . I was held up." Henry shook his head unhappily. "I'm so sorry. But I promise you—"

"No!" I forgot to whisper. "Don't make any promises you can't keep. Next time you may be held up again, or the time after that, and then . . ." I was on the point of bursting into tears again. Lottie and Mia were staring at me, wide-eyed. They were probably wondering what drugs I'd taken before going to sleep.

"And then Arthur will put his threat into practice," I said all the same, ending with a sob, although it was cut short by the kitchen door banging open.

"No, he won't!" It was Grayson, standing in the doorway and breathing heavily.

I felt guilty because I'd completely forgotten him since he broke into a thousand icy splinters in the dream. But it was good to see him. Now we were all together.

He came closer and dropped something on the table in front of us.

"Is that what I think it is?" asked Henry slowly.

"Yup," Grayson said grimly. "It is."

We were looking at Mia's spotted gray glove.

Lottie put her hands on her hips. "Is this some kind of competition? Finding out who can wander around out of doors the longest without a jacket in the middle of the night? Do you boys know how stupid that is? Apart from which, you have school tomorrow!" Shaking her head, she turned back to her vanilla crescents.

"And what were you doing with my glove, Grayson?" asked Mia, bewildered. "It won't fit you. Anyway, there isn't a complete pair because I lost the other one."

"This *is* the other one," said Grayson, dropping into a chair.

"What? Really and truly? Where did you find it?"

Grayson was opening his mouth to answer, but I quickly interrupted him. "Mia, could you make Grayson and Henry some hot chocolate?"

"Sure. I'd like some more myself. How about you, Lottie?"

"No, thanks," said Lottie, turning to us. "But would you switch the oven on, Mia dear? Three hundred and seventy-five degrees."

I waited until Lottie and Mia were busy again, and the coffee machine was hissing and bubbling loud enough. Then I leaned forward and asked quickly, "Have you been with *Arthur*, Grayson?"

Grayson nodded. "I'd had about enough of it, understand? I'd really had enough of it."

"You got the glove away from him!" For the first time that night, I saw Henry smile. "Grayson, you're amazing!" He held his hand out, palm facing Grayson, and they did a high five.

"But how did you do it?" I asked breathlessly. "What happened?"

Grayson leaned back. "Well, I went there and I punched him on the nose. End of the show."

"Just like that?"

"Just like that."

I began to laugh, and after all those tears, it felt peculiar, almost a little painful. And very likely hysterical, because I couldn't stop.

It was such . . . such a stroke of *genius*! While Henry and I were fighting off stupid energy fields in the dream world, Grayson had done the only right thing. Punching Arthur might not work in a dream, but in reality it was totally different.

"I was just so angry." Grayson's eyebrows came grimly together. Like Henry, he looked really disheveled and frozen at the same time. The milk-foaming device was still hissing loudly enough for us to go on talking undisturbed. "When I came out of the dream because that bastard had turned me into an ice sculpture, for God's sake, I simply had to do something. So I got on my bike, rode off to Arthur's place, and climbed the wall. I took the key to the back door out of its hiding place in the swimming pool building, and I—well, I didn't mind if I was caught. I'd just have said I was drunk. Arthur was lying in bed asleep. The bastard!" Grayson picked the glove up from the table and shook it. "He was wearing this. And he was smiling in his sleep—I swear he was. I've never been angrier in my life."

I could understand that. I could understand it very well indeed.

"And then?" asked Henry expectantly.

"Then?" Grayson repeated. "Like I said, then I grabbed hold of him and gave him a punch on the nose." He rubbed the palm of his left hand over the knuckles on his right hand. "Well, to be honest, not just one. Could be that I broke it for him." He grinned. "After that I picked up the glove and went back the same way I'd come." Here he glanced expectantly at the door. "So don't be surprised if the police turn up to arrest me for breaking and entering. And grievous bodily harm," he added.

Henry looked as if he could kiss Grayson, but I did it for him. I stood up, put my arms around Grayson and dropped a kiss on his hair as he sat on the bench. And then another, and another. "Guess what—you're my hero."

"Mine too," Henry told him.

I let go of Grayson, who was looking slightly embarrassed, and sat down again. "But what does that mean?"

"It means that Arthur will leave Mia in peace for the time

being." Henry linked his hands behind his head. "He doesn't have any personal possession of hers now. Which isn't to say he won't find ways and means of getting another one."

"Or something belonging to someone else," said Grayson. "But I think we're in the clear for the moment. Although we'll have to keep a very close eye on Arthur. And on all our own belongings." He looked up and glanced at the stove. Lottie had just put the first baking sheet into the oven. "Oh God, that smells marvelous. What is it?"

"Lottie's all-the-year-round comfort vanilla crescents." Mia put the steaming cups of chocolate on the table. "And let me make one thing clear, she's baking them for *me*, and Liv can have a couple as well because she was so worried about me that she burst into tears. I walked in my sleep again, you see, and I almost jumped out of the window. I only woke because Liv threw some smelly valerian tea in my face." She sat down and grinned cheerfully at the company. "So if you can't top that, I'm afraid you'll just have to watch while we eat the vanilla crescents."

Henry was grinning as well. "Oh, no, we can't top that," he said. "Can we, Grayson?"

Grayson shook his head. He was looking very satisfied. "No, no one could top that story. But if I don't get a vanilla crescent, I'm afraid I'll burst into tears too."

"There's plenty for everyone," said Lottie, putting another sheet in the oven.

'INCREDIBLE,' SAID MIA, staring at the polished black stone slab in the front garden of the villa in Elms Walk.

"Absolutely," I agreed. So that was what the Boker had bought with our savings: a tombstone for the topiary peacock.

She didn't call it a tombstone—she called it a memorial tablet. All she wanted, she claimed, was to be constantly reminded of the transitory nature of plant life, the destructive power of certain individuals, and the necessity of opposing that destructive power energetically.

"In memory of Mr. Snuggles, Buxus sempervirens 'Myrtifolia,' slaughtered in a single night after twenty-five years of tireless growth," Mia read aloud. "I suppose we should be glad she didn't have our names carved on it as well."

"No, Buttercup! Bad dog!" I hastily hauled Buttercup out of the flower bed, although she was in the middle of lifting her leg to do the only right thing to the memorial tablet. "We'll have to find another way to the park when we take her for a walk. I'll never be able to look at this tablet without dreaming of our phone."

"I'd hoped so much that Grayson would get a new iPhone. Then we could have had his old one," said Mia.

Today was the twins' birthday, and Mia's heavy sigh reminded me that I still didn't know what to wear for this evening's party, which was thankfully to be held at home and not at the Boker's after all. Florence had had the "amusing" idea of sending a dress code out with the invitations. All guests related to Grayson and Florence were to come in blue; other students from our school in red; the people whom Florence knew from her charity work (a soup kitchen for the homeless) in green; white for all partners included in the guests' invitations; and black for everyone who came into none of those categories.

Persephone was beside herself. She not only couldn't wear her new blue Missoni skirt, she also thought that red didn't suit her. Only when she thought of asking Gabriel to bring her as his partner (to which he had no objection) was she happy again.

My problem was different: I didn't know which color would be right in my case. Apart from white and green, I could really have come in any of them. But Mia thought Florence would probably be furious if we wore anything blue. And for lack of anything red (Persephone had a point: red suits very few people, and I'm not one of them), I finally put on my black shirtdress, which did for almost any occasion, and jazzed it up a bit with tights in black and colored stripes. The last time I'd worn it was for a neighbor's funeral in South Africa, and then it had been knee-length. Now it was a minidress, and a bit tighter, so presumably too sexy for a funeral but just right for this evening.

The best thing about the dress was the little pocket sewn

to one side of it, which was the perfect size for a snuffbox from the rococo period.

The party was really meant to start at eight, but when I came downstairs at seven thirty, there were already a great many guests there. The soup-kitchen people in green had come early, many of them in the afternoon to help with clearing the living room and dining room. A lot of the furniture was now in the garage and the garden shed, leaving room for the small platform for the cover band that Ernest had provided as a surprise present for Florence and Grayson. The band was called the Chords, and Persephone claimed that they were known as a support band for Avec, but the fact was that neither name meant anything to me. However, they played well, and that was what mattered. The band had already arrived and gone through the mysterious and complicated ritual of tuning their instruments, which always makes musicians look as if human life were at stake.

Grayson and Florence were fully occupied welcoming the guests, who were now streaming in. Florence was smiling radiantly and looked beautiful in her new green dress, which I supposed she was wearing to show solidarity with her soup-kitchen colleagues. Grayson waved to me, and I was relieved to see him looking so relaxed. And glad that for the sake of a quiet life he'd put on a blue striped shirt instead of the white one he was wearing earlier. Florence had thrown a fit over the white shirt in the afternoon. "White! Are you trying to turn me into a nervous wreck? If you wear that, everyone will think you're only one of the guests' partners," she had snapped at him, adding dramatically, "Can't you do as I want just for once?"

Well, he obviously could. Although blue might not be the

perfect color choice—on the other hand, of course he was related to Florence.

I strolled into the kitchen where the buffet delivered in the afternoon had been laid out. Mia heaped a large helping on a plate to take it upstairs with her in secret. I saw, to my relief, that it was normal party food and not jellified seaweed patties echoing the colors of the evening. I was ready to believe anything of Florence (and the Boker, who had paid for the catering as a present).

I looked around surreptitiously for Henry. In passing, a good-looking young guy in a blue T-shirt (a cousin of the Spencers?) pressed a glass of champagne into my hand. I passed it straight on to Persephone, who in her turn gave it to her elder sister, Pandora.

"How sensible of you to avoid alcohol," said Emily, who had come up beside me unnoticed. "I'm sure you can manage to make an exhibition of yourself even stone-cold sober." She was wearing a plain, high-necked but close-fitting red dress, and I had to admit that she was one of those few people who really looked good in that color.

"Wow," I said. "You look super, Emily."

"Am I supposed to feel flattered?" She favored me with a scornful look as she moved on, and I was already regretting my spontaneous compliment. On the other hand, I felt a little sorry for her—over the last week or so it had been obvious that she'd do anything to get Grayson back. But she hadn't succeeded, even with the backing of Florence and Mrs. Spencer combined.

Well, perhaps she'd do it this evening. In *that* dress . . .

I hoped Grayson would stand firm.

Meanwhile the band had begun to play. I heard "Here

Comes the Weekend" from the living room, and the singer sounded almost like P!nk. Persephone had found us two glasses of punch and gave me one of them before we made our way into the living room, where the first couples were already dancing. We leaned back against the bookshelves (from which Mom had removed her first editions of Oscar Wilde and Emily Dickinson, to be on the safe side), and Persephone smoothed down her white dress with a happy sigh.

"I bet Jasper is sorry he has to be in France right now," I shouted against the music, smiling at her.

"Jasper who?" cried Persephone, but then she laughed. "I couldn't care less about Jasper today. Just for once, life is good."

In any case, it had certainly been much worse. And there was so much to be grateful for.

For instance, the fact that Grayson hadn't been arrested for breaking and entering and grievous bodily harm, simply because Arthur hadn't told anyone about the incident. But I was grateful all the same, because otherwise Grayson might have spent his eighteenth birthday in a police cell, or maybe in the nuthouse.

There was a heartrending story in the Tittle-Tattle blog about Arthur, and how he had tried to rescue a poor little puppy being tormented by four bad characters. In spite of being outnumbered, brave Arthur had finally saved the puppy—but he had suffered a broken nose, two black eyes, and a cut on his eyebrow (Grayson must really have been *very* angry).

Extraordinarily, everyone at Frognal Academy seemed to believe this sentimental story without reservations. Brave

Arthur, the rescuer of little dogs, was the school's new hero. And the girls in Mia's class sighed louder than ever when they saw him in the corridors.

However, it would be some time before all traces of the fight had faded, and every time I saw Arthur, it gave me a certain satisfaction to see them still there. Even though I guessed that he was planning cruel revenge for every single bruise.

He had spoken to me only once, when we ran into each other by the chemistry lab, and I was turning to leave immediately when he took hold of my arm and held it firmly. "Don't rejoice too soon, Liv Silver. I haven't finished with you yet," he had said, darting me glances of such hatred that his sighing fan club of girls would surely have lost faith in him. But there was no one else there to see Arthur's real face.

What he said didn't surprise me. I was only surprised that it left me cold. "I haven't finished with you either," I replied, and I meant it. I would never forgive him for what he'd tried to do to my sister. "And now let go of me, if you don't want Secrecy to have another accident to report."

In dreams, Arthur would have grinned viciously and tried turning me to stone, but this was real life, and in real life, I was the one who could do kung fu. Furthermore, a group of students was just coming around the corner. So he let go of me.

"We'll meet again," he snapped at me.

"Oh, Arthur?" I called after him. "What happened to that poor little puppy in the end?"

But there was even more that I had to be grateful for: Mia hadn't walked in her sleep once since that night. And without asking too many questions, she'd promised to watch her personal possessions like a hawk, particularly in school. I was also grateful that I could talk to Henry again without bursting into tears or shouting at him—in fact, we were getting on quite well. Maybe because we deliberately avoided all difficult subjects when we met.

Oh, and somehow I was glad that Charles and Lottie were on the dance floor together, looking amorously into each other's eyes. They made a lovely couple. Well, Lottie was lovely, Charles was . . . just Charles. The main thing was that they were happy. I wasn't quite sure that I could stand much more love in the household right now, because at the moment Ernest and Mom were going in for so much deep, soppy happiness that Mia was toying with the thought of moving out early. Today they'd offered to look after Buttercup and Spot in Lottie's rooms up on the third floor, where they were probably making out on the sofa while Buttercup and Spot put their paws over their eyes.

The Boker still hadn't recovered from her elder son's engagement and probably never would. At every possible opportunity, she pointed out what a drop in social status his second marriage would mean for Ernest—after all, his first wife had been 201st in line for the British throne. But of course that wasn't the reason why she'd decided to stay home today. "This is a party for the young, and I don't want to be in the way," she had said modestly when Florence invited her, but I was sure the real reason she wasn't here was that blue didn't suit her. If family members had been told to come in beige, she'd have been the first to show up.

"Here comes Henry!" Persephone dug her elbow into my ribs. "Amazing—he looks good even in a lumberjack shirt."

"It's not a lumberjack shirt; it's just a check pattern,"

Henry put her right. "I don't like it. But it was the only red thing in my wardrobe except for a Norwegian sweater with reindeer knitted into it. Anyway, I could never outdo your dress, Persephone."

"I know! Looks super, don't you think? And see how the skirt swings out!" She turned on her own axis and blew us a kiss. "I'm going to look for Gabriel!"

Henry took her place beside me leaning on the bookshelves and watched her go. "Amazing similarity to a coconut meringue pie. A coconut meringue pie that's had a bit of an accident."

"So much for the quality of your compliments." I sighed.

"I suppose that means if I said you're looking wonderful this evening, you wouldn't believe me?" He smiled at me, and in my present good mood, I smiled back. Over the last few days, he'd seemed much more relaxed than for weeks before, and as if he'd been sleeping better.

People were crowding into the living room now. Someone had opened the door to the terrace, and pleasantly cold night air came in from outside. The band went over to "Narcotic" by Liquido, and I took Henry's arm and drew him out into the corridor, where we sat down on the stairs, a vantage point from which we could watch the party.

"You look somehow . . . happy," I said after a while. *And terribly attractive.* (Of course I didn't say that, I just thought it.)

"I am." His eyes lingered very briefly on my mouth. "Well, not necessarily happy. But anyway, I have one thing less to worry about."

I cautiously felt the snuffbox in my pocket. "Really?"

He nodded. "At the moment things at home . . ." He

stopped. "Well, I told you I'd been having trouble with my father. To put it mildly. About the trust fund."

Yes. He'd mentioned it.

"But all that has come to nothing."

"What, the trust fund?" I asked, although of course I knew better.

"No, the trouble. My father has given up that stupid idea of investing it. At least for now."

"That sounds very sensible," I said, avoiding a green elbow going upstairs past us on the way to the bathroom. A few guests were still arriving, and I wondered how many Florence had invited. And how many people could do charitable work in a single soup kitchen.

"To be honest, I never expected my father to think better of it." Henry leaned back. "He wouldn't listen to anything I said."

"Maybe he just needed someone to appeal to his conscience," I said, and I handed Henry the snuffbox. "Here. I think this belongs to your family."

I'd known Henry for some time now, but I'd never seen him so taken aback. I'd never known him to stammer either.

"Is . . . is . . . is . . . th-that by any chance . . . ?"

"The snuffbox that Milo borrowed from your father, yes," I said, enjoying the look on his face. "I'd have kept it, only I don't take snuff."

Henry's mouth was still slightly open. He looked from the snuffbox to me and back again. "You were the . . . How did you . . . ?"

I allowed myself a mysterious smile. "Well, it's not as if I'd learned nothing from you. And like I said, your father only needed to have a few basic principles explained to him. It was easy."

Easy, ha-ha! It had taken me days just to find his father's dream door. Unfortunately it wasn't, as I'd assumed, anywhere close to B's door (why not, I wondered?) but in a drafty corridor off to one side of it. And I'd really found it only because it had his initials carved in the wood: R.H. for Ronald Harper.

And then the real challenge began: Harper wasn't the type of man to listen to other people telling him how to run his business projects, and he'd had no intention of changing his mind about investing his children's trust in a high-risk hedge fund run by dubious private bankers. I'd had to pull out all the stops, four nights running. Only when I haunted him as the Ghost of Christmas Yet to Come did he crack. I'd rather have tried a version of the late Henry Harper Senior, but that wasn't going to work because I knew nothing about the appearance and character of Henry's grandfather. Instead I had to use the ghost out of *A Christmas Carol*, and I was prepared for it because I'd taken that part in a Christmas play three years ago in Berkeley. Apart from a small slipup— literally, because I nearly fell over the hem of my long, scary, hooded gray cloak—I thought I played it very well. And thanks to Charles Dickens, there's nothing like showing a man his own gravestone to convince him that his life is on the wrong track.

I felt really proud now that my trouble had been worthwhile. Don't let anyone say dreams can never alter reality.

Henry slipped the snuffbox into the pocket of his jeans and gave me that very special Henry smile that was kept only for me—and made me go weak at the knees. "I swear I'll get you to tell me the whole story sometime," he said, standing up and putting out his hand to me. "But for now it will be enough if you'll dance with me."

I laid my hand in his and smiled. The band played "Dream On" by Aerosmith. It couldn't be a coincidence.

TITTLE-TATTLE BLOG

The Frognal Academy Tittle-Tattle Blog, with all the latest gossip, the best rumors, and the hottest scandals from our school.

ABOUT ME:
My name is Secrecy—I'm right here among you, and I know *all* your secrets.

18 February

Eleven minutes! Jasper Grant's relationship status on Facebook had been "single" for exactly eleven minutes when Persephone dumped Gabriel. She's a fast worker.

A little too fast, unfortunately, as it turned out. Because after twelve minutes Jasper's profile said "In a relationship" again.

Good-bye, Lily, hi there, Louise. An excellent choice, judging by the bikini-clad photos in Louise's profile. And if the villa, the pool, and the palm trees visible beyond the bikini belong to Louise's parents, then Jasper is to be congratulated. He's using his time abroad to make friends forever with a holiday home on the Côte d'Azur—so much more important than a good grade in French, don't you think?

So now Persephone will have to spend the time until Easter knocking her head against the wall. And, Gabriel, you stand firm—you really do deserve something better.

However, now for our breaking news: I've only just heard that Anabel Scott came out of the psychiatric hospital on Friday. Obviously acute polymorphic psychotic disorder can be cured, and the schizophrenia must have been a wrong diagnosis. One way or another, Anabel is back! She's been discharged, and she'll probably spend a little while convalescing at home before returning to her studies. At the moment we can only speculate on whether she and Arthur will pick up their relationship again—they were certainly the best-looking couple that Frognal ever had. What am I saying? The best-looking couple the world had ever seen, and I wouldn't grudge it to them. But after so long, I guess getting back together isn't easy.

We'll have to wait and see.

See you soon!

Love from Secrecy

PS—In case you're waiting to hear the latest scandals from Florence and Grayson Spencer's birthday party: Sorry to disappoint you. The party was a scandal-free zone. Delicious food, super band, fantastic atmosphere—like Florence, the party was just perfect.

On That Same Night . . .

ANABEL WAS WEARING a short black dress and looked more beautiful than ever as she walked toward us in the corridor. The faint light played around her slender body, and all we needed was the right background music to put the finishing touch to her appearance in the part of a fallen angel.

"How was the party?" She put her head on one side and smiled at us. "So stupid that I got left off the invitation list."

What an idiot I was. What a silly idiot! The evening so far had been perfect, and I'd just wanted it to go on a little longer. So after a moment's hesitation, I'd gone out through my green door, officially to look in on Mia and make sure she was all right. Henry, Grayson, and I had made it our business to do that these last few weeks. But who did I think I was kidding?

Not Henry for one—he was already waiting for me.

"How about a little visit to Amy?" He'd smiled when he saw me. "And then you can tell me, at your leisure, how you fixed everything with my father."

I wasn't about to do that, for sure. But anything seemed

possible in Amy's brightly colored, peaceful dream world. Even that Henry and I might . . . "Okay," I said quickly.

However, it was at that precise moment, of course, that London's number one demon fan appeared in front of us, newly discharged from the psychiatric hospital, without a doubt after being given the all clear for mental health by a doctor who was either as crazy as Anabel herself or had been manipulated in his dreams.

"Anabel!" I crossed my arms. "How did you get Dr. Anderson to discharge you?"

"Dr. Anderson?" Anabel raised an eyebrow. "Oh, he has nothing to do with my discharge. No, the good doctor is asleep," she cheerfully explained. "Asleep for . . . well, I'm afraid it will be *forever*."

"He's dead?" I asked, horrified. I remembered Anabel's threat at our last meeting and the way Senator Tod had disappeared without a trace. It looked very much as if Anabel had been as good—or bad—as her word. I suddenly felt icy cold.

Anabel laughed. "Oh, no! He really is asleep. And the best of it is, he thinks he's awake."

Oh God, that sounded kind of familiar to me. I felt goose bumps coming up all over myself.

"I've locked him into his own dream," Anabel went on. "He's been sleeping for two whole weeks now, and no one can wake him."

"That is really . . . ," Henry murmured. I reached for his hand.

"Brilliant, yes," Anabel finished the sentence for him. "I know. The doctors can't explain what's the matter with him.

All his vital functions are working perfectly. Well, not quite all of them. He has to be artificially fed, but he doesn't know about that. He lies peacefully in bed and thinks his life is going on as usual. He has no idea that he's still dreaming."

A groan escaped me. Why had we had to go this way? Why hadn't I simply enjoyed the lovely evening, which could have given me the illusion that everything was all right, and left it at that?

Anabel gave me an understanding look. "You're not feeling sorry for him, are you? It's all he deserves. Unlike your sister." She glanced at Mia's forget-me-not-blue door and the grim figure of Mr. Wu standing outside it. "Arthur's plans for her were really horrible. And I hope you all realize he'll be pursuing them with more determination than ever."

"Yes," said Henry, sighing. "Arthur is as persistent as you are."

"With the difference being that he does it to get revenge," said Anabel. "He has a score to settle with me too. And I'm afraid that now I've been discharged from the hospital he'll want me to pay it."

Henry and I exchanged a glance. Was he thinking what had just crossed my own mind? That it would be a good thing if Arthur and Anabel destroyed each other?

"You've seen what perfect command he has over dreams now," Anabel went on. "But I'm even better. And it would be clever of you to work with me. Together, we can keep Arthur . . . at bay."

Henry's grasp of my hand tightened. Was Anabel seriously offering to do a deal with us?

"Maybe——" she began, but the squeal of door hinges

interrupted her. The sound came from Grayson's door, which obviously needed oiling. However, it wasn't Grayson who came out and carefully closed the door.

"Emily?" I cried incredulously. I didn't believe it! This must be Arthur making himself look like Emily.

Emily stared at us in alarm. She looked like a child caught in the act of stealing candy. "Oh, it's you two," she murmured. "And, Anabel . . . I didn't know that you were another . . ." Then she pulled herself together and assumed her most arrogant governessy expression. "Well, if you're standing around looking stupid, maybe you can tell me where to find Grayson's grandmother's door."

It really was Emily. She knew about the corridors. And she'd been in Grayson's dream, the nasty creature! Presumably not for the first time.

"You—" I began, but Henry let go of my hand and interrupted me. "Mrs. Spencer's door? Turn left twice, then right—at least, that's where it was recently. It's the ocher door with gold fittings. And there's a clipped box bush in a tub outside it."

"Oh, good. Thanks." Emily tossed back her gleaming hair and stalked away.

Bewildered, I watched her disappear. "Why did you let her go? And what . . . ?"

Anabel laughed again. She wound a strand of her golden hair around one finger. "Arthur is clever. He's looking for allies who are in the same boat. All of us ought to do that. It wasn't a bad choice to let Emily in on the secret. She may not have much imagination, but she certainly has plenty of motive. If only on account of Grayson."

"Arthur and Emily?" I asked.

"Looks like it," said Henry. "It makes me wonder who else we're going to meet here."

Anabel turned to go. "As I said, time to take a stand. Think about my offer. What is it they say? My enemy's enemy is my friend." She turned back to us once more and winked at me. "And it's only just begun."

THE RULE BOOK OF DREAMS

Would you like to visit your friends in their dreams?
No problem—the rules are easy.

1. You need something personal belonging to the person you want to visit. When you go to sleep, you must have it somewhere on your body. (So it's best to choose something small, not a bicycle or anything like that, which would make it crowded in your bed. And uncomfortable.)

2. In the dream, you must look out for your own personal dream door—only you know what it looks like. This is a little tricky, because only when you touch the door in your dream will you realize that you are in a state known as *lucid dreaming.*

3. Now it's up to you: Will you dare to go through that door? It will take you into the corridors into which all the dream doors of everyone in the world lead. There are countless passages and branching corridors, so be careful not to lose

your way. And take good notice of what your door looks like!

4. Next you must find the door of the person you want to visit. Although dream doors often change their places, those of the people closest to us are usually near our own. And generally they reflect the true characters of their owners—so now you will find out how well you really know your friends.

5. When you have found the right door, you sometimes have an obstacle to overcome. Many people's subconscious minds feel a need to protect their doors from intruders. If you know your friend well, however, you will probably get through the door easily enough. It is different if the dreamer is protecting his or her own door deliberately, something that I would recommend you do as well while you are about it. Unfortunately we never know who else is roaming the corridor, and I don't suppose you want uninvited guests in your dreams, do you?

6. In your friend's dream, and also in your own, you can take on any shape you like. If you're really good at it, you can even make yourself completely invisible. However, you can also appear as yourself and do all the things that you wouldn't dare to do awake in daytime. As a rule, the other person won't remember anything about the dream on waking; we remember only a small part of our dreams. And go carefully: if the other person wakes while you are in his or her dream, it will be uncomfortable. The dream

collapses, and you fall into a kind of black hole and won't be able to breathe until you are awake again yourself.

7. Of course it's not very nice to spy on someone's dreams in secret—it's better for you and your friend to meet in the corridor and decide whose dream to visit. The best of it is that in a dream you can travel anywhere, to any place in the world, and you can even think up places that don't really exist. You can do simply anything.

8. Have fun! But don't overdo it: sleep is not very refreshing while you are having lucid dreams, and if you do it all night, you could drop off to sleep in school and dribble on your math book—and no one really wants to do that.

9. Oh yes, and if you happen to meet Anabel or Arthur, run for it as fast as you can.

Lottie's All-the-Year-Round Comfort Vanilla Crescents

You will need:
1 stick plus 6 tablespoons softened butter
Scant ½ cup sugar
1 vanilla pod
1¾ cup flour
Scant ½ cup ground almonds
After baking:
¼ cup confectioner's sugar
¼ cup of vanilla sugar (optional)

These ingredients will make about 40 small vanilla crescents.

Heat the oven to 375° F. Cream the butter and sugar together until the mixture is smooth. Slit the vanilla pod lengthwise, scrape out the inside of it, and add to the butter mixture. Sift in the flour, add the ground almonds, and work it all together. (Using your hands is the best way.) Form the dough into a ball, wrap it in foil or plastic wrap, and let it rest in the fridge for an hour. (Leave out this stage only in an emergency.) Then roll the dough into a sausage shape and cut into pieces about one inch wide. Shape the little pieces into crescents and put them on a baking sheet lined with parchment paper.

Bake the crescents on the middle rack for 10 minutes, until light brown. Mix the confectioner's sugar and vanilla sugar (if using), and sprinkle over the hot crescents. Let them cool entirely on the baking sheet; these cookies are very fragile.

Then feed them fast to everyone in need of comfort, along with friendly remarks like "Everything will be all right." (Or you can put them in a tin where they will keep crisp, and they can be eaten all week to comfort people.)

Have a good time!

CAST OF CHARACTERS

Liv Silver, goes on having lucid dreams

Mia Silver, Liv's younger sister, has no idea what goes on in her dreams

Ann Matthews, Liv's mother

Lottie Wastlhuber, Liv and Mia's German au pair

Ernest Spencer, wants to marry Ann

Grayson Spencer, Ernest's son, twin brother of Florence

Florence Spencer, Ernest's daughter, twin sister of Grayson

Charles Spencer, Ernest's brother, dentist

Mrs. Spencer, also known as the Boker, resembles Snow White's wicked stepmother thirty years on

Henry Harper, likes dreaming with Liv, most of the time, anyway

Milo Harper, Henry's younger brother

Ronald Harper, Henry's father

B, a naked woman in a whirlpool

Biljana, lingerie model and Henry's father's girlfriend

Arthur Hamilton, ex-friend of Anabel Scott, Henry, and Grayson

Persephone Porter-Peregrin, has decided to be Liv's best friend

Anabel Scott, Arthur's ex-girlfriend, has been in a psychiatric hospital since the end of Book 1

Emily Clark, Grayson's girlfriend, kindred spirit of Mrs. Spencer

Senator Tod, a man who talks in anagrams

Princess Buttercup, the family dog

Spot, the Spencers' cat

Mr. Snuggles, now kindling, formerly a topiary peacock

And of course *Secrecy* . . .

Brief guest appearances by: *Sam*, Emily's younger brother, and his girlfriend, *Itsy* (whose real name I'm afraid we don't know); a waiter (not surprised by anything); *Mrs. Lawrence*, the French teacher (surprised by a lot of things); *Eric* and *Gabriel*, lunchtime friends in school; *Jasper Grant* (staying abroad this time); *Mr. Wu* (a genuine hero, makes only a short appearance); *Amy Harper* (Henry's little sister, very cute); and various animals (not at all cute, but disgusting, poisonous, eight-legged, or prickly, and hopefully locked into the realm of dreams forever. But who can tell?).

Author's Note

Hello, all you dreamers out there—I hope you felt you'd enjoyed this book when you closed it, although of course it's annoying of Anabel to end it with the same words as in the first book. But she's right; the story really isn't over yet. In Book 1, I ended by starting to tell you something about Book 2. Stupidly, some of what I said then never happened: no curse, no veterinarian, oh dear! That's how it is: I make up my mind to write about something, and then in the end I write about something else. (Although I haven't given up on the veterinarian yet.) So this time I will say only that in the third book of The Silver Trilogy, whatever else happens, there will be a big wedding party. And as well as the dreamers we already know, there will be some more, so a good deal will be going on in the corridors outside the dream doors. And . . . no, I'd better stop there. But one thing is for sure: at the end of Book 3 we'll know who is hiding behind the name of Secrecy. I'll be very interested to know how many of you have guessed right all along.

See you soon!

Love from *Kerstin Gier*

GO FISH

Kerstin Gier

© Arena Portrait

What's your favorite part about writing for teens?
I always wanted to write books for children and teens so that I wouldn't forget what it feels like to be fourteen. However, I have since realized that there's really no need to worry. Even my mom acts like a fourteen-year-old every now and then. And she's seventy-five!

What makes you laugh?
Sometimes it can take a while, but I can usually laugh about anything.

What do you do on a rainy day?
My favorite thing to do on a rainy day is this: sitting in the lobby of the Covent Garden Hotel in London with a nice cup of tea in my hand and watching all the umbrellas on the enchanting Monmouth Street. What I end up doing instead: getting the wet cats off the couch, yelling at my son, Lennart, to take his wellies and wet raincoat off the expensive rug, and pleading with the universe that the sun will be out again soon.

If you were stranded on a desert island, who would you want for company?

My husband, my son, and, of course, we won't forget the cats.

If you could travel in time, where would you go and what would you do?

Well, I chicken out easily. I wouldn't dare to go back very far. And in any case, I wouldn't stay long. Just the idea of not having a modern flushing toilet really gives me the creeps. But I imagine being in England during the Regency period must have been very charming somehow, even with the outhouses and all that. Just like a Jane Austen movie. And if I get dressed up for the trip by Madam Rossini, then I wouldn't even mind going back to the seventeenth or eighteenth century—maybe without the wig.

Do you ever get writer's block? What do you do to get back on track?

Writer's block is one thing I just can't afford to have. But if things don't go so well and if I have enough time, I'll just do something else that day. Other than that, turning up the music and dancing around the room has helped in the past.

What do you want readers to remember about your books?

Life is fun if you can manage to appreciate it with all its weirdness.

Liv has solved mysteries, unearthed difficult truths, fought madmen, and escaped life-threatening peril, all from the comfort of her own bed. But, unfortunately for her, Liv's troubles are far from over, and she's in more danger than ever before. . . .

KEEP READING FOR AN EXCERPT.

˙SO LET'S TALK about your demon. Have you heard his voice this week?" He leaned back, folded his hands over his stomach, and looked expectantly at her. She peered back at him out of those unusual turquoise-colored eyes that had captivated him from the first. Like everything about her, as it happened. Without a doubt, Anabel Scott was the most attractive patient he had ever treated, but that wasn't what fascinated him so much. It was the fact that even after so many hours of therapy, he still couldn't figure her out. She always managed to surprise him, to get him to drop his guard, and he hated it. Every time she made him feel he was inferior to her, he was upset—after all, he was the qualified psychotherapist, and she was only eighteen years old, and severely disturbed.

But it was going well today. Today he was in control.

"He's not *my* demon," she replied, looking down. Her eyelashes were so long that they cast shadows on her cheeks. "And no, I haven't heard anything. Or sensed anything."

"Then that makes it—let's see—sixteen weeks since you

saw or heard the demon, or sensed his presence, am I right?"
He intentionally let his voice sound a little superior, knowing that he was provoking her that way.

"Yes," she said.

He liked her meek tone of voice and allowed himself a
small smile. "So why do you think your hallucinations have
gone away?"

"I guess it could be . . ." She bit her lower lip.

"Yes? Speak up."

She sighed and put a strand of her gleaming golden hair
back from her forehead. "I guess it could be the pills," she
admitted.

"Very good." He leaned forward to scribble a note: *ak,
d.s., v., hr, vk.* They were nonsense abbreviations; he was just
making them up as he went along. Because he knew that she
was reading them upside down and trying to work out what
on earth they meant. With difficulty, he suppressed a triumphant grin. Yes, she had certainly aroused a sadistic streak
in him, and yes, given up the proper professional approach
to treating her long ago. But that didn't matter to him. Anabel
was no ordinary patient. He wanted her to acknowledge his
authority at long last. He was Dr. Otto Anderson, and one
day he would be medical director of this psychiatric hospital. The institution where she was presumably going to
spend the rest of her life. "Pills are essential in the treatment of a case of polymorphous psychotic disorder like
yours," he went on as he leaned back again, relishing the
expression on her face. "Therapeutically, however, we have
done much more than that. We have identified your childhood
traumas and analyzed the causes of your false memories."
That was a great exaggeration. He knew from the girl's father

that she had spent her first three years of life with a dubious sect that performed rites of black magic, but Anabel herself couldn't remember anything. And his attempts to find out more by means of hypnotism—which he had used even though it wasn't really allowed—had not been successful either. In fact, they knew no more than they had at the beginning of her treatment. He wasn't even sure whether the causes of Anabel's psychotic disturbance really did lie in her childhood; he wasn't sure of anything about her. But never mind—what mattered was that she saw him as the experienced psychiatrist who could read her mind, the man to whom she owed all her insights. "So at last you are ready to accept that your demon existed only in your imagination."

"Stop calling him my demon." She pushed her chair back and stood up.

"Anabel!" he said sternly. And it had been going so well. "Our session isn't over yet."

"Oh, yes it is, dear doctor," she replied. "My alarm clock will go off any moment now. I have a date to see a course adviser about my studies, and I mustn't oversleep and miss it. You'll laugh, but I want to study medicine so that I can specialize in forensic psychiatry later."

"Don't talk nonsense, Anabel!" A strange feeling came over him. Something was wrong. With her. With him. With this room. And why was the air full of the scent of his mother's lily-of-the-valley perfume all of a sudden? He nervously reached for his pen. A date to see a course adviser about her studies? Ridiculous. They were in the closed department of the hospital, and Anabel couldn't go anywhere without his permission, not even out onto the grounds. "Sit down again at once. You know the rules. Only I can end our sessions."

Anabel smiled pityingly. "You poor thing. Don't you realize yet that your rules mean no more here than—what did you call them?—false memories?"

He felt his heart miss a beat. There was something buried deep inside him, a thought or a recollection, information that he must bring to the surface. That was urgent because it was important. A matter of life or death. But somehow he couldn't get at it.

"Don't look so shocked." Anabel was already at the door, laughing quietly. "I really must go, but I'll come and see you again next week. That's a promise. So until then, sweet dreams."

Before he could say any more, she had closed the door behind her, and he heard her steps going away down the corridor. The little monster knew perfectly well that he wasn't going to give himself away by running after her, thus showing everyone that he couldn't control his patient. But this was the last time she'd act up with him that way. She wouldn't end the session against his will again. Next time he'd enlist the support of some of the male nurses. Maybe he'd have her strapped down—there were a number of methods that he hadn't exhausted yet.

When he closed Anabel's file and put it back in the drawer, he still had that faint lily-of-the-valley perfume in his nostrils, the scent that reminded him of his mother. And for a split second, he thought he even heard his mother sobbing as she called his name.

But then the voice and the perfume both went away, and everything was the same as usual.

DESSERT WAS TAPIOCA pudding, which would have taken my appetite right away if the Rasmus problem hadn't done it already.

"Aren't you going to eat that, Liv?" Grayson pointed to my tapioca, pale, translucent, and wobbly in its glass dish in front of me. He'd already wolfed down his own helping of lumpy slime with pineapple jam.

I pushed the dish his way. "No, you're welcome to it. One more British tradition that hasn't swept me off my feet yet."

"Ignoramus," said Grayson with his mouth full, and Henry laughed.

It was a Tuesday at the beginning of March, and the sun shone in through the tall, poorly cleaned windows of the school cafeteria. It cast a delicate striped pattern on walls and faces, bathing everything in warm light. I even imagined I could catch the smell of spring in the air, but maybe that was just the large bunch of daffodils lying on the teachers' table, where my French teacher, Mrs. Lawrence, had just sat down. She looked as if she'd slept even worse than me.

So there was spring in the air; Grayson, Henry, and I had grabbed our favorite table in the sunny corner near the exit; and I'd heard a little while ago that there wouldn't be a history test tomorrow after all. In short, everything would have been just wonderful, if I hadn't had the aforesaid Rasmus problem on my mind.

"Sometimes tapioca pudding can be delicious." Henry, who had sensibly skipped dessert, smiled at me, and for a few seconds, I forgot our troubles and smiled back. Maybe things would turn out all right. What did Lottie always say? *There are no such things as problems, only challenges.*

Exactly. Think how boring life would be without any challenges. Not that it had been absolutely necessary to add an extra challenge to the pile of them already facing me, anyway. Unfortunately that was the very thing I'd done.

It had happened on the evening of the day before yesterday, and I still had no idea how I was going to wriggle out of it.

Henry and Grayson had been studying for a math test at our house, and when they'd finished, Henry had taken a little detour to my room to say good night to me on his way to the front door. It was late, and the house had been quiet for some time. Even Grayson thought Henry had already left for home.

I was genuinely surprised to see Henry, not just because it was the middle of the night, but also because we still hadn't gotten around to officially changing our relationship status from "unhappily separated" to "happily reconciled." Over the last few weeks, we had silently gone back to holding hands, and we'd also kissed a couple of times, so you could have thought everything was back to the same as before, or at least well on the way there—but that wasn't it. The experiences of recent months, and things that Grayson had told me about Henry's love life before I came on the scene, had left their mark on me in the form of a persistent inferiority complex about my sexual inexperience (or "being so backward," as my mother put it).

If I hadn't been so happy that we were close to each other again, maybe I'd have taken the trouble to analyze the feelings smoldering under my happy infatuation more closely, and if I'd done that, maybe I wouldn't have thought up Rasmus in the first place.

But as it was, I'd put my foot in it.

When Henry had looked around the door, I was just putting in the new mouth guard for my teeth. My dentist, a.k.a. Charles Spencer, had discovered that I obviously ground my teeth in my sleep (and I immediately believed him), so the mouth guard was to keep me from wearing the enamel of my teeth away at night. I couldn't tell whether it was working; mainly it seemed to make my mouth water a lot, so I thought of it as my silly drooling thingy.

At the sight of Henry, I immediately tucked it between the mattress and the bedstead, without letting him notice. It was bad enough that my pajama top and bottoms didn't match, and didn't suit me all that well either, although Henry said he thought checked flannel was amazingly sexy. Which led to me kissing him, kind of as a reward for the nice compliment, and that kiss led to the next one, which lasted rather longer, and finally (by now I'd lost some of my sense of time and place) we were lying on my bed whispering things that sounded like lines from soppy song lyrics, although right at that moment they didn't seem to me soppy at all.

So our relationship status was clearly heading for "happily in love," and I was inclined to believe that Henry really did think I looked sexy in checked flannel.

But then he stopped in the middle of what he was doing, pushed a strand of my hair back from my forehead, and said I didn't need to be afraid.

"Afraid of what?" I asked, still feeling a bit dazed from all the kissing. It took me a couple of seconds to realize that it had just happened in real life, and not, as usual, in a dream where no one could disturb us. Which was probably why it felt so much more intense than usual too.

Henry propped himself on his elbows. "You know what. Afraid it might all happen too quickly. Or I might expect too much from you. Or want you to do something before you're ready for it. We truly do have as long as you like before your first time."

And then it happened. Now, in the bright light of the school cafeteria on a fine spring day, I couldn't explain it to myself . . . well, I could explain it, sure, but unfortunately that made things no better. Anyway, Henry's choice of words was to blame. That infuriating *your first time*.

It was the cue that brought my inferiority complex into play, and it also dragged its friend, my injured pride, along with it. They were both firmly convinced that Henry was somehow sorry for me because of my inexperience, or at least the expression on his face sometimes very much resembled pity.

Like at that exact moment, for instance.

"Oh. So you think I've never . . . never slept with a boy?" I sat up and wrapped the bedspread more tightly around me. "I see what you mean now." I laughed a little. "You took that virginity stuff seriously when you and the others were play-ing your demon game, did you?"

"Er, yes." Henry sat up as well.

"But I only said I was a virgin so that I could play the game with you." My injured pride was making me say things that surprised me as much as they surprised Henry. Meanwhile, my inferiority complex was applauding enthusiastically.

I really liked the confusion on Henry's face, and the way he raised one eyebrow. Not a trace of pity now.

"We never really talked about it before," I babbled, almost forgetting that I was telling downright lies, my voice sounded so convincing. "Of course I didn't have as many boyfriends as you've had girlfriends, but well, there was . . . this boy that I went out with. In Pretoria."

Since Henry didn't respond but just looked at me expec-tantly, I went on. "It wasn't a great love or anything like that, and we only went out for three months, but sex with him was . . ." At this point, my injured pride suddenly switched off (damn it), and I was on my own again.

And hating myself horribly. Why had I done it? Instead of using the opportunity for a genuine conversation, I was simply making everything worse. I instantly went bright red in the face because I saw no way of ending the sentence I'd just begun. *Sex with him was* . . . hello? Only now did I notice how intently Henry was looking into my eyes all this time. "Was . . . okay," I muttered with the last of my strength.

"Okay," repeated Henry slowly. "And . . . what was this guy's name?"

Yes, you stupid injured pride, what was it? I ought to have thought of that before. The longer you hesitate before telling a lie, the less convincing it is. Any child knows that.

So I said, quickly, "Rasmus." Because it was the first name to occur to me when I thought of South Africa. And because I actually was a pretty good liar.

Rasmus had been the name of our neighbor's asthmatic chow. I used to dog-sit him, and for a hundred rands an hour, I took him and a pug called Sir Barksalot for walks with our own dog, Buttercup.

"Rasmus," repeated Henry, and I nodded, relieved. It sounded good. There could be worse names for imaginary ex-boyfriends. Sir Barksalot, for instance.

To my surprise, Henry changed the subject at this point, although I'd already prepared myself for an interrogation. Or to be precise, he didn't actually change the subject, he began kissing me again. As if he wanted to prove that he was better at it than Rasmus. It wouldn't have made any difference if Rasmus had been real—no Rasmus in the world could kiss better than Henry.